THE DEVIL'S TRINITY

By the same author

NORTH SLOPE
SHADOW OF THE WOLF
HELL'S GATE
THE EAGLE'S COVENANT

To my darling wife, Patricia.

I would like to thank my son Terry Parker, ex Royal Air Force Harrier Test Pilot, for refining my flying techniques, and David Kennedy, ex United States Navy test pilot for putting me right on American naval matters and procedure. I would also like to thank my dear friend, Lynn Gough for reading the manuscript for me; not the best of jobs I must admit. For all their efforts I take full responsibility for any mistakes.

THE DEVIL'S TRINITY

Michael Parker

ROBERT HALE · LONDON

ISBN 978-0-7090-8564-5

Robert Hale Limited
Clerkenwell House
Clerkenwell Green
London EC1R 0HT

www.halebooks.com

2 4 6 8 10 9 7 5 3 1

WORCESTERSHIRE COUNTY COUNCIL	
828	
Bertrams	25.05.08
T	£18.99
WO	

Typeset in 10.25/13.5pt Sabon
Printed and bound in Great Britain by
Biddles Limited, King's Lynn

CHAPTER ONE

Harry Marsham, who was known as Marsh to his friends, should have died that night. His lifelong friend and business partner in their underwater exploration business, Greg Walsh was not so lucky. When the freighter loomed up out of the darkness and struck their yacht, the *Ocean Quest*, it caught it amidships and rolled it over into the dark waters of the sea, crushing the boat like matchwood. Luck was on Marsh's side that night; he had a marginally better chance than Walsh because he was standing on the open deck. He was waiting to climb the main mast to check a faulty riding light, which had failed for no apparent reason. Walsh was rummaging about below decks. He had gone there to look for a torch and spare bulbs, and to see if he could figure out why the battery power had failed.

The two men were on their yacht about 800 miles south-east of Cuba, in the Caribbean Sea. It was past midnight, but the stars were no longer visible because of the low cloud cover. The sea was calm and the air was hot and oppressive, with the heat being clamped in by the clouds, and there was no breeze to give them respite from the heat. The yacht was becalmed, its sails hanging limp.

They drifted gently on the ocean, invisible, unseen and unseeing. There was no urgency in either of the men's movements. The slight swell of the sea lifted the *Ocean Quest* gently. Marsh peered up the mast, waiting for Walsh to bring up a torch. He couldn't see much, but he felt he was doing something positive, as if just standing there looking was sufficient.

Then a sound reached his ear that was different. Despite the calm, the yacht pitched and fell gently, but suddenly there was a subtle change in the rhythm. The sound made him turn his head and look into the inky blackness.

He could see nothing. He kept his hand on the mast and felt the rise and fall of the yacht beneath the soles of his deck shoes. But the yacht moved slightly abeam. The breeze chilled his legs and the hairs on his neck began to lift. He peered again, this time more intently. Was there something out there? Was there a whale beneath the surface, swimming close by? His hand dropped away from the mast and he took a step forward and that was when he saw the ship looming like a colossus, coming straight at them out of the night.

Marsh opened his mouth to scream out a warning to Walsh, but the warning cry stopped in his throat, cut off by the raw fear and disbelief that buried itself deep into his conscience and rendered him momentarily speechless. He tried to shout again but the freighter struck, and in an instant the *Ocean Quest* lifted. A shudder ran through the boat as the huge, scarred prow of the ship smashed through the hull, split the yacht in two and pitched Marsh out into the dark waters of the ocean.

He felt his world spinning as the ship cut through the yacht, crushing everything in its path, turning the sea into a maelstrom of shattered timber and boiling, foaming water.

Marsh knew he was about to die. It was inescapable; he knew that there was nothing he could do that could save him as the yacht disintegrated and the sea enveloped him, filling his mouth and lungs with its salty bitterness.

An indescribable force spun him over and over and he could feel the cold steel of the ship's hull raking his flesh. Hard, ripping barnacles tore at his skin, slashing his clothing and opening up a thousand cuts all over his body. His instant, uncontrollable reflexes made him scream out in pain, but no sound came because his mouth was filled instantly with water, and his soul filled with unimaginable fear. He coughed and choked, fighting like a madman, thrashing his arms about in a tremendous battle to get away from the steel hull of the ship to the life-giving air on the surface.

Marsh had never considered himself a brave man although all his working life he had devoted himself to the sea and the world that lay beneath it. The sea was like a second home to him. He loved it. He had seen and experienced its vagaries, its power and its tranquillity, and he had never feared it; he had always respected it. And he had always known that he could die in it. Now it threatened to engulf him and drag him deep into its depths; no longer a friend but a mortal enemy.

He kicked out desperately as the hull of the ship banged into him again and blind panic seized him. His own, inherent fear drove him into frenzied anger, responding like a trapped animal fighting for its life. He thought he had forced himself away from the danger but again he felt the hull of the ship and knew he could be pulled in by the power of the ship's screws. He pushed hard with both legs and struck out with a superhuman effort to draw himself away from the pull of the swirling water and the fear of being drawn into the threshing screws.

How long he was under the water he didn't know, but it felt like an eternity to Marsh. The reality was that he had been under for little more than thirty seconds, which for a man of Marsh's experience was of no consequence, but the pain and violence seemed to go on for ever. Eventually he broke clear of the surface in a fit of choking and coughing. Each indrawn breath closed his throat like a trap, shutting out the sweet, blessed air. He trod water and tried desperately to control his breathing, but his natural life-preserving instincts kept him gasping like a drowning man. Slowly the coughing subsided and at last he felt some measure of control returning.

Marsh trod water as he turned round, looking for the ship that had just run them down. He saw it slide by like a moving mountain, no more than twenty metres from him. He backed away and swam further into calmer water. Then he stopped and looked back at the ship, its bulk merging with the night. Then a wave sloshed over his head and he lost sight of it.

He thought suddenly of his friend and forgot everything about the ship. He called out Walsh's name, spinning round, searching for him in the swell of the water. The wash from the ship kept splashing over him. The salt was beginning to sting his eyes and from time to time he would suddenly drop beneath the water. But despite that, he kept calling out his friend's name.

He could see very little, just the phosphorescence of the sloughing wave tops. He kept calling until his voice became quite hoarse and he realized that it was pointless; Walsh wasn't there. He felt an overwhelming sadness engulf him when the reality dawned on him. He also felt a gnawing disbelief and anger that fate had been so cruel that in the vast expanse of that ocean, they should end up becalmed right in the path of that ship. But the noise and the violence were over now. It was quiet and he was quite alone.

It took Marsh quite some time to calm down and think of the dangerous situation he was in. He was beginning to feel the stinging effects of the salt water on his cuts, and knew there was a distinct possibility that the smell of his blood would attract any sharks in the vicinity. There was nothing he could do, he realized that. If the sharks took him, that would be the end. There would be no rescue; no miraculous survival.

What he could do though was to consider exactly what his position was and what chance he had of being rescued. But it was all pointless and the thought disappeared from his head as quickly as it had entered; he had no chance.

He twisted round, letting the dying swell lift him. He knew he was about 500 miles south-east of Jamaica and about 800 miles south-east of Cuba. But he knew he could have been in the middle of the Atlantic Ocean for all the difference it would make; he was miles from land and would probably drown before any hope of rescue came.

Marsh didn't really know why Greg Walsh had chosen to sail this far from their base in Freeport in the Bahamas. It wasn't unusual for the two of them and Walsh's wife, Helen, to go off sailing for a few days, particularly when business was slack. Walsh had been unusually reticent about his plans, simply telling Marsh that he felt like a longer cruise this time and not simply a quick jaunt around the islands. Marsh was relieved that Helen had chosen to remain at the boatyard and catch up on paperwork and a little shopping in Freeport.

He looked up at the sky, hoping to see a star; some small, bleak light of comfort, a small crumb. His only hope now lay in the ship that had run them down. He knew it would take some distance for the ship to stop and lower a boat. For that was surely what they would do. He knew there was no way the crew on watch could have failed to see them, even though the *Ocean Quest* was without navigation lights. The noise and sudden impact would not have gone unnoticed anyway. They would certainly turn back and begin a search of the area.

He slipped beneath the surface. The water was suddenly cold on his face. It startled him and he kicked out, bursting through the surface, blowing the water out of his nose and mouth. The salt stung his throat. He dragged a hand over his face, pushing the hair away from his eyes. As the water lapped over his shoulders he began stroking out vigorously. Marsh knew he could only do this for so long, then exhaustion would overtake him and he would succumb and drown.

He searched again, but he was trying to search through almost total darkness. And at sea level, he would only be able to see a few metres. It meant that any boat launched to find them would fail because they would also be limited by their field of vision. He decided to swim in the direction the ship was heading, but then realized that he was too disorientated to figure out which way to go. And there was no moonlight either. He did think of searching round for some of the debris from the *Ocean Quest*. Perhaps he could cling to some flotsam. But come daylight he would probably have become shark meat.

Then, quite suddenly, just for a brief moment he thought he saw the ship. He tried to concentrate and focus his vision in the area the silhouette of the ship appeared to be. He started swimming towards it, hope against hope.

He soon realized that the silhouette was indeed no vision; the ship was there and she was stationary. Strangely though she was much closer than he would have expected, given the distance a ship needs to come to a halt. Then he realized why he could not see the ship clearly in the darkness: she was carrying no lights!

Marsh stopped swimming. Apprehension and curiosity began to tease at his mind. Why would the ship be carrying no lights? And because she was so close and stationary, did that mean she was already stopping when she smashed into the *Ocean Quest*?

He began swimming again, cautiously this time. But whatever the reasons for this mystery, that ship was Marsh's only hope of survival and he had to take it. As he swam he called out, shouting as loud as he could, but his voice was like a thin reed in a non-existent breeze, and it barely carried across the water.

For a while he thought his brain was playing tricks on him and the ship was still moving. The distance between him and the freighter was difficult to judge. He was making little progress and the ship didn't seem to be getting any closer. But he could see no tell-tale phosphorescent wake from the ship, which meant the screws were not turning. It lifted his spirits again and he swam more strongly even though the apprehension hadn't left him.

Marsh had been in the water for about thirty minutes when he reached the stern of the ship. He had hoped to hear the sound of voices as a boat was lowered to search for survivors of the collision, but there was nothing, no movement, no lights of any kind, just silence.

He cupped his hands to his mouth and called out. The sound carried up to the ship but seemed to bounce off the hull. He called again but still the ship seemed lifeless. It was as though there was not a soul on board. He thought of the old mariners' stories of ghost ships. But that's all they ever were to Marsh, just stories.

He frowned as he thought back to that moment on the *Ocean Quest*'s deck, just before the crushing impact of the ship. It was strange that there had been no sound; nothing to warn of the coming disaster. And, as he bounced along the punishing hull, there had been no force drawing him down into the threshing screws. He thought of how quickly he had reached the ship in the circumstances. It meant only one thing to Marsh: when the ship struck the *Ocean Quest*, she was not under way. She was already stopping!

Marsh couldn't accept it; there was no rational explanation. Not yet! He didn't believe this ship was another *Mary Celeste*, another one of those ghost ships; there had to be life on board. He called out again.

'Ahoy there; you on board!'

There was no answer. He waited, treading water, his face turned upwards expectantly. He was getting cold too, despite the comparative warmth of the water. And tired; his limbs were beginning to protest and the stinging pain from the cuts on his body seemed to be multiplying.

He called out again but there was still no response. He felt anger rising inside him now. The apprehension he had felt earlier was leaving him and he thrashed at the water furiously.

'For God's sake,' he called out desperately, 'if you have any compassion, answer me!'

But there was still silence.

A sense of futility and desperation was creeping over him and he began swimming, intending to circle the ship with the hope of finding some way on board, although how he expected to climb the sheer sides, he had no idea.

Then he heard voices.

The relief was crushing and overwhelming. Tears filled his eyes and he brushed them away. He guessed that his voice must have carried up to whoever was on watch at the time. He waited, listening to the gentle lapping of the water against the hull. The voices were stronger now, but in a language Marsh did not understand. Not that he cared.

He raised his arm above the water and called out. He expected to see some lights come on and he hoped that the whiteness of his hand would stand out in the beam of a searchlight. But for some inexplicable reason the decks remained cloaked in darkness.

Marsh began to sense a strange, uneasy doubt; an uncertainty that was marching against the feeling of relief he had experienced moments earlier. He knew there was all manner of illegal traffic in the Caribbean: drugs, arms, people smugglers. People like that would not be interested in somebody like him; his life would be of little worth to them. But on a ship this size he doubted if it was engaged in anything illegal.

Suddenly a light snapped on, its beam directed down towards the surface of the water. It moved rapidly, searching for him. Marsh called out, waving his arms furiously. As the beam moved towards him, Marsh swam into its small, comforting circle of light. It was quite intense and he had to shield his eyes from the glare. He shouted up at the unseen crew member holding the light.

'Ahoy there!'

He almost laughed then, a nervous, falsetto laugh; here at last was sanctuary.

Then, without warning, there was the sound of a rifle shot. The bullet zipped through the still night air, popping into the water. Then another shot followed instantly by a 'pop' as another bullet slammed into the sea beside him.

It was probably a couple of seconds before Marsh realized what was happening, but for him it seemed to be an unreal moment suspended in time before the awful truth dawned on him.

'Oh my God,' he cried. 'No!'

The bullets punctured the water throwing up small columns as they peppered the pool of light on the surface. Marsh screamed and spun away from the circle, clawing madly in a desperate attempt to escape the creeping, deadly shots. The gun barked out its shattering message, each slap of the water moving inevitably towards him as the circle of light maintained its deadly grip on his desperate struggle.

He dived beneath the surface as a bullet ripped into his leg behind the knee. The pain was excruciating but Marsh knew he had to ignore it and pull himself down deeper beneath the water. He could still hear the plucking sounds as the bullets spent their energy just above his desperate struggle for survival.

He stopped well below the surface and turned towards the hull of the ship. The pain in his leg was becoming almost too much to bear. He didn't know what to do for his own survival, and all he could think of was to swim towards the belly of the freighter and find a dubious sanctuary.

As he touched the cold, metal surface of the ship, he paused and let himself drift slowly upwards until his head cleared the water. He stopped and pressed his cheek against the cold steel. He reached down and fingered the wound in his leg. He guessed that he wasn't seriously injured; perhaps it was because the water had absorbed much of the bullet's energy. But for all that, it still felt as if his leg had been severed. He knew the blood would be oozing from it and once more the fear of sharks crept up his spine.

Marsh looked back towards the circle of light. It was still moving about, still searching for him. There was no shooting now and the uncanny silence had returned. He trod water, keeping his eyes fixed firmly on the light. He had no idea what to do now; if he swam away from the ship he would eventually drown; if he gave himself up and threw himself on their mercy ... No, they would kill him before he had even asked for sanctuary.

He heard a sudden splash, the sound of something entering the water. A boat perhaps? The sound came from the stern. Marsh was roughly amidships. The voices returned, shouting from the deck. They sounded agitated, but they were quick, clear, unmistakable words of command and they flew from the deck above down to the men in the boat.

Marsh tensed, pulled his elbows in and let himself sink deeper until his nose was barely clear of the surface. His common sense told him he was in a trap from which there was no chance of escape. Swim away and drown, or remain by the ship and be slaughtered. He knew he had little choice but to swim away, but where to?

Suddenly he heard another voice calling out excitedly. It was coming from the boat, and the man calling out was shouting wildly. The wavering beam of light stopped and moved rapidly across to the boat. It picked out some of the floating wreckage of the *Ocean Quest*. Now everybody seemed to be getting excited and there were voices issuing commands from everywhere. Marsh inched his way carefully along the hull, moving towards the bow. He intended to use the current distraction to make his way clear of the ship and as far away from it as possible.

Then a hand reached up out of the water and touched him.

Marsh gasped in sheer fright. His spine went rigid and a massive shudder plunged down his back. He spun round and instinctively lunged with his elbow. It thudded into something soft. He went rigid then as he saw Walsh's corpse roll over and the pale, dead face came up from beneath the dark surface.

He almost lost the will to live then. His nerves were strung so taught they were almost at breaking point, and only a superhuman effort of will stopped him from screaming in uncontrollable terror. Seeing his friend float up from the deep like an underworld spectre, his white face masked in the appalling rictus of death was almost too much for Marsh's singing nerves to take.

His spine loosened in another massive shudder and he pushed the corpse away. The cadaver refused to move and he lunged at it, feeling sick. He pulled his good leg up and gave the body a massive kick. It drifted from him, face up, away from the hull of the ship. Marsh clawed at the steel hull and pulled himself away from Walsh's drifting body.

Suddenly there was a cry of exultation from the deck and a rapid succession of shots. Marsh could hear the bullets thudding into Walsh's body. He saw it roll over under the thudding impact and the shooting stopped.

He was stunned by the horror of it all. He felt sick and weakened, and his strength seemed to be slipping away from him. The water lapped over his face and he felt lethargic and weak. Marsh knew the sea well; he had lived with it most of his life. It had always been a source of immense pleasure to him and he knew how it could turn suddenly and become a threat. He knew that to weaken was to succumb to its inherent menace and had learned to live with the dangers.

He now had to call on those years of experience and his own strength of will to restore his capacity for survival. There was still considerable danger and Marsh knew that he had to recognize that in order to cope with it and survive. There was still a great deal of shouting going on and he could see the men now in the rubber dinghy, shrouded in a circle of light, around Walsh's body. It was an ironic twist of fate, he thought, that Walsh had saved him that night, even in death.

He considered his situation and knew it was hopeless; there was nothing he could do to resolve it. There would be no sanctuary on the ship and the sea offered no hope. He was hundreds of miles from land. To the north lay the island of Haiti. North-west was Jamaica and beyond that the yawning gap between the Yucatan Peninsula and Cuba. Jamaica might just as well have been on the moon for all the good it was going to do him. Whatever he tried, he would be dead within hours. If nothing else, the sharks would see to that.

He edged his way towards the bow of the ship, clinging to the hull, still not knowing what he would do. While the ship was there it was a floating sanctuary; a tangible hope, but all in the mind now.

He swam to the forward end of the freighter and round to the other side. Then he pushed away from the ship, knowing that the crew would only be interested in what was happening elsewhere and not in the darkness where he was. They had their quarry and would be seeking no more. He was about five metres from the ship when he suddenly swam into the anchor chain.

And that was when he saw the other ship!

He held on to the anchor chain, his mouth open in complete shock. He tried gathering his senses and marshalling his fading strength to make sense out of all this. To see the other ship was certainly a complete shock, but, as he reflected on it, he soon realized that it was not as surprising as he had first thought; it was almost certainly a transfer of cargo that was about to take place and probably a haul of drugs or illicit arms. And whatever the reason was for these two ships to come together, it did not bode well for him.

And then he thought about Greg Walsh and his unusual decision to sail this far from Freeport for no other reason than he said he fancied a longer trip. Could it be possible, Marsh wondered, that Walsh expected these two ships to be here? And was his long-standing friend and business partner involved in something covert and illegal? Whatever the answer was, Marsh realized that there was very little chance of finding out, because he was unlikely to survive much longer. Unless he could get on board the second ship unseen.

The second vessel was a lot smaller than the freighter that had smashed through the *Ocean Quest*, no more than about 6000 tons by Marsh's reckoning. Because she was smaller, her draught was lower and offered him a better chance of getting on board and concealing himself.

He knew there was no way he could get up on to the deck of the freighter, although he had contemplated climbing up the anchor chain. To attempt it would have been suicidal. The smaller ship offered him a marginally better hope.

He began to edge his way carefully towards the stern of the freighter until he was able to pick out the name on the prow of the other ship. It was the *Taliba*.

Marsh stopped. He knew the boat and he knew who owned it, but there was no way in a million years that he would ever have suspected the man to be involved in something as dangerous as this. And that little knot of truth began to grow in him that his partner, Greg Walsh, might have had foreknowledge of what these two ships would be doing here at this precise time and position. And it was that knowledge that meant he had not been killed in a tragic accident at sea.

He had been murdered!

CHAPTER TWO

About a week before the *Ocean Quest* had been sunk by the freighter, Remo Francesini of the American security service, the CIA, had stood in the waiting-room of the military hospital at Cape Canaveral in Florida. He was waiting for a doctor to take him along to an isolation ward where a young man lay sick and dying. He was deep in thought and was concerned, not for the young man but for something else that weighed much heavier on his mind.

Francesini was a big man, over six feet tall and weighed about 200 pounds. He had always prided himself on his fitness, much of which was a result of serving in the United States Marine Corps and subsequently as a member of the Navy Seals; the covert group of specialists who worked behind enemy lines on operations that required courage, stealth and a philosophical attitude to whatever fate had in store for them and to whatever their masters ordered them to do.

Today he was at the hospital in his capacity as head of the Mission Support Office, which was responsible for collecting and collating intelligence information and reporting directly to the Deputy Director of Operations of the CIA at Langley in West Virginia. Francesini's boss was Admiral James Starling and it was the admiral who had insisted that he, Remo Francesini, should visit the dying man at the hospital and not one of Remo's subordinates, which would normally have been the case.

He was the only person in the waiting-room. He was wearing green coveralls, a surgeon's cap on his head and covers over his shoes. A Havana cigar, illegal in the United States but to which his bosses turned a blind eye, was clamped between his teeth. It was unlit because smoking was now banned in all American hospitals, so he contented himself with thinking about the reasons why he was there and where he would sooner be.

It was quiet and the walls, which were almost bare save for a couple of naval prints, seemed to reflect a melancholy that fused with his own. There was a small table in the room and a couple of chairs. There was no reading material.

Since the attacks on the World Trade Centre in New York, in September 2001 by the Muslim terrorist organization al-Qaeda, the whole of the CIA and the White House had become jumpy at the slightest hint of another terrorist operation on American soil. The bosses at the top of the pile were more nervous than their underlings because it would be their heads and jobs on the line if their departments screwed up.

Admiral Starling was no different, except that he had the CIA Director of Operations bearing down on him who in turn had to contend with the Oval Office in the White House.

The melancholy feeling that settled in Francesini's mind was the result of hopelessness and a fear that he could not prevent another terror attack by al-Qaeda because their attacks were so difficult to predict or detect, despite the most sophisticated technology available and the magnificent and selfless efforts of the CIA agents in the field.

Home-grown terrorism was another factor that troubled him and the unbelievable willingness of second and third generation Arab Americans to support their Middle Eastern cousins in their appalling acts of murder.

A sixth sense told him that what he was about to see and hopefully hear, was a warning that had dropped into their laps by sheer good fortune. But even then, Francesini hadn't a clue just how significant the warning would prove to be; his task was to glean as much from this as was humanly possible and pray that another atrocity would be avoided.

Sadly, the melancholy in him hid his usual countenance of good humour and confidence. He had a charisma that people usually warmed to, which meant never suspecting for a minute that his worries were ably hidden and could quite easily have been their worries.

A door opened and a naval officer stepped into the room. He was dressed in a similar fashion to Francesini.

'You can see him now, sir.'

Francesini walked towards the open door. 'Any improvement?' he asked the young naval officer without any real hope.

The young man shook his head. 'He'll be lucky to last another month. Try not to tax him too much.'

'Has he said anything?'

Again the shake of the head. 'No, nothing of significance, but you can still try; you might get something out of him.'

Francesini nodded and followed the officer out of the room. The tap of their heels echoed round the walls of the long corridor, intruding into the silence. At the far end of the corridor, the naval officer pushed opened a pair of swing doors that opened into another passage. He stopped by the first door and beckoned Francesini, opening the door for him.

The room looked clinical and efficient. Beside the bed was an array of monitoring equipment humming quietly, interrupted rhythmically by a pulsing sound from a heart monitor. The green trace on the monitor screen looked irregular and the spikes were erratic.

He paused at the bedside and looked down at the man lying on the bed. There were two bottles hanging from a stainless steel contraption with tubes branching down to the patient's arms. He was in his thirties. Francesini knew that from the man's notes he had read when he had arrived at the hospital. There was an oxygen bottle beside the man's bed, but at the moment it was not in use.

Most of his hair had fallen out and what was left hung in small, wispy clumps from his scalp. One eye was closed. The other eye was open but red and angry and weeping. He had suppurating sores on his face and neck and they continued unseen down his body to the soles of his feet.

Francesini knew the man was suffering from bone calcium deficiency, leukaemia and dysentery. He felt desperately sorry for him, not because he was dying, but because of the long and painful end to the poor man's life: he was dying from radiation sickness.

Francesini pulled a chair over and sat beside the bed. He studied the man for a while and wondered if he would learn anything because the poor wretch looked comatose. The dying man had been picked up somewhere along the Florida Keys, wandering aimlessly along the road. The police had been called by some concerned citizen who described the man as looking like he had been in a road accident. It was true and he had been in a sorry state even then when the police picked him up. He had no identity papers on him and did not look like an American, although that in itself was not significant. So the local authorities had put him into hospital until the Immigration Department could deal with him.

The poor man had lain there for several days before a retired army doctor chanced by. What the doctor saw reminded him of clinical notes he had studied in his early days as a junior army doctor. The notes were comprehensive and were of Japan after the atomic bomb. And what the sharp old medic suggested to the Pentagon sent shivers down their spines and set the alarm bells ringing all the way to the White House. The sick man was immediately transferred to the isolation wing where he was now.

'I wish you would say something,' Francesini muttered. 'You're not being much help to yourself. You came to us but you won't say why. The doctor says you could be OK, but you need something to give you hope.' It was a lie and it rolled glibly off his tongue.

The man's eye moved and he turned his face a little. Francesini was encouraged.

'If you have a family, we can let them know. We can bring them here for you.' He leaned forward, getting closer. 'It doesn't matter where they are; we can get them.'

The man's lips moved as he tried to form a word. Francesini watched closely as the blistered lips trembled, the blood from the sores on his mouth was still wet. Suddenly the man's hand reached out and grabbed Francesini's wrist and a word tumbled out. His voice was faint and cracked. It was virtually hopeless. Francesini shook his head knowing he could do nothing for him unless he knew more.

The strength in the man's grip ebbed away and he relaxed. Francesini took hold of his hand and held it.

'How did you get the burns?' he asked, not expecting an answer. 'What are they doing? What are they up to?' Francesini didn't even know who 'they' were!

The frustration threatened to tip the quiet calm into boiling emotion. He wanted to wring the truth from the man and bully him into answering his questions. But he never did; he just sat there and talked softly.

He left the room after twenty minutes, discarding his protective clothing in a bin that was outside the door. He called at the reception desk to tell them that the dying man was asleep, and would they inform the doctor that he was leaving.

It was a bright, uplifting day outside the hospital and the warm sun on his face gave Francesini a reason to feel a little better as he stepped out into the sunshine. He took a cigar from his pocket. He lit it and drew in a lungful of smoke.

'Taliban,' he muttered to himself. Was that the word the dying man had been trying to say, Taliban? Muslim fanatics who used to hold the reins of power in Afghanistan?

'I thought we had thrown them out,' he muttered to himself.

Then he shook his head, blew the cigar smoke out leisurely and wondered what Admiral Starling would have to say.

Marsh shivered. He felt cold, but that didn't concern him too much; it was a warm night and the chill would soon pass. He thought about his own situation and what he could do and how he could get out of it. The irony of it did not escape him; he made his living getting wet and avoiding death. This time he wasn't enjoying it, neither was he getting paid!

The self-indulgence passed and despair crowded in, swarming over him as he recalled the terrifying moments surrounding Walsh's death. It was the nature of it and the following circumstances that horrified him. He wondered if he would ever get home to Freeport to report everything to the police. He thought too of Helen, Walsh's widow, and how he would tell her. In fact, *what* he would tell her.

Marsh had been a partner in their underwater survey business with Walsh and his widow, Helen for a good number of years. They owned a boatyard in Freeport and also their own, underwater survey vessel. Although business had been good over the years they still struggled to pay off their short-term loans and the mortgage on the yard and the submersible.

He had seen the *Taliba*, the ship now alongside the freighter, in Freeport. It was shortly before Greg Walsh had agreed to work on a relatively short commission for its owner, Hakeem Khan.

Khan was a wealthy oceanographer and explorer. He was well known among oceanographers the world over. And he was well respected. Walsh had worked on that commission for a few months, but it had not involved Marsh or Helen. Marsh could never figure out why Walsh had excluded him. It hadn't been a contentious issue really, and, in fact, had given Marsh an opportunity to spend some free time on his own in Europe, taking in the old capital cities and doing some skiing and getting in *après ski* in the best traditions of a bachelor.

Shortly after completing the commission, Walsh had begun to act strangely and a little secretively. Marsh hadn't realized it at first, but slowly it had generated some friction between them. It never reached the extent where they had fallen out, but it was a little difficult for Marsh and Helen to understand. Helen had tried to question her husband several times, but had never been able to get anything from him.

But whatever it was that was troubling Walsh, it always seemed to go back to the work he had completed for Hakeem Khan. And Marsh was now rapidly piecing together some seemingly irrelevant parts of a jigsaw that worried him.

But the most important thing on Marsh's mind at that moment was how to secure his own safety in what was now an extremely dangerous position.

His mind went back to the smaller of the two vessels, the *Taliba*. It was an Arabic word meaning 'seeker of knowledge'. It had been operating in the Caribbean Sea and the Gulf of Mexico for a couple of years now. Walsh told him it was operating on an oil exploration licence.

He looked up at the colossus that was the freighter, then at the *Taliba*. Of the two ships, he knew that the smaller craft was his only hope.

He had swum to the stern end of the *Taliba* and had been there for some minutes going through the useless exercise of trying to figure out exactly what the ship was doing there in the first place. He cursed himself and brought his mind back to how he was going to make best use of the opportunity that had presented itself.

Marsh knew that clambering aboard the boat would not be difficult because the crew of the *Taliba* all had their attention focused on the freighter and what was apparently the preparation to transfer cargo. It was only Marsh's weakened state that might jeopardize his attempt to climb up on to the aft deck of the *Taliba*.

He kicked with his legs, ignoring the pain from the bullet wound and reached up for the diving platform which had been hoisted into its stowage position. His fingers touched the framework and he grabbed and held on. Then he slowly pulled himself clear of the water. He felt a little rush of adrenalin and a sense of euphoria swept over him on this initial success, but he knew his chances of survival were still slim. He had to be careful.

Once he was on the aft deck, he lay prone and remained perfectly still. He lay like that for several minutes and allowed his pulse rate to settle, taking advantage of the brief respite he had been given.

As he lay there, Marsh could hear rather than see, the work going on at the forward end of the *Taliba*. It was also clear that the hatch covers were being hoisted clear on the forward deck of the freighter. Although neither ship was carrying lights, which of course was illegal, Marsh could see the flicker of torchlight on the deck of the freighter and could just about make out silhouettes of men on the wings of both ships.

Suddenly the winch motor on the freighter burst into life and within moments a large crate appeared as it was swung from the hatch of the freighter to the forward deck of the *Taliba*.

A breeze suddenly sprang up and ran like a lizard across his back. He shivered and began to cast around for somewhere to conceal himself. He needed to do it quickly while both crews were engaged in the transfer of whatever cargo it was. And the noise of the transfer was loud enough to mask any noise that Marsh made while he looked for his bolthole.

But before he went looking for that bolthole, Marsh thought again about Hakeem Khan the respected member of that breed of oceanographers who work in the oceans of the world, and who were never happier than when they were doing just that.

So what the hell was he doing here?

Hakeem Khan watched the loading dispassionately from the bridge of the *Taliba*. If he was nervous, he did not appear so. He stood with his legs apart and his hands locked together behind his back. He stared out of the windows of the bridge through dark eyes beneath a heavy frown. He was quite bulky, but none of it was fat because of his lifestyle at sea. Despite his apparent fitness however, Khan was not a well man.

He was there on the bridge because he was not disposed to letting his captain oversee the operation. Nevertheless he managed to display a detached interest. His head moved in a spontaneous nod of satisfaction as the sling, now divested of its burden, moved upward like the long tail of a firefly. His eyes followed it until it disappeared into the darkness above the freighter. He then turned to a huge man standing beside him.

'We are in Allah's hands now, Malik,' he said quietly.

Malik nodded his huge head. 'May He be praised.'

There were two other men on the bridge with Khan and Malik: the ship's captain, Jose Maria de Leon, who was a Cuban, and the duty wheelman. Khan spoke to the captain.

'It is done. Lock it away, Señor de Leon. I will be in my cabin.'

De Leon moved towards the bridge telephone, but before he could pick it up, the operator called through from the wireless room.

De Leon and Khan exchanged glances. De Leon stepped through into the wireless room. A few moments later he called to Khan, 'You had better take this, sir. They have a problem.'

Khan frowned and walked into the wireless room. The captain handed him the headset which he pressed to his ear. De Leon watched intently.

'When was this?' Khan asked sharply. 'And you have the body on board?'

He lifted up his face and shook his head in despair.

'And he has papers on him?' He listened. 'His name?'

The others watched Khan as his face froze.

'Mother of God.' He looked at de Leon. 'Get the cage ready.'

He threw the headset on to the radio table. 'Tell them to stand by,' he ordered the operator. 'I'm going on board.' He turned to Malik. 'You too.'

There was just a hint of dawn breaking on the far horizon as Marsh thought he could see movement on the bridge of the *Taliba*. Two figures moved hurriedly down the stairway from the bridge to the lower deck. Beyond them he saw the cage being hooked up to the derrick crane. It was a shark cage, used to allow divers to study shark behaviour in safety. The two figures stepped inside the cage and it was lifted up and swung across to the deck of the freighter.

One of them looked like Khan. He didn't recognize the second figure.

Marsh assumed this was part of the illegal business that was being conducted. Perhaps Khan was going over to the freighter to pay for whatever contraband had been delivered; for Marsh was convinced it had to be contraband of one kind or another. As the cage disappeared from Marsh's view he pushed the thought from his mind and began to consider his own position and what he could do.

On the deck of the freighter, Khan stood over the dead body of Greg Walsh. Water still dripped from Greg Walsh's body, forming small, red pools on the deck of the freighter. He had been laid on his back and, in the torchlight, could be clearly seen small blossoms of flowering red on his clothing. Khan stared at it.

'There was no one else?' he asked at length.

The captain of the freighter glanced up. 'No.'

Khan's eyes just flickered towards him; then they were back on the pale, dead face.

'Why?' he muttered softly to himself. 'Why were you here?'

Malik heard the whisper and sensed the urgent query in Khan's voice.

'Coincidence?' he offered. 'A chance in a thousand?'

Khan looked at him. 'We would like to think so, wouldn't we, Malik? But I fear that is not the case.' He waved his hand dismissively. 'Throw him back into the sea and let his secrets go with him. The sharks will not go hungry.'

He stared at Walsh's dead face for a little longer. Then he knelt down and placed the tip of his finger on Walsh's chin.

'Why were you here, Walsh? Why?'

He stood up and walked back to the cage in silence. Malik followed.

As they swung back over to the *Taliba*, Khan's face was fused into a deep scowl. A small pain nagged at his chest, the familiar pain that the doctors had warned him about. He lifted his hand and massaged his chest.

A single doubt now lay in his mind. For the first time in many weeks it occurred to him that others might know.

Marsh had been transfixed by the comings and goings between the two ships, but now he knew he had little time; he had to find some-where to conceal himself. Khan was unlikely to be on the freighter too long completing whatever business it was he was conducting; the ships would have to move on soon. Certainly once Khan was back on board.

There were two lifeboats secured on their davits, one either side of the ship. Choosing the lifeboat furthest away from the freighter, and away from the direction most eyes might look, Marsh ran at a crouch towards the boat. He climbed up on to the steelwork of the davits and slipped beneath the tarpaulin covering the boat.

The darkness closed in on him as he settled down in the bottom of the lifeboat. He had no plan and didn't know what he was going to do. He certainly had no hope of rescue. Whatever happened now would be in the hands of God.

Or in the hands of Hakeem Khan.

CHAPTER THREE

Francesini drew heavily on the Cuban cigar and leaned back in his chair. On his desk in front of him was an open folder. It was the detail gathered on the unfortunate man he had seen in the hospital at Cape Canaveral, dying of radiation sickness. The man's fingerprints and DNA had revealed nothing at all from an extensive search in the CIA files. Neither had the check that Francesini had ordered on all suspected Taliban operatives in the United States. He had pulled the man's file because he had been told the man was dead, and this meant he was of no further use to Francesini, except to continue worrying the life out of him.

The phone rang. He blew the smoke out of his mouth and picked up the receiver.

'Francesini.'

'Starling here. My office please, Remo.' The gravelly voice had just time enough to resonate in his ear before the phone went dead. James Starling could be laconic when he wanted to be. Telephone conversations for him were always apt to be short; he preferred face-to-face chats.

Francesini knew the rules. He put the phone down and put his cigar in the ashtray, carefully removing the glowing ember. He then took the files from his desk and locked them away in his safe. Satisfied that he had left nothing on view, he locked the door and made his way to Admiral Starling's office. He knocked and walked in.

There were two men in the room with James Starling. Francesini recognized them immediately. One was Hamilton Ford who worked for the Directorate of Science and Technology, the department in the CIA responsible for gathering external intelligence from technical resources. The other was Jimmy Navarro, a senior intelligence analyst who worked with Ford. Admiral Starling was sitting at his desk, dominating the room. He waved Francesini to a vacant chair.

'Sit down, Remo. Thanks for coming over.' As if Francesini had any option.

'You know Hamilton and Jimmy, so no introductions necessary.' Francesini made himself as comfortable as possible in the remaining empty chair. Starling waited until he was still.

'We have a problem, Remo. Homeland Security knows about this but I've asked Washington to back off until we've had a chance to deal with it. If we don't, the crap's gonna hit the fan.'

Homeland Security was the department set up by President George W. Bush shortly after the suicide attacks by the al-Qaeda fanatics on the World Trade Centre in New York, which meant different security organizations with different agendas all pulling in different directions.

'We have some satellite imagery here of the border between Uzbekistan and Afghanistan. It was taken three weeks ago. Jimmy will fill you in.' He nodded at Navarro.

Starling's office was a reflection of the man. It had the air of efficiency and durability about it. There was a photograph of him with President Clinton. The admiral was in full uniform in the picture, taller than the President. It flattered the President more than it did the admiral. Starling was a former US Navy pilot and an unspoken legend in military intelligence. So much so that he was practically ambushed into taking up a position with the CIA. The framed picture hung on the wall behind his desk.

There were two computers in the room plus a whiteboard on the wall next to a pull down screen. There was a projector positioned conveniently in front of it, but Francesini had known the admiral to use the blank wall.

The desk around which they were all sitting was almost certainly older than Starling although the rest of the furniture was more in keeping with the image of the CIA. There were no ashtrays, much to Francesini's dismay.

Navarro passed two satellite photographs across the desk to Francesini. He then got up from his chair and stood behind him, looking over his shoulder.

'These were taken by our Quickbird satellite. Resolution is down to five hundred yards. What you see are heat transmissions and on-board, computer-enhanced images. They were taken at two o'clock in the morning. The sky was slightly overcast but with a full moon it gave us a good picture.'

Francesini looked at the black and white grainy images. It was reasonably clear that what he was looking at was a collection of vehicles. There were probably about thirty men around them. He handed the photographs back to Navarro.

'Why don't you tell me what it is I'm really looking at?' he suggested.

Navarro took the photographs back and put them on the desk in front of his chair. He didn't sit down.

'We had a report from the British who have an SAS team in the area,' he explained. 'There has been some unusual activity lately, which they have been monitoring. We asked them to, because we had some intelligence from a reasonably reliable source,' he added unnecessarily. 'We checked on it and came up with this.'

He pulled a photograph from a folder and handed it to Francesini.

'About one hundred miles north, in Uzbekistan, we picked up this convoy of trucks. Small stuff really, but it was heading south.' The photograph showed the convoy quite clearly, although the resolution was not the same as the Quickbird satellite imagery. 'Interestingly, there was another convoy coming up from the south, in Afghanistan, about the same size.' He pulled another photograph.

Francesini gave the pictures the once over. 'An exchange of weapons perhaps?' he suggested. 'A consignment of drugs?'

'Well, of course, we know that is a possible option,' Navarro said, 'but with the intelligence we received, we think it may have been an exchange of weapons.'

'What kind of weapons?' Francesini asked carefully.

James Starling leaned forward, his fingers interlocked. Navarro saw the admiral lean forward and resumed his seat.

'You will recall, Remo,' the admiral began, 'that the intelligence we have gathered thus far, both human and satellite, makes it pretty certain that a nuclear bomb has been shipped out of the Ukraine?'

Francesini felt his jaw stiffen and his teeth clenched together. He had an uncomfortable feeling about the outcome of this conversation because the admiral's demeanour indicated that he was building up to something more sinister. And Francesini had already made an assumption that scared the living daylights out of him, particularly with the information he had but had not yet shared with Admiral Starling.

He looked sharply at the admiral. He knew that his field of responsibility included any foreign intelligence on nuclear hardware and nuclear capability of potentially unstable regimes.

Francesini picked up on the admiral's words. 'Pretty certain is right, sir. There's always that ten per cent which is intuitive guesswork.' He pointed at the satellite photographs. 'And without human intelligence we've no idea what's in those trucks.'

Ford spoke up then, shrugging his shoulders. 'You're right, Remo, but we do know that the Ukranians are selling off their nukes. Sure, they deny it; blame it on the Mafia, but there are a lot of wealthy politicians in what is a relatively poor country with no productive infrastructure.'

Francesini grinned. 'There are wealthy politicians in ours, but not through selling nukes. Trouble is, Hamilton, the terrorists need delivery systems, and there are none of those in Afghanistan or Iran. So I don't suppose for one minute that the Taliban or al-Qaeda have suddenly found that they are capable of launching a nuclear attack against the West.'

Ford went on, 'An exchange was made at the border, but they didn't load anything into the southern convoy. According to the SAS team on the ground and our Quickbird imagery, a helicopter arrived, a transfer was made and the convoys dispersed.'

Francesini sat forward, the warning signals screaming inside his head. 'So what was the second convoy for? And which way did the helicopter go?'

Ford pushed another satellite photo across the desk. He tapped it with his finger. 'The second convoy, we believe was delivering some of the pay-off; probably a consignment of drugs. Part payment no doubt for the nuke. As for the helicopter it was tracked on a south-west heading.'

Francesini pictured the map in his mind. 'Towards Iran?'

Ford nodded, but didn't take his eyes off Francesini. There was silence for a while. Francesini was conscious of the three men looking at him. It was his remit to have his finger on the nuclear pulse, so to speak.

'Why do I think that's not it? That there's more to come?' Francesini asked no one in particular.

Starling took over then. 'The helicopter was tracked as far as the Iranian border, but unfortunately we lost it there.'

'So it's inconclusive,' Francesini put in hopefully. 'And it may not have been a nuke.'

'Maybe not, but the trouble is, Remo, we can't always deal in facts,' Ford said generously. 'Can we? Hard intelligence is difficult to come by at the best of times. But we do have some hard facts here. One of which is that we know a nuke has gone missing. When that happens we normally locate it fairly quickly, but I'm afraid this one has vanished into thin air.

'Or into Iran,' Francesini said dispassionately.

'We're not sure Iran has it,' Starling said. 'As much as they would like to have a nuclear deterrent, they're not ready yet.' He held his hand up. 'I know they are now processing pure grade uranium, and our intelligence on the ground supports their worst-kept secret that they plan to manufacture a nuke soon.'

'So you think a terrorist organization has the nuke? And they're backed by Iran?'

Starling studied his deputy for some time. 'No,' he said eventually. 'We are confident that Iran does not have any nukes.'

'So is it a terrorist organization?' Francesini queried. 'And do they have a nuke?'

Starling shook his head.

'Not one,' he answered. 'Three!'

Marsh woke up. He opened his eyes and looked around the inside of the lifeboat, wondering where the hell he was. And then it dawned on him. Around him was a cocoon of heat and semi-darkness. His body raged in discomfort and his skin felt like canvas stretched over a tight frame. He moved and the pain in his knee made him gasp out loud. He remembered the rifle shots and reached down to rub at the joint. It was swollen and very tender to the touch.

His mind dragged itself from a feeling of lethargy and fed small nuggets of painful memory into his brain. Pictures opened up for him and he recalled the horrific scenes that had brought him to his present predicament. Each event played itself out like a scene from a nightmare and he sagged mentally when he realized he was still in mortal danger and he knew that he had to get off the ship.

When Marsh had crawled into the lifeboat, it had offered sanctuary, albeit temporary. Now it was hot and airless and he knew he was in danger of dehydrating seriously. He already had a raging thirst and hunger pains shot through his belly adding to his discomfort.

He moved and straightened his legs in an effort to find some comfort on the hard boards. The effort and subsequent flash of pain almost made him pass out. He abandoned the task and lay there gasping with his mouth open in a silent cry of pain and anguish.

After several minutes, when he felt some strength return to him, Marsh gingerly lifted up the edge of the tarpaulin. The sunlight burst through like a brilliant flare and he was forced to close his eyes against it. He lowered the tarpaulin and kept his eyes closed for a while.

He tried again, but this time he inched up the tarpaulin and squinted against the glare until he was able to look around and take stock of his surroundings. He could see the aft deck of the *Taliba* was deserted, but that did not mean there was nobody about. He looked towards midships and saw a couple of the crew leaning on the ship's rail in quiet conversation. Behind them was the superstructure of the bridge and accommodation block. There was one person on the starboard side of the bridge out on the wing, looking across the water at something.

Marsh moved to the other side of the lifeboat and lifted the tarpaulin cover gently. He could see a scattering of islands in the distance, which was probably what the figure on the bridge was looking at. Marsh had no idea what islands they were. But this was the Caribbean and islands meant boats and pleasure craft.

It was then that Marsh realized that the *Taliba* was heading towards the land.

He began thinking ahead: should he chance it or not? He could die here on Khan's boat or take his chances out there in the sea. Only the latter offered an extremely slim advantage, but that depended on how close to the land the *Taliba* would sail.

He lowered the tarpaulin and started to think.

To remain where he was, inside the stifling heat of the lifeboat, was not an option. If he gave himself up to the ship's crew, he would be killed and dumped overboard. If he waited until nightfall before leaving his hiding place he would almost certainly have drifted into unconsciousness because of serious dehydration. After considering all the alternatives, Marsh knew there was only one option: he had to get off the ship. There was no choice, but he knew he couldn't go just then; he had to wait until the ship was close enough to shore to give him a fair chance. He pulled a lifejacket from one of the lifeboat's lockers and lay down on his back, closing his eyes and thinking how his luck was panning out. The sea had tried to claim him once, and now it might get the chance to claim him again.

It was sometime later when Marsh woke. The heat was stifling but after looking out from beneath the tarpaulin, he could see the sun was lower in the sky and the ship was much closer to land. By his reckoning the ship was about five miles from the shore.

He eased the tarpaulin up and slid carefully from the lifeboat. Keeping the bulk of it between him and the bridge to avoid detection, he edged towards the ship's rail. The pain in his knee was almost unbearable, but the thought of what might happen to him if he was caught, was even more so. He leaned over the rail and rolled forward, dropping into the sea.

He hit the water with a smack and was immediately drawn under and spewed out into the ship's wake, thankfully clear of the propellers. He wanted to gasp in deep draughts of air but tried to keep himself below the waterline for as long as he possibly could before surfacing.

His wounded leg still hurt like blazes, but Marsh kept himself afloat while struggling into the lifejacket by treading water with his good leg. He felt refreshed by the plunge into the sea but knew it would not last long, so he turned towards the direction of the land and began swimming.

Francesini had placed the satellite photographs on his desk and was studying them when Starling walked in. When the admiral had told him that there was a chance that al-Qaeda had three nukes, Francesini asked Hamilton Ford and his sidekick, Navarro to leave the office for a while, then had what could only be described as a heated discussion with the admiral.

Starling's excuse was that the evidence had not been available to him until shortly before he had asked Francesini to come to his office. He apologized for the discourtesy but blamed it on Washington; always a good source at which to lay the blame.

'What do you make of it, Remo?' the admiral asked. As he put the question, he walked over to the coffee pot that Francesini always kept hot on the bureau and poured himself a cup.

Francesini looked up. 'Well, you tell me that two nukes have gone missing within the space of three weeks and now another one. If al-Qaeda has them, how on earth can they expect to get them into America without being detected? We've got this country sewn up tighter than a duck's arse.'

'It's a big country, Remo,' Starling offered unhelpfully as he lifted the cup to his mouth. 'There are lots of ways.'

'So tell me. They can't fly them over and drop them from a hijacked airliner. The delivery system needed for a nuke attack is too sophisticated for a hijack operation. If they smuggle them in by road, the chances are we'll pick up and stop them. But if they do manage to get them into the country, the odds are they will put them where they will do the most damage, in any one of our major cities. But the technique used to explode a nuke is quite sophisticated; you can't just leave them in the trunk of a car in a parking-lot and blow them up. It doesn't make sense.'

'It never does.' He sipped his coffee thoughtfully. Eventually he asked Francesini about the man they had picked up dying from radiation burns. 'We never came up with anything, did we?'

Francesini sighed deeply and gathered up the photographs. 'You think there might be a connection?'

'I'm clutching at straws, Remo. Who was he? Where did he come from? Remember, the first two bombs went missing some weeks ago. Where are they?' He didn't expect any answers. 'Tell me again about the fellow.'

Francesini shovelled the photographs into a folder and locked them away in a filing cabinet. 'He was found wandering down in the Florida Keys area. His DNA profile puts him in the Middle East, Arab origin. Aged about thirty-five. Looked like he'd been in the water for some time. We couldn't put out a missing persons enquiry because of the security implications.'

'So he was found in the Keys,' Starling conjectured. 'Obviously he'd been in the water. Did he fall from a ship? If so, where was the ship from? How many ships have been in the Gulf and the Caribbean in the last month?' He held his hand up defensively. 'I know; too many to account for. It could be Cuba, Remo.'

Francesini laughed. 'Unlikely sir; we've got more agents there than the Castro faithful. All promised a future in the good ol' US of A after so many years of loyal service, etcetera, etcetera. We would know if al-Qaeda was in league with the Cubans, no doubt about it.'

Starling put his cup down. 'We need to know, Remo,' he said rather seriously. 'I've got Ford and Navarro working on it, and I want you to pull out all the stops. Anything you need, anything, let me know. If al-Qaeda has those bombs, we could be in serious trouble.'

Francesini looked at him from his chair, rocking slightly. 'So could a lot of people, sir. So could a lot of people.'

He couldn't tell Starling what he already knew because his boss would only deal in facts, not conjecture, and the only fact he had was that he had one person working on something that really *was* pure conjecture. But it was really too preposterous for him to reveal to Starling. His boss would probably laugh him out of the office.

He had that 'preposterous' supposition locked in his safe. A proposition brought to him in a roundabout way by the man who had died when the *Ocean Quest* sank, although at the moment Francesini was unaware of the man's death.

That man was Greg Walsh.

Marsh began to swim boldly, striking out for the land. He had waited for a while until the *Taliba* was far enough away to avoid being seen by anyone onboard who might have seen him go over the side. Marsh was a strong swimmer, but the lifejacket hindered him because he hadn't been able put the thing on properly, so from time to time he rested up and allowed himself to drift with the current. He switched from swimming to drifting but soon realized that he was achieving very little, and the shoreline remained ever distant.

He was weakening a lot quicker than he had bargained for, his strength draining from him with each stroke. The lifejacket kept slipping above his head and he had to struggle to keep it beneath his chin. Each time he struggled, he slipped under the water and would surface, coughing and spluttering, and cursing.

Marsh could feel the battle slipping away. The shoreline never seemed to be getting any closer and all he wanted to do now was rest. He pushed the thought to the back of his mind and struggled on, but he so desperately wanted to close his eyes and sleep.

He knew the game was over; he was losing and the fight now was just to keep going until, mercifully, he would succumb and sink below the surface.

Marsh suddenly realized that he no longer had the lifejacket. It must have bobbed away when he had slipped beneath the surface. The fact that it was gone garnered a little strength for him, but it was too little, too late.

He heard voices in his head and knew the end was now very close, and he slipped beneath the surface again.

The voices disappeared and there was now no hope. He had no strength, no will.

He didn't hear anybody dive into the water, but he was vaguely conscious of an arm going round his neck. He opened his eyes and looked into a round face. He tried to say something but the face filled his vision and something closed over his mouth. He could feel his lungs expanding under some strange force and his heart started pumping life into him as he passed out.

CHAPTER FOUR

Hakeem Khan's dark eyes moved restlessly but he saw nothing because his mind was filled with a thundering and worrying curiosity. The man they had pulled out of the water, Greg Walsh; was it a coincidence or not? Why had he been there?

The *Taliba* had left Jamaica and was heading for the wide expanse of the Gulf of Mexico. The reason the ship called in at Kingston was that Khan wanted to achieve a sense of normality to any observers. It was paramount that no suspicion should fall on him or the *Taliba*, and it also meant the opportunity to restock with fresh produce and take on fuel.

But now Khan was troubled because he had not been able to put the discovery of Walsh's body out of his mind, and he was persuaded by his own fears that the sense of normality he had been hoping to achieve was already under threat.

The broad expanse of ocean before him was now his hiding place; a great void in which to run. His hands were linked together behind his back and his bull head was thrust out on hard, square shoulders. He was leaning forward, holding himself steady on the balls of his feet. Although Khan was a small man in height, his stature and presence dwarfed everyone around him. His dark eyebrows, almost satanic looking, added to his intimidating demeanour.

Captain de Leon and Malik were on the bridge with him, waiting for him to continue the dialogue he had started.

'After Walsh had worked for me on the commission in the Gulf, I had hoped he would have continued to work with us, but he pulled out for some reason.' He said nothing for a while. They waited. 'Why would he show up at that precise moment?'

'Do you think he knew something, sir?' de Leon asked.

Khan shook his head. 'Only Allah can tell us that. But we have to assume the worst. We have to assume that somehow Walsh expected us to be there. Nothing else makes sense.'

'Perhaps he went to the Americans,' Malik suggested.

Khan looked at Malik. 'Perhaps, but there is no point in dwelling on the imponderable,' he stated, and left it at that.

'Then I think we must assume he went to the Americans and therefore we must act accordingly,' de Leon said after a while.

Khan agreed. 'Yes, it's the wisest course. From now on we have to remain extra vigilant.' He sighed deeply. 'Captain, I want you to prepare a plan of action for the crew. If we are to assume the Americans have a suspicion of our intentions, then the crew have to be aware of their responsibilities. If we are stopped at all it will be because the Americans wish to board us, and we must not let them find what they are looking for; we must drop the device on to the sea-bed.'

'Recovery might be difficult,' de Leon admitted.

'Nevertheless, it must be done. We can use the sea gallery.'

The sea gallery that Khan referred to was a large chamber, about eighty square metres in area, within the bowels of the ship that had bottom doors which opened up from the floor of the chamber. It was used for diver recovery during inclement weather. The gallery was on a level with the sea so that when the doors were open, the sea did not flood into the large chamber. It was also convenient for lowering diving bells from within the ship. As a safeguard during stormy weather, and whenever the bottom doors were open, the doors in the bulkheads were watertight, and they could not be opened when the bottom doors were in use.

'Make provision for it,' he told the captain. 'And pray to Allah that we never have to use it,' he added.

He left the two men on the bridge and went down to his cabin. As he reached the door, he felt a sharp pain across his chest. He cursed and clutched at himself with both hands, leaning his body against the bulkhead for support. He closed his eyes and breathed in deeply, drawing in long, careful draughts of air. As the pain subsided he opened his cabin door and went straight to a medicine cabinet in his bathroom. He took two pills from a small bottle and swallowed them with a drink of water.

After about ten minutes, Khan felt a little more comfortable. He sat at his desk and looked out of the forward facing windows. He stared at the Galeazzi Tower that was clamped to the forward deck. This was a tall, domed diving bell used in all deep dives. It could be suspended up to 1000 feet below the surface of the water and used by a team of divers on a saturation dive. This requires divers to breathe a mixture of helium and oxygen to guard against nitrogen narcosis; a kind of euphoria in which a diver is unable to comprehend the physical dangers that exist at such depths. The mind hallucinates and the result is usually death.

Khan stared at it, fixed securely midway between the bridge and the fo'c'sle head. Was it all coincidence? he asked himself. Does someone know?

He got up from the desk and sat on the edge of his bed, removed his shoes and gave up pondering the imponderable. He settled back on the bed as the pain in his chest subsided and very soon was asleep.

About an hour later Khan was woken by a knock on the cabin door. It was de Leon. Khan called him in.

'We have received a reply,' de Leon began, 'but I'm afraid it isn't good news. We cannot get a pilot for the *Challenger*.'

The *Challenger* was a deep-sea diving vessel, designed for underwater survey and exploration work. It was currently at the port of Havana in Cuba undergoing some essential maintenance under the watchful eye of Khan's chief diver, Julio Batista.

Khan sat up and swung his legs off the bed. He ran his hand over his face. 'It doesn't surprise me,' he said. 'We're not exactly overrun with submersible pilots in this game.' He slipped on his shoes and stood up.

'You will have to pilot her. You were going to anyway,' de Leon told him.

Khan shot him a stern look. 'You know I cannot; the risk would be too high.'

The pain in his chest was never far away. To risk a complicated dive could put too much strain on his heart. To attempt the three dives that they needed would almost certainly end in disaster, and their plan would certainly fail.

He walked over to his desk and switched on the light. Sitting there, with the light throwing a shadow over his features, it added an uncomfortable menace to his already dominant nature.

'Who is there who could pilot the *Challenger*?' de Leon asked him.

Khan considered that for a moment. 'Only two; Riker, the American, but he's currently working somewhere in the Pacific on a commission for the Woods Hole Institute. And the other is Harry Marsham. He is, or was,' he corrected himself, 'a partner in the underwater business run by Greg Walsh. They own the *Helena*, the sister ship to our *Challenger*. Trouble is, if he was with Walsh he'll be dead.'

'How long would it take to train someone?' De Leon asked.

Khan shrugged. 'Depending on the weather conditions, a competent submersible pilot could be trained within two weeks. But we would need to do test dives. And we don't have the time. The weather is deteriorating, and we have been warned to expect a hurricane.' He shook his head irritably. 'The longer we are kept from completing our task, the more likely it is that the Americans will learn the truth and stop us.'

'If we cannot find another pilot, you will have to do it.'

Khan's eyes hardened. They were like deep pools of water crystallizing into ice. His hand strayed to his chest and his fingers gently touched the silk of his shirt.

'If only the accident had not happened,' he muttered angrily, looking up at de Leon. 'The accident to Habib, I mean.'

Habib was the man that Remo Francesini had found dying in the hospital in Miami.

'The bomb incident was unfortunate and costly,' de Leon observed. 'We were lucky your group were able to locate another.'

Khan nodded. 'Replacing the bomb will turn out to be easier than replacing Habib.' His hand fell away from his chest. 'But we must find another diver. We must!'

Francesini thought he had hit the equivalent of pay dirt – pure gold. But he had been in the game too long to count his chickens. The poor, unfortunate wretch who had been lying near death through radiation burns had whispered one word: Taliban. Or so Francesini had thought.

A report from the United States Coast Guard had linked the name of a man pulled out of the sea with a gunshot wound in his leg to that of the Ocean Quest Underwater Survey Company, operating out of the Bahamas. The man's name was Harry Marsham, one of the directors of the company. The other two directors were Helen Walsh and her husband, Greg.

Francesini had flagged Walsh's name on the CIA computers when Walsh's suppositions and fears had landed on his desk. It wasn't necessary to give a reason; simply a request to feed through anything that came into the CIA network that might be of interest to a particular department.

It wasn't until he recalled the information he had in a file on Greg Walsh that the truth hit him. Coupled with the seemingly outrageous supposition by Walsh, one that he could not trust himself to divulge to Admiral Starling, was the appearance in the report of the word *Taliba*.

Was that, he wondered, the name the dying man had whispered to him in the hospital? *Taliba*?

Francesini read the summation of his own, written discourse and tried not to let his imagination run away with him. If the dead man had come from the ship, *Taliba*, and was dying from radiation burns because of his association with that vessel, then he had a duty to put a high priority on it.

But he had to be careful.

And he had to be right.

Marsh opened his eyes, blinked briefly and stared into the face of a man sitting beside his bed. It was a pleasant face. His expression was cheerful; a countenance conspired probably to cheer the patient up. Marsh thought he could smell cigar smoke, but the man was not smoking.

'Hi.' Marsh felt tenderness in his throat and knew he would have to speak softly. He looked around the room. It was aesthetically clean, as though its sterility was forced, demanding to be seen without prejudice. Marsh frowned but welcomed the small vase of flowers that added a touch of contrasting colour.

'Who are you?'

The man smiled. It was a pleasant smile. 'My name is Remo Francesini, but my friends call me Remo.' He shrugged. 'Some even call me Frankie. And you're Harry Marsham. Do I call you Harry?'

Marsh liked him immediately. There was no affectation in his manner and he appeared relaxed and friendly.

'No, Marsh will do. Where am I?' he asked.

'Guantanamo Bay Naval hospital.'

Marsh lifted his head off the pillow. 'How the hell did I get here?' he asked. 'Did you pull me out of the water?'

'Hell no, the only time I get near water is when I take a shower.' He leaned a little closer, his expression changing a little. 'Look, I said I would let them know if you woke up, OK?' He got up from the chair. 'Just a few minutes, then I'll be back.'

He left Marsh alone. It was quiet, and that slight smell of cigar smoke reminded him he was back with the living. He wondered how he was going to explain Greg's death to Helen. Why they were actually where they were when the freighter struck. It was Greg's insistence that they sailed out to that point, but he never did give a reason. It wasn't unusual for the two of them to spend a day or two out sailing, but they would often have Helen with them. This time, Greg had persuaded Marsh that they should leave Helen behind. For some reason, it didn't seem to bother her.

He put his thoughts back to how he would explain such bizarre circumstances surrounding Greg's death. Was it an accident? If he told her that the action of the ship that struck them was definitely hostile, would she believe him? Would anybody for that matter? And could he prove it?

During his life and death struggle, Marsh had wanted to get back on dry land and report everything to the authorities. But how could he explain it? Why would the crew of the freighter open fire on him? No doubt the authorities would put it down to smugglers where weapons were *de rigeur*. But more worryingly, if he made it known publicly what he had witnessed on the *Taliba*, and the switch of cargo, he knew without doubt he would put his own life in danger.

There was a noise outside in the corridor. The door swung open and a doctor came into the room with a nurse. Marsh gave up worrying about his immediate problem and let the doctor examine him.

'You're still quite weak, Mr Marsham,' the doctor told him. 'You've taken a terrible battering.' He flexed Marsh's knee gently. 'How on earth did you get this?'

Marsh shook his head. 'I can't remember,' he lied.

The doctor straightened. 'Well, no matter. Our job is to fix you up and get you out of here. The military police here will want to talk to you, I'm sure. Couple of days and you should be OK to leave. We'll give you a sedative later this evening. Help you rest.'

When the doctor and nurse had left, Francesini popped his head round the door.

'Everything OK?'

Marsh smiled, 'I'll get by.'

Francesini closed the door behind him and sat down beside the bed.

'Right,' he said, 'where shall we begin?'

'Well, how about you tell me who you are and what it is you want,' Marsh suggested.

Francesini opened his hands apologetically. 'Good idea. I'm from the United States Immigration Department,' he lied. 'We thought it important to ask you a few questions, informally so to speak. That will give you a chance to get your strength up before we sit you down and take a statement.'

He made himself more comfortable. 'We're concerned, naturally, about the gunshot wound to your knee. How you got it.' He held his hand up. 'No need to answer that yet. We would also like to know what happened. What we know is that you and your friend Walsh were out sailing. The boat has disappeared and you've turned up on your own, without your partner.'

Marsh stopped him. 'How did you know I was sailing with Greg?'

'You had your wallet on you when you were pulled out of the water. Your business cards told us who you were. So, we contacted your boatyard in Freeport. Mrs Walsh has told us that you and her husband, Greg Walsh, went out sailing a couple of days ago.'

Marsh said 'Oh', and laid back on his pillow.

'Naturally she's very distressed. So, as soon as we have the right answers, we can get you back to Freeport.' He was quiet for a while. 'So, what happened?'

'We ran into something,' Marsh explained evenly. It was almost the truth.

'Where?'

Marsh almost told him then, but there was no way he could have made it from the middle of the Caribbean Sea, 800 miles from Cuba without help, and he didn't feel that he could explain the truth to this man. Not yet.

'It happened a few miles offshore, just south of Jamaica.' He brought his hand up to his head. 'I can't remember much about it.' He hoped that Jamaica sounded about right because he really didn't have a clue what landfall it was he saw from the lifeboat on board the *Taliba*, it was simply his own version of dead reckoning.

'What about the gunshot wound?'

Marsh shook his head. 'It's like I told you, Remo; I can't remember.'

A thoughtful expression clouded Francesini's face. 'Your partner's death will have to be explained considering you've been shot. It could mean a delay before you can get back home.'

'What kind of a delay?'

Francesini shrugged. 'Well, because your boat must have sunk close to Jamaican territorial waters and you got yourself shot, it could be a matter for the local Jamaican authorities. Someone will want to know what happened to Walsh. Was there a gunfight? Were you attacked by pirates? There are several possibilities of course.' He lifted his hands in an empty gesture. 'The police there might want to keep you in custody for a week, minimum. They could release you on bail, I suppose.'

Francesini hoped he was piling on the pressure enough to force Marsh to open up about what really happened. Because he had more of an insight into Walsh's affairs than Marsh probably knew, he had to drag every possible gem from the man that he could.

Marsh felt he was getting into something quite messy. Because he had lied when he said the *Ocean Quest* had sunk just off the coast of Jamaica, he had put himself into a difficult situation. If he changed his story now, the police would probably think he was lying anyway just to save his own skin. He wondered if he would be able to stand extensive interrogation and keep coming up with the same story.

He had been lying on his back, propped up by his pillows. He struggled to sit up. Francesini leaned forward and helped him.

'So why is the Immigration Department interested in me?' he asked.

Francesini gave that some thought; now it was his turn to be careful. 'Well,' he said eventually, 'you're on American soil at the moment. After all, it was the Coast Guard that picked you up.'

Marsh realized that his visitor hadn't answered the question, so he decided to stall a little.

'Look, I can't wait around for this mess to be sorted out; I've far too much to do.'

'Like what?'

Marsh looked at him. 'Once we get over this, Helen and I, that's Greg's wife, sorry, widow, still have a business to run. We have a lot of investment in our boatyard. Greg's affairs have to be put in order. You get me home and I'll go to the police myself. I'm certainly not going to hide from anyone.'

Francesini ignored him. 'You're financed through the bank, right?'

'Yes,' Marsh replied warily, wondering where this was going. 'Usually when we take on a commission we ask the bank for a short-term loan. At the moment we have no loans and only a mortgage to service. Why do you ask?'

Once again Francesini ignored him. 'So, what's your business? Fishing trips, cruises, that kind of thing?'

Marsh laughed. 'Goodness me, no; we are an underwater exploration company: Ocean Quest. We take commissions from some of the biggest institutions in the world. We do survey work for oil companies. Underwater geological surveys for construction companies. We sometimes do a commission for international magazines like the *National Geographic*. Our equipment is expensive to buy, expensive to run and expensive to maintain.'

'Have you been doing much work lately?' Francesini asked Marsh.

Marsh glanced at him and shook his head. 'No. Why?'

'Why not?'

Marsh didn't answer for a while. Just lately, Walsh had been putting off some of the smaller commissions that had been coming in. At first it hadn't bothered Marsh, but soon it became something of a stand-off between the two of them. Helen had noticed the tension developing and occasionally Marsh had seen her arguing furiously with her husband.

'I don't know why not,' Marsh replied.

'So what do you do when you don't have any work coming in?'

Deep dives was the answer that Marsh should have said, but not for any institution. For a few weeks now, Walsh had wanted Marsh and Helen to help him on some deep-water compression dives, dives that had something to do with the survey work Walsh had carried out for Hakeem Khan. He had been quite evasive about the reason why he wanted to go over work that had already been completed and paid for, but often muttered something about not being convinced that their figures had been accurate and it wouldn't do to give clients erroneous figures, particularly when they had paid handsomely.

'Oh, we do maintenance around the yard, chase up new business; that kind of thing.' It was a poor effort.

'Did you and Walsh always work on the same jobs?' Francesini asked him.

Marsh shook his head. 'Why?'

'If you worked separately, would you talk to each other about your work?'

'Sometimes, but not always. It would depend on customer privilege and privacy. As long as the money rolled in, we were quite happy.' He wondered where this was going.

'Mercenaries,' Francesini said lightly.

Marsh laughed again. 'Yes, you could say that. But we were never armed.'

'Could anything you or Walsh have done recently be the reason for you getting shot?'

The question went straight to Marsh's heart, like a bullet finding its target. The answer was yes, Marsh was convinced of that now, but he couldn't say why, nor could he explain to Francesini what was running through his mind right then, and the seeds of panic growing inside him.

He decided to get rid of his visitor and try desperately hard to recall some of the many conversations and arguments between him and Walsh in the last few months. Only then would he be able to understand the surprising turn of events his life had taken. He made his excuses to Francesini.

'Look, I'm tired. Can we continue this some other day?'

Francesini nodded and stood up. 'Sure thing.' He put his hand out. Marsh shook it. 'You take care now and I'll see you again.'

He closed the door behind him as he left and Marsh stared at it for ages.

Whoever he said he was, thought Marsh, he was not from the Immigration Department, and the web that he was convinced that

Walsh had been weaving was beginning to unravel with disastrous and dangerous consequences.

Khan stepped into the access hatch through the upper watertight door on the submersible, the *Challenger*. It was in the centre of the submersible and opened into a vertical shaft. At the bottom of this shaft was the watertight door. It was locked mechanically and while the *Challenger* was submerged, the door could not be opened against the pressure of the water until the shaft was flooded. It was the same with the upper hatch door through which Khan was now descending.

He climbed down the ladder and stopped beside a small platform which could be raised into a recess in the curved bulkhead wall of the shaft. Just above him was a small door set flush into the curved wall. He opened it. Inside was a steel snap-hook attached to a metal cable, five millimetres thick. This cable snaked round two pulleys and dropped vertically into a concealed cable drum.

Attached to one of the pulley wheels was a strain gauge. It was a self-contained, waterproof electronic unit converted to read a distance in metres. Khan examined the assembly carefully. It was pivoted so that it could be swung out into the vertical shaft. The pivot and locking pins were as thick as a man's thumb.

Looking down, Khan slipped his feet into two, recessed openings in the chamber wall and raised the platform, carefully latching it into place. He continued his descent until he was at the bottom of the shaft. He spun the locking wheel of the lower door and allowed it to swing open against a small counterweight.

Beneath him he could see the metal plates of the *Taliba*'s forward deck. A small ladder had been attached to the underside of the *Challenger*'s hull at the point where an underskirt would normally be fitted. He went down the ladder and ducked beneath the ballast tanks, then straightened and looked into the brilliant sunshine.

Julio Batista, his chief diver was standing there. He could see that Khan was satisfied with the modifications that had been carried out. Batista was smiling. He was always smiling. A young man, twenty-eight years of age, he had lived most of his life in or around the sea. It was his life. Whether he was surfing, belly-boarding, scuba diving or just swimming, he was never happier. He was a little over six feet tall, well muscled because of his lifestyle and, unusually for a Spaniard, he had tight, blond curly hair.

Julio Batista had worked for Khan now for about three years and was very fond of his boss. Khan trusted him, and he trusted Khan. As much a professional as Batista was, he was also unscrupulous and would work for anybody if the money was right. And as far as he was concerned, Hakeem Khan was the most generous man he had ever worked for. He waited for his boss to speak.

'The modifications are fine, Julio. Perfect.' He put his arm round Batista's shoulder. 'Now I have to ask you to do something for me. I want you to go to Freeport at Grand Bahama, to Greg Walsh's boat-yard. I am hoping you will find Harry Marsham there. There has been an accident that cannot be explained, and his partner, Walsh, is dead. I want you to ask him to pilot the *Challenger*.' Batista was unaware of the 'accident' because he had not been on board the *Taliba* when the freighter collided with the yacht *Ocean Quest*.

Khan knew that Marsh had survived the sinking of the *Ocean Quest* because the news of his rescue had been reported in the *Freeport Press* and on the website of that newspaper.

Batista arched his eyebrows in surprise. 'I thought you would be piloting the *Challenger*.'

Khan nodded. 'I know, I know. But my heart will not allow me to risk it. Marsham is the only man who can do it without training. And you know him; you have worked with him.'

Batista had worked on deep dives with both Marsh and Greg Walsh, several years earlier. He was already an experienced diver when he met them and had always got on well with them. He didn't know that Greg Walsh had died.

'As you say; I know him. I knew Walsh too, of course. I didn't realize he had died.'

Khan gave Batista a friendly pat on the shoulder and looked up at the *Challenger*.

'This is a dangerous business, Julio. Men die.' He looked at the *Challenger* again. 'You have done well, Julio. Allah will sing your praises as he does with all his soldiers. Now go and get Marsham.'

CHAPTER FIVE

Marsh opened his eyes and immediately thought of Helen. He had been dreaming about her and was now able to give substance to the dream. He had always had affection for Helen, but because she was married to Walsh, he had only ever been able to show the normal signs of friendship towards her, despite wishing that he could have known her more intimately. And now he felt guilt because he was giving free rein to his feelings for her despite the fact she had been a widow barely a few days.

It was true that Helen and Greg had argued a great deal lately. Marsh usually put this down to the fact that there was something of a cash-flow problem in the company. Although the three of them were partners in the business, there had never been any formal contracts drawn up between them, and it had always been accepted that Greg was the senior partner.

There had been talk, a few years earlier, of getting round to sorting out their respective roles and legalizing them, but they hadn't been in any hurry. The company had grown from a small outfit to the reputable business it was now. The uniqueness of Ocean Quest, and their extreme professionalism lent itself to the company's success.

Their prize possession was the submersible, *Helena*. It had been named after Helen and built by the McDonnell Douglas Aircraft Corporation in America. Designed by Marsh and Walsh, it had been built for use in the field of geological marine exploration primarily, particularly around deep water wellheads and deep sea rigs.

To recover some of the substantial amount of the cost which had been initially borne by the bank, they had sold the designs to the McDonnell Douglas Corporation after their successful sea trials. Despite that, they still owed the bank a great deal of money.

Now Marsh lay in bed, thinking of Helen and wondering what they were going to do. Once the two of them had got over Greg's death, if that was ever possible, he knew they would have to address the problem of how to continue with the business before the banks foreclosed on them. Their yacht, the *Ocean Quest*, had been an essential part of their assets and would have to be replaced. Another diver would have to be recruited and trained. Contracts would then be required to protect the new recruit.

But, more importantly, and only Marsh knew this, how was he going to deal with the fact that someone on that freighter, in league with Khan, was responsible for Greg's death. And there was no way he could tell Helen.

Helen Walsh stared through the window of her spacious villa, absently watching the gulls weave and turn in the sky above Freeport Harbour. The air conditioning hummed quietly behind her to combat the day's high temperatures. In the garden below her, a gecko scampered across the green lawn and disappeared into the undergrowth beneath the wild jasmine and pink orchids.

Helen was an attractive woman, and the sadness in her face did little to hide her beauty. The peace and tranquillity of the scene that lay spread out before her offered no comfort. In her hand she was holding a copy of the *Freeport News*. It was folded at the article now uppermost in her mind.

Sitting in the room behind her was Inspector Horatio Bain of the Bahamian CID. It was he who had brought the news to her a couple of days earlier of Greg's death. The newspaper had lain on her table since that visit and she had not been able to read it. The inspector picked the paper up and read the article out loud.

'Wreckage has been sighted believed to be the missing yacht *Ocean Quest*, which sailed out of Freeport a few days ago. On board were the two well-known local oceanographers, Greg Walsh and his partner Harry Marsham, owners of the underwater exploration company, Ocean Quest. Harry Marsham was picked up by the US Coast Guard and is recovering in hospital at the Guantanamo Naval Base in Cuba. Hope for Walsh is fading fast although his wife, Helen Walsh, refuses to believe anything has happened to him.' He had folded the paper then and laid it back on the table.

Helen turned away from the window. 'There must be some word, Inspector,' she pleaded. 'I can't believe Greg has not been found. He must have been picked up.'

The inspector sighed. 'I wish there was something I could say which might possibly give you hope. But there has been no report of any ship picking up your husband. Whatever happened must have happened very quickly.' He held his hands out. Like his wishes, they were empty.

'What have you tried?' she demanded to know. 'Perhaps he is already in some hospital somewhere. Maybe he is suffering from amnesia.' She sounded desperate, clutching at unlikely straws.

Despite her anguish there was still an unaffected sexual attractiveness in her which the inspector found impossible to deny and, in the circumstances was totally shameful.

'We have contacted all the countries bordering the Caribbean,' he assured her. 'No one answering your husband's description, has turned up in any medical institution, believe me.' He stood up, anxious now to get away. 'I am sorry, Mrs Walsh, but you have to prepare yourself for the worst.'

Helen's shoulders dropped. She turned away from the window. 'Of course, Inspector, but I can't give up hope.' She looked up, expectantly. 'You won't give up trying though, will you?'

He smiled. 'Of course not,' he answered. 'But it would have been helpful if we had known their plans. As it is, we're guessing.'

'I don't think they intended going anywhere in particular,' she muttered.

'I know; you told us that when you heard the dreadful news.' He was glad to talk, to avoid the more constraining atmosphere.

'And you have checked, haven't you?'

The question was unnecessary, and she had already asked it.

He nodded. 'Of course. There is still a search going on, but we have received no further reports. The Americans are still searching.' He left it at that. There was really nothing more he could say.

Helen knew it, too, and it was pointless talking it round. She saved him further embarrassment by releasing him from his self-imposed obligation.

'Well, thank you, Inspector Bain. I know you will keep looking. And I'm sure you will let me know as soon as you have anything positive.'

She walked to the door with him. Outside in the bright sunshine he paused on the front porch and offered Helen his sympathies. She thanked him and closed the door.

Admiral Starling glowered across his desk at Francesini. His mood was best described as 'concerned'. And when Starling was concerned about something, being close to him was not the most sensible place to be. Francesini was glad that he had the desk between himself and his boss.

'So we've lost it,' Francesini said.

Starling peered at him from beneath dark eyebrows. 'Our intelligence on the ground in Iran insists the bomb was transferred from the helicopter, just inside the border and taken down to the coast.'

'Which means the Iranians probably knew about it?'

'Exactly, but why take it down to the coast?'

'To ship it out.'

Francesini's concern about nuclear devices was always the nightmare scenario that one would be smuggled into the United States and be detonated with all the horrendous consequences. But the best brains in CIA Intelligence played their own war games and were always able to offer up their best guess at how the terrorists would penetrate American security, and get a nuclear bomb inside, and he was reasonably confident that every angle had been covered. Reasonably confident.

But this wasn't one of the CIA's 'best guess' scenarios; Iran was not about to export nuclear bombs to commit a terrorist act. In her present state, she had too much to lose.

'Our human intelligence on the ground in Iran,' Starling told him, 'is spread fairly thin south of the Straits of Hormuz, which is where we believe the device ended up.' He drummed his fingers on the table.

'Remo, this one bothers me. And I'm not getting the right signals from you. If you have anything I should know about, no matter how flimsy, I want to know. Understand? We've got to know where that nuke is heading.'

Francesini nodded. 'Anything that crosses my desk that might be worth you looking at, sir, I'll let you know.'

Starling leaned threateningly across the desk. 'I said "anything however flimsy", Remo, not "anything that might cross your desk".'

He paused. 'I've known you a long time, Remo, and I know how you work. Don't mess me around. Don't play your silly little games where you keep your cards close to your chest. If I thought you were shafting me for some petty, selfish reason; afraid that some other department might get a look at the deck you're holding, so help me, Remo I'd run you through myself. And I mean it. Do I make myself clear?'

So Francesini told him. And, as he opened up on the flimsiest of detail, of how Walsh first came to him, how Walsh eventually agreed to work for him and why a man named Harry Marsham was being kept in hospital in Guantanamo, Starling's expression changed from one of utter astonishment to menacing and threatening intensity.

Marsh felt well enough to go home now. When he had asked the doctor how long he would be kept in, the doctor said that he didn't know. Marsh decided the only way he could leave would be to discharge himself, but he was aware that he was more or less in military custody, which meant leaving the hospital would mean breaking the law – whatever law on Guantanamo Bay Naval Station he would be breaking. And where would he go if he walked out of the hospital?

Marsh was fast coming to the conclusion that there was no legal reason for keeping him there and was determined to leave as soon as he possibly could, but he needed the willing co-operation of the Americans. Just then the door opened and Francesini walked in with another man.

Francesini greeted him cheerfully. 'Good morning, Mr Marsham. How are you this morning? I've brought a colleague with me. James Starling.'

Marsh was surprised at seeing a second man with the so-called man from the Immigration Department. It was definitely becoming intriguing.

'And what do I call you?' Marsh asked, holding out his hand to the admiral.

'Jim,' Starling answered warmly, shaking Marsh's offered hand. 'Most folks do,' he added, ignoring Francesini's sideways glance at him.

The two men drew up chairs and placed them beside Marsh's bed, settling themselves into them.

'And how can I help you?' Marsh asked, expecting Francesini to say something, but Starling continued.

'As I understand it, you and your partner, Greg Walsh, were sailing when your yacht was in collision with something else; possibly a submerged object.'

A not very impressive beginning, Marsh concluded.

'And unfortunately your partner is still missing.' Marsh nodded. Starling pressed on, 'Was there a reason why you were sailing in that area? Where you were hit?'

Marsh shook his head. 'Why do you ask?'

'We are trying to establish a reason for your friend's death.'

'Who said he was dead?'

Starling seemed slightly taken aback at Marsh's response. 'I'm sorry; it was an assumption.' Francesini glanced at his boss. He seemed to be enjoying Starling's lumbering efforts at getting to the point, if indeed there was a point to be got to!

'Were you out fishing? Were you out as some part of a business contract? There has to be a straightforward explanation.'

We weren't fishing, thought Marsh, but he is. Why?

'What kind of straightforward explanation do you want? We were out fishing and I was cleaning my rifle when something struck our boat and I ended up with a bullet in my leg. Will that do?'

Starling stiffened, affronted by Marsh's acerbic response. 'I think you're playing games with us, Mr Marsham.'

Marsh shook his head. 'Seriously, but aren't we all playing games then?'

Starling and Francesini exchanged glances. 'What do you mean?' Francesini asked.

'What I mean is that you are no more from the Immigration Department than I am from the moon.'

This seemed to stun the two men. Then Starling relaxed, realizing that Marsh was too astute to be fooled for too long. 'Why do you say that?'

Marsh shifted his position, pushing the pillows up behind his back. 'Well, first of all, two men in suits do not come visiting from the Immigration Department over an incident which is outside their jurisdiction; an incident which occurred outside territorial waters and one in which there are no witnesses.'

'You told me you were sunk just off the coast,' Francesini complained.

'So I lied. No different to what you two are doing. Now, do you want to tell me who you really are and why you want to talk to me, or do I discharge myself and go home?'

Starling seemed to consider this for a few moments. 'OK, Mr Marsham,' he said eventually. 'We're from the CIA. And yes, you are right; we have no hold over you. Whatever happened to you and your friend is a matter for the Jamaican authorities, and I assume they will almost certainly want to pass it on to your own people. But we are deeply interested in your partner, Walsh.'

This caught Marsh by surprise and another piece of the jigsaw slipped into place.

'Greg? Why?'

'Before I answer that, can you tell me if he has been acting differently lately?'

Greg was on to something, Marsh was sure of that now.

'In what way?' he asked.

Francesini sat forward and held his hand up towards Starling, preferring to take over the conversation.

'Greg Walsh came to me a few months ago. He apparently had completed some oceanographic work for a leading oceanographer by the name of Hakeem Khan although he wouldn't tell me who the guy was at first because he was still honouring client confidentiality. But he was concerned with the figures he was coming up with and what he euphemistically described as "other things".'

'Why would he come to you?'

'Well, he didn't exactly come to me; it was in a kind of roundabout way. He couldn't take his doubts to the Bahamian authorities because he couldn't rely on their security. Plus the fact that he didn't think they would take him seriously. Those were his words, not mine. So he contacted someone he knew who had past links with us; a retired agent.'

Marsh nodded knowingly. 'That would be old Mancini.'

'You know him?'

'Knew him,' Marsh said. 'He died a couple of months ago. Natural causes,' he added. 'So, what then?'

'What he spoke to me about was what you might call low-grade material. But he was quite convinced of his fears. I think he was a bit paranoid. I agreed to put it on file and "keep an eye on it".' He lifted his finger and touched the side of his head. 'But what he told me began to nag away at me. So I contacted him and asked him to do some more probing. Trouble was that his contract with the client had finished.'

Starling stood up and walked to the end of Marsh's bed. He stood there, arms stiff, holding the end of the bed, facing Marsh. 'We want to know if he took you into his confidence. After all, you are his business partner.' He waited, but when he saw Marsh shake his head, he carried on, 'I have to accept that you are telling me the truth, but can you tell me if there is anything that Greg Walsh kept on file that you have access to that might give us a look into his affairs?'

'Like what?' Marsh asked.

'Computer files, hard copies. Something locked away; anything that he would have kept separate from the business. If you can give us his cell phone number, we can check the records of all his calls.'

Marsh knew he wouldn't be able to help them. If Greg had been up to something secret, well, he sure as hell kept it secret from him. Unless Helen knew.

'Look,' he said to the two of them, 'I really don't know that I can help you.'

'You could look through his papers,' Starling told him. 'Look for anything that might connect with—'

'His paranoia? His low-grade intelligence?' Marsh reminded him.

Starling got serious then. 'Marsh, please don't trivialize this. We cannot tell you what it is we are looking for and why. All we can do is ask you to co-operate in any way you can. And I can tell you that your friend's low-grade intelligence has been upgraded. It is now extremely important.'

Marsh knew that this was his ticket home. Once there he could do some rummaging around through Greg's things and tell the CIA there was nothing to be found. He hoped! But now he was beginning to get just a little bit scared. Greg was dead and he had been shot. It just might be a good idea to have the might of the CIA on his side.

'OK,' he said after a while. 'What do you want me to do?'

CHAPTER SIX

Marsh walked into the arrivals lounge at the Grand Bahama International Airport at Freeport wearing a fresh set of clothes that Francesini had bought for him in the navy shop at Guantanamo Bay. The CIA man had used some of the money from Marsh's wallet, which he had had to change for Marsh because of the state it was in after its long immersion in the ocean. He had also arranged for the renewal of Marsh's credit cards, driving licence etc, which had also suffered. Marsh had picked up a few other personal items at the shop on the base which included the small flight bag he was carrying. The whole business meant Marsh had been kept at the base a couple of days longer than he would have liked, but under the circumstances there was little he could do.

He felt happy and relieved to see the sunshine flooding in through the airport windows; he was home now. He was walking with a slight limp, but the doctor had assured him that because it was little more than a flesh wound, there would be no lasting damage and he would be fine within a week or so.

As he walked through the arrival doors into the main lounge, he saw Helen in the crowd. Just the sight of her made his pulse quicken. She was searching the faces of the arriving passengers, her dark hair shimmering as she moved her head. Although Marsh had no luggage and had cleared Customs before his fellow passengers, he was still caught up with those people emerging from other flights.

Suddenly her face brightened as she saw him. She thrust her hand in the air and waved furiously, then moved quickly towards the point where Marsh would come through into the main concourse. He wanted to sweep her into his arms but had to remember she had been widowed barely a week. He smiled and put his arms around her, kissing her warmly on her cheek.

Helen flung her arms around him.

'Oh, Marsh,' she said, 'it's so good to see you.'

She held him very tightly, so much so that he could feel her body pressing into him. It felt so comforting, so natural.

He pulled away and looked at her full in the face. He was aware of the general movement of people around them, most of them being met by loved ones, friends and relatives. How many, he wondered were arriving under the shadow of a death in the family?

'Helen, I don't know what to say.'

She touched his lips with the tips of her fingers. 'Don't say anything.'

She turned, taking hold of his hand. 'Come on,' she said, and together they walked out of the airport into the Bahamian sunshine.

It was two hours later that Marsh had gone through part of his rehabilitation. Helen had insisted that he come back to her villa so she could give him a meal and they could talk about the tragic events that had so swiftly overtaken them both and perhaps make up their minds what they would do.

He had enjoyed a hot bath followed by a cool shower, then a shave and a meal. It was never far from his mind that he was in Greg's house, using Greg's things. While he had been in the bathroom he had been constantly aware of the heady scent of Helen's cosmetics; her soap, bath salts, talcum powder. It reminded him of the time once, years ago, when he had lived with a girl – those heady, lovely days of a golden youth.

They had finished their meal and Marsh was sipping his wine when Helen asked him what he was going to do. He didn't want to spoil the moment by going into detail about the conversation he had had with Francesini and Starling at the hospital, but he felt it was only fair that they, he and Helen, talked about what plans they would make about their own futures and that of the company; whether they should continue as a partnership, sell up, that kind of thing. But first the question of what he had to do immediately had to be dealt with.

'I have to see Inspector Bain,' he told her. 'No doubt he will want to question me about Greg and what happened. He is expecting me, isn't he?'

'Tomorrow,' she told him. 'He said he trusts you otherwise he would have been waiting for you at the airport.'

'I'm honoured,' he said. 'Better than being wanted.'

'You are wanted,' she said suddenly. She lowered her eyes and looked into her hands. Marsh wondered if she had made a mistake; an unintentional statement. She lifted her head, her eyes looking at him directly as though she had reached a decision and was about to tell him something of great importance.

'Marsh, there's something you should know.' She interlocked her fingers and stared down at her empty palms. 'Greg and I were not really very close. Oh, I loved him once, but that was a long time ago.' She looked up and Marsh could see tears on her cheeks. 'Don't misunderstand me, please, Marsh; you can't share your life with a man and not lose something when the love goes and your life begins to break apart. And when he dies, it's still painful. We were good friends once, but lately ...' She paused, struggling to put into words what was in her mind. Marsh waited, knowing how difficult it must be for her. Helen straightened suddenly, as though summoning up the courage to carry on. Her voice softened when she spoke again.

'Marsh, when Inspector Bain told me that one of you had survived, I prayed that it was you.'

She dropped her face into her hands and burst into a flood of tears.

Marsh felt something uncanny surge through his whole body, almost like an electric shock. When Helen spoke those last words, she had been looking directly at him, saying with her eyes what lay deep in her heart. Her admission of her true feelings for him rendered him speechless, and he felt an embarrassing sense of guilt and shame that he was the one she had prayed for in such terrible circumstances.

He realized that Greg's death had been the unkind release she had wanted and now she was ridding herself of the lie they had been living. Now her true feelings for Marsh were out in the open. Helen would not have been callous enough to wish her husband dead, but fate had intervened and she could mourn him as a dear, lost friend and try to pick up the fragments of her shattered life.

Marsh stood up and walked round the table to her. He put his hand on her arm and she stood and reached up to him. They held each other tightly, staying that way for some time, not moving, not saying a word. He could feel her sobbing against him and was content to let her cry.

Soon she pulled away and brushed her tears away with her hands. Then she brushed the front of Marsh's chest in a vain effort to remove the tear stains from his shirt.

'Thank you, Marsh.' She pulled away from him and began clearing the table. 'Things to do,' she said with a sigh. Then she was about to say something else when the phone rang. She stopped what she was doing and walked over to a small bureau and picked up the phone. Marsh waited while she spoke. When she put the phone down, she had a puzzled look on her face.

'That was Mac at the boatyard. There's a man there calling himself Batista; says he would like to speak to you.'

Nothing happened for a moment because the name took a few moments to register. When it did Marsh felt a small shudder run down his spine.

'Julio Batista,' he said, more to himself than to Helen. 'One of Khan's divers.'

Helen still had her hand on the phone even though she had put it back in its cradle.

'Hakeem Khan?' she said. 'Isn't that the guy Greg worked for some time ago?'

He didn't answer because his mind was racing at the implications. What could Batista want with him? He thought about Francesini, the CIA and Greg, and didn't like the answers that were popping into his mind. Then he thought about Helen and realized that any fears he might have could unsettle her if she became aware of them. So he decided to play it out; see what Batista wanted and then worry about it.

'Yes,' he said eventually. 'He commissioned Greg. But we weren't involved, remember...?' His voice tailed off and his mind went on to the figures that Greg had been concerned about after the commission. He put the thought from his mind. 'Well, whatever, let's go and see what Batista wants.'

Helen began to tidy up taking the dirty dishes to the dishwasher. She spent a few minutes making sure everything was in its place, put a vase of flowers back on the table and did a quick check to make sure everything was to her satisfaction. Marsh recalled how Greg would often moan about Helen's mania for making sure the house was tidy before they left.

They walked out of the villa and climbed into Helen's yellow Chevrolet pick-up truck. Helen gunned the motor into life and pulled out of the driveway.

And as they left, neither of them noticed two men sitting in a black sedan watching the house.

Julio Batista thought the boatyard looked slack; no sign of any real work being carried out. The yard was at Hawksbill Creek, right in the heart of the Freeport waterfront. The sights and sounds of the different yards, the gulls flying overhead, boats pulling away from their moorings, the pop-pop of marine diesels, all these were so familiar to Batista, but here at Ocean Quest's boatyard there was an eerie emptiness, as though an invisible hand had covered the yard and shut out all the other sounds.

At the far end of the yard, at the top of a slipway, was the submersible, *Helena*. Batista could see someone working on the 'neck' of the submersible. It was the section that connected the pilot's cockpit – a large, bubble shaped orb of tough acrylic polymer – to the forward section of the sub's pressure hull. The cockpit gave the pilot of the submersible almost perfect, all round vision.

Batista could see no one else in the yard. He had checked the office which was locked. He walked down to the slipway towards the submersible, looking round as he covered the short distance, taking in all the sights and sound. He reached the submersible and called up to the mechanic.

The man stopped working and glanced up to see who was calling. When he saw Batista he acknowledged him. 'Couple of minutes,' he said, 'and I'll be with you.'

The mechanic was actually working on the explosive collar. This was a steel ring, hinged so that it opened in order to clamp it round the neck of the submersible that separated the cockpit from the main body. It had a watertight connector that located firmly into a connecting socket when the ring was locked in place. The collar contained explosive charges. It was fitted around the neck, or thorax as Marsh often called it, and was designed to explode and sever the neck and allow the polymer cockpit to detach itself from the sub and rise to the surface in the event of an emergency.

The collar was always removed after two years, replaced with another, and returned to the manufacturer for inspection and verification. Batista waited until the mechanic had completed the refit and then told him why he was there. The man told him his boss wasn't there but would phone the house. Would he wait? Batista said yes, he would.

It was about thirty minutes later when Batista heard the Chevrolet pick-up drive in to the yard. He had been waiting in the small reception area of the office reading a diving magazine. He put it down and stood up as Helen and Marsh walked in.

Helen introduced herself and Marsh, shaking hands with Batista. She thought how young and good-looking he was. He was casually dressed in clothes that showed a taste for designer fashion. He was tanned from long exposure to the sun, not from a sun bed. The overall effect was of someone of unaffected charm and warmth.

'Hallo Julio,' Marsh said, extending his hand. 'Long time no see. I remember you now.'

Batista smiled and shook Marsh by the hand. 'I was a lot younger then. And the weather was worse than this.'

'You don't look much older now,' Marsh told him with a chuckle.

Batista acknowledged that, and then offered his condolences to Helen. 'Your mechanic has told me what happened; such a terrible loss. I am so sorry.'

Helen thanked him and offered him a drink which he declined.

'So, what is it you want to see us about?' she asked.

'Well, it's Marsh I want to talk to,' he told her.

Helen glanced at Marsh who immediately saw an opportunity to cut Helen out of the conversation on the pretext that it might be something confidential. The truth was that Marsh had a bad feeling about this and didn't want Helen to learn too much. He suggested to Batista that they talk in the office. Helen seemed to pick up on this and said she would talk to Mac about the work on the *Helena*, while the two men got down to the reason for Batista's visit.

Ten minutes later, Helen saw Batista leave the office and walk out of the yard. He waved at her and disappeared through the open gates. Marsh came out of the office and walked down the yard to the slipway where Helen and Mac were in deep conversation.

'Well,' she asked when he reached her, 'do I get to know what he wanted?'

'He offered me a job,' he told her.

'And?'

He shook his head. 'I turned it down.'

Francesini looked across his desk at James Starling. His boss stared back from beneath a deep frown, the mechanics of what Francesini had put to him slowly locking into place. The sunlight filtered through the Venetian blinds, and the sounds of everyday normality could just be heard penetrating the double-glazed windows.

The reality outside the glass was what the CIA swore to protect. The reality inside the room was the truth of how hard and dangerous that protection was to come by. While lunatics and terrorists, mad-hats and wicked regimes threatened the freedoms America had fought for so often in the past, men like Starling and Francesini, and their subordinates, toiled ceaselessly to keep the American dream safe and alive.

And Starling was still trying to come to terms not so much with what Francesini had said, but with what he hadn't said.

'Let me get this straight, Remo,' Starling said, shifting his position in the chair. His finger jabbed the air as he ticked off the step-by-step account of Francesini's dissertation.

'This guy Greg, whom you never knew and who came your way through the retired CIA agent, Mancini in the Bahamas, gets worried about some survey details he has been commissioned to provide, but has nothing to back it up except something based on his own knowl-edge, gut feeling and hearsay.' Francesini nodded; it was about right. Starling continued, 'He was commissioned by someone he wouldn't name at first because of client confidentiality, although he would have done if you'd taken it further at the time. Correct?' Francesini nodded again.

'Greg is talking about oil exploration in the Florida Narrows, right?' Again the nod from the other side of the desk. 'And he talks about explosive drilling? Like drilling through bedrock, shoving in some sticks of dynamite and blowing the rock up. Makes it easier to drill, right?'

'Something like that,' Francesini said at last.

'But we're not talking about the side of a mountain, are we? We're talking about the sea bed. So why are we worried? We know it happens; these are new drilling techniques.' He leaned forward, putting his elbow on the desk and held his hand up, like he was offering a bowl to Francesini. 'But you're worried, aren't you, Remo? Not because of Greg Walsh's figures, the gut feeling and the hearsay bit, but because of that guy who ended up in hospital dying of radiation sickness.' Francesini said nothing this time, so Starling encouraged him. 'Don't leave me in limbo, Remo, remind me.'

Francesini had been smoking a cigar, and for a while it had burned quietly in the ashtray on his desk. He picked it up and drew heavily on it. Starling frowned, he disapproved of smoking, but believed Francesini could do what he wanted in his own office. Although he had to admit to himself that the cigars his subordinate chose to smoke had quite a pleasant smell to them.

'We understand Walsh's concerns,' Francesini began, 'more now than we did when he first came to us. He had nothing to substantiate his worries really. His logic was sound but difficult to accept. Sticks of dynamite didn't come into his reckoning at all, but something bigger and more deadly.' He lifted his hands in a throw away motion. 'But what could we do? He wouldn't tell us who his client was until we agreed to get heavily involved and to keep his name out of it, which we couldn't. Then we found that guy dying of radiation sickness, and the only word he spoke was "Taliba".'

'The name of the yacht belonging to Hakeem Khan,' Starling added for him.

Francesini nodded. 'Quite. We know two nukes have already disappeared and now a third one has been spirited out of the Ukraine. I've been putting two and two together and I don't like what I'm coming up with.'

'Have you run a check on Khan?'

'I did. He appears to be beyond corruption; he's a well-respected oceanographer among his peer group and apparently very good at his job. He doesn't come across as a political extremist, quite the opposite in fact; he's as clean as a whistle.'

'Where is he now?' Starling asked.

'On the *Taliba* somewhere in the south Santaren Channel, about a hundred miles off the Florida coast.'

'And you're keeping an eye on him.' It was a statement. Francesini said nothing.

Starling got up from the desk and walked over to the far side of the office. He picked up the coffee percolator, poured himself a cup, and drank thoughtfully, his mind somewhere in the Santaren Channel. Francesini knew what his boss was like and knew he would be fired up inside, damning Greg Walsh to hell for being so correct about client confidentiality, and damning Khan to hell even though there was nothing at all to pin on Khan. Yet!

Starling put the cup down.

'Remo, I'm going to take this to the President. We've got to board the *Taliba* and check it out. But it will have to be done very carefully.'

'What if the President says no?' Francesini asked.

'If he says no, we'll do it anyway. All I have to lose is my job.'

When Helen pulled up outside her villa, she hadn't given a great deal of thought to Marsh's refusal to work with Batista. It wasn't a prime consideration at the moment, and she felt much happier at the prospect of having him around for some time to come. She knew that they both understood the need to move on with the business, but there were certain legal considerations to deal with before they could begin to re-establish themselves in the unique, dangerous and compelling world of oceanography.

She opened the front door, stepped inside the hall and tossed her car keys on to a small side table. They landed next to a vase of fresh flowers. She turned her head a little as Marsh followed her in. The thoughts that flowed through her mind were rather mixed, but she knew she had to put them aside and begin the task of reaching decisions that would affect both her and Marsh.

She walked though the lounge and into the American-style kitchen.

'Drink?' she called out, peering into the tall refrigerator.

'Coke will do thanks.'

Helen poured a couple of cokes on ice and placed them on the breakfast bar.

Then she stopped and stared at the wall opposite with a strange expression on her face.

Marsh looked at her quizzically. 'What's up?'

Helen was looking beyond him, her eyes fixed on something in the room. He turned but there was nothing he could see. Nothing obvious anyway.

'What is it?' He looked back at her. 'What's up?'

Helen pointed. 'That picture.'

He turned and looked in the direction she was pointing. On the far wall was a framed photograph of their yacht, *Ocean Quest*. It had been taken shortly after the yacht had been delivered to the yard about two years earlier.

'What about it?'

'It's straight,' she told him.

'What do you mean, it's straight? It's supposed to be.'

Helen walked round the breakfast bar and crossed the room. She stopped by the picture.

'This picture never hangs straight, Marsh. Every morning I straighten it and by the end of the day it's crooked again. I used to nag Greg about it. He promised to fix it for me.'

'So? Perhaps you got lucky this time.'

She said nothing but began looking around the room. Then she walked across to a desk beneath a window that had panoramic views of the harbour. She began opening the drawers, one at a time, and carefully searching through them.

As she walked past the small table on which she had tossed her car keys, she stopped.

'The flowers,' she said, 'I never position them that way.'

Then she walked out of the room and Marsh followed.

She was rummaging through her bathroom cabinet when he reached her.

'Helen, what's happened?'

'Bastards!' was all she said, as she brushed past him and went into the bedroom.

Again Marsh followed her and watched as she went through the drawers in her dressing table.

'Have you been robbed?' he asked eventually.

She straightened and shook her head. 'No, I don't think so.' she replied, with a puzzled expression on her face. 'But I'm pretty sure someone has searched the house.'

He frowned. 'How do you know?'

'I know, Marsh,' she said sharply. 'That picture is never straight. I never set my flowers the way they are now. Someone has been searching for something and they have been very professional at it. Well, almost.'

She walked past him and went back into the lounge.

'I know it, Marsh,' she said as he reappeared. 'I know it.'

'Helen,' he said quietly, 'if you're right, then whoever did this will probably have searched my place too.'

'I am right, Marsh.' Her voice was controlled now; not so tense. 'Believe me, I know I am right; but why? What do I have that can be of any interest to...?' She didn't know how to complete the question. 'Well, to whoever has been here?'

Marsh began to feel a little unsettled. Unseen forces were entering into their lives and he didn't like the feel of it one bit.

'I'd better go,' he said quietly. 'I'll need your car.'

Helen nodded towards the keys on the table, but said nothing. Marsh left her standing there, albeit reluctantly, picked up the keys and went outside. He climbed into the pick-up truck, started the motor and roared out of the drive.

The President of the United States sat behind his desk, known as the Resolute desk because it was crafted from the ancient timbers of the old British warship HMS Resolute. He was in the Oval Office of the White House, his National Security Adviser and Chief of Staff with him. They were facing Admiral Hal Maycock, Chief of Defence Staff at the Pentagon, Admiral Dan Gutteridge, Operations Commandant for the United States Coast Guard, James Starling and Remo Francesini. There was an atmosphere of absolute intensity right there in the political heart of America, and if any one of them was at all fazed by the assorted company, it had to be Francesini, because these men were gathered here on the strength of his unbending belief that there could be a draconian threat from a terrorist organization that he had not been able to positively identify and all based on the fears of a dead man and one word from a foreigner dying from radiation sickness.

'Where's the *Taliba* now?' the President asked.

'She's in the Santaren Channel, Mr President,' Starling answered.

'You're sitting on it?'

'Yes, sir. We have her on satellite observation and Strategic Air Command is over flying as well.'

'What do we know of her owner,' – he glanced at a notepad – 'Hakeem Khan?'

'Top man, Mr President,' Francesini answered. 'Clean as a whistle. Been involved with some of the best names in oceanography for many years. He has worked with most of the top institutions here and in Europe.'

'Nationality?'

'He was born in Saudi Arabia. Place called Khamis Mushayt. Little town in the south-west of the country. No political leanings. Considered almost Western in his thinking because of his long association with organizations in the West. Very wealthy man, self made. Sort of man you would be quite happy to invite to the White House, Mr President.'

The President looked at his National Security Adviser. 'What do you think, Jack?'

Jack Corby studied the backs of his hands for a moment. 'Seems to me, Mr President that we're caught between a rock and a hard place. We could lift this Mr Khan and take him away to Guantanamo for questioning, but we'd get so much flak from the international community, particularly the Arabs, we'd have to let him go. If we leave him alone, and he is up to something, and that's a big "if", we could be in serious trouble. We could get the Coast Guard to run a check on the *Taliba* under the pretext of drugs. After all, we're doing it all the time. But probably most important is to get someone who's working with him to tell us what's happening.' He turned his hands up in an empty gesture. 'But how the hell do we get on the inside? What do we know of his crew, their allegiances? What kind of persuasion can we use? After all, if they're all terrorists, and fanatical too, we would be wasting our time.'

Clive Merton, the Chief of Staff came up with a suggestion. 'Why don't we arrange an accident? A collision at sea. Shouldn't be too difficult.'

The admiral reminded him of something he seemed to have forgotten. 'If he has those nukes on board, we could be in serious trouble. God knows what would happen in a collision. After all, an accident like that would not be precise science. No telling if he's got them wired for such an eventuality. He could be planning to steam into port and detonate the bastards. We've got to be so careful. And if it got in to the public domain that there were nukes involved in a collision we'd staged, the Press would have a field day and some heavyweight senators would be waving impeachment papers around. It's far too risky.'

'Mr President?' Francesini lifted a hand. The President nodded. Francesini had the floor. 'I think we should board the *Taliba* and carry out a complete search. We can take the political flak at that level, and it would all blow over anyway. The point is, if he has those nukes on board, he would refuse us permission to board. That would immediately put our tails up and we could sit on his ass and watch every move he makes. We could even put it that a refusal is tantamount to an admission of guilt. A man of his standing wouldn't like that.'

The President looked over at the Admiral Gutteridge. 'Dan?'

'Not a problem, Mr President. You authorize it, the Coast Guard will execute it.'

The President looked back at Francesini. 'What is your gut feeling then, Remo?'

This made Francesini a little nervous. Almost like starting a war on a hunch.

'If I've made a mistake I will be hugely embarrassed and Admiral Starling will sack me. But we know two nukes are missing and we also know a third one has now been officially declared missing. If that third nuke is on it way to the Caribbean, to the *Taliba*, we want to be around when they try to deliver it. But first we have to make sure we're not running up blind alleyways. The *Taliba* could be a red herring of our own making. Of *my* making,' he corrected himself. 'But I sure as hell would want to know,' he added, 'one way or the other.'

CHAPTER SEVEN

James Starling was satisfied with the outcome of the meeting with the President and his advisers. But although he appeared relaxed as he sat in the back of the big Ford sedan as it swept away from the White House, he was far from it. Sitting beside him in the relative peace and quiet of the car, Francesini appeared thoughtful; the memory of his meeting with the President burning fresh in his mind as though he was still in the Oval Office. Perhaps he should have felt nervous and apprehensive because he had staked his entire future career and personal credibility on a hunch; and there was no bigger person to gamble that hunch with than the President himself.

What Francesini had persuaded the President to agree to, meant that he had committed the American Government to an act of what could only be conceived as piracy, without having much more than a credible argument. The famous scientist, Albert Einstein once said that if the theory doesn't fit the facts, change the facts. Well, in this case, Francesini's theory was based on facts that he was unable to change, and if his theory got into the hands of the American Press and hence the public domain there would be more at stake than Francesini's reputation and career. And if he was right, the lives of thousands of Americans could be forfeit if the President failed to act.

Through the blackened, one-way glass of the car windows, he watched the buildings of Capitol Hill flashing past. People hurried along the sidewalks, their lives and destiny probably under their own control, but without giving a thought to people like him and Starling; unconsciously relying on them to let the President know of any threat, real or imagined, that might devastate their very normal, controlled lives.

Mr and Mrs average American. Did they really have two point four children? Who cared anyway whether they had a whole football team; their lives were not there to be played ball with by politicians and security agents who could not do their jobs properly.

The phone rang. Starling picked it up, grunted and handed the phone to Francesini, listening carefully to his subordinate's responses.

'Anything? Nothing? Nothing at all?' He looked up and cursed softly.

Starling watched Francesini pause for a moment, obviously thinking through to the next decision he was going to make. He put the phone back to his ear.

'I'll be over. Set up a meeting with Inspector Bain; he's head of the Bahamian CID tomorrow, first thing.'

He handed the phone back to Starling who put it back in its resting place beside him, and waited for Francesini to tell him what it was all about.

'I had two of my guys search Greg Walsh's home at Freeport; see if they could find anything relating to Walsh's commission with Khan. Marsh's place too. They found nothing.'

The car stopped for a red light. Starling watched the pedestrians crossing, some running, some with their heads down; others deep in conversation with whoever was beside them. It was so normal. It was a beautiful day out there and he would have given anything to be sitting with his wife in their garden, relaxing and their only concern would be what they would be having for their evening meal.

'So why am I not surprised?' he asked, putting the thought away.

Francesini looked at him briefly, and then studied the closely shaved head of the driver in front of him.

'Because you think this is a wild goose chase?' he asked.

Starling chuckled. 'If only.' The car moved off, accelerating quickly. 'If only this was a dream and we could wake up. You forget, Remo, I know you and your hunches; that's one of the reasons I employ you. Whatever Walsh had, if he thought it was important, really important, he would have kept it in the bank or some secure safe somewhere else. And remember, Marsh promised to see if he could find anything in his partner's belongings that could help us.'

It was Francesini's turn to chuckle. 'Sir, have you ever put something away for safe-keeping and when you wanted it, you just couldn't remember where you'd put it? And no amount of searching would turn it up?'

'If I had to admit to that under oath Remo, I would,' he joked.

'Well, I figured that no amount of searching from an amateur like Marsh would unearth it. That's why I decided to get my men to do it.'

'And they found nothing.'

Francesini nodded lamely. 'That's why I'm going over there.'

Marsh phoned Helen and told her that his place had been searched as well, but he didn't think anything had been taken. There was little else for him to do there so he drove back to Helen's place. She took Marsh into town and dropped him off near his bank. She gave him a kiss on the cheek and Marsh agreed to phone her the following day. He watched the pick-up truck disappear and walked into the bank.

About two hours later, Marsh was back at his house when there was a knock on the door. He had almost finished a meal and wondered if it might have been Helen, but it was more wishful thinking than anything else. He opened the door and his heart dropped when he saw Julio Batista standing there. Beside him was one of the biggest men Marsh had ever seen in his life.

'Hallo, Julio,' he said, the surprise evident in his voice. 'What are you doing here?'

'Hallo, Marsh,' Batista replied. He turned slightly and gestured towards the giant standing beside him. 'Allow me to introduce my friend, Malik.'

Marsh looked up at him. 'Malik, just that?' The big man nodded. 'So what do you want, Julio?'

'May we come in?'

Marsh knew from their body language that this was not going to be a social call. He tried to put them off.

'I'm afraid it isn't convenient,' he told them.

Batista shrugged. 'No matter, I can tell you what I want just as easy standing out here.'

'So what do you want?' Marsh asked, the irritation clear in his voice.

'Someone wishes to meet you.' He gestured. 'We have a car. It's only a short drive and we will not take up too much of your time.'

The warning bells began to sound clearly in Marsh's head, but there was nothing in Batista's manner that was threatening. Perhaps that last statement was meant to put him at ease.

'Who wants to see me?'

'My employer, Hakeem Khan,' Batista told him.

Marsh looked at Malik and felt just a slight shiver of apprehension slither down his spine. 'I have already told you, Julio, I don't want a job. I'm sure Mr Khan will find somebody else suitable for whatever it is.'

'He wants you,' Batista insisted. 'And he would prefer to hear your refusal himself.'

'And what makes Mr Khan think I want a job?' Marsh wondered how far this would go before Malik was brought into the discussion, because he was quite certain that was the reason he was there. 'I have plenty to do here.'

Batista shrugged. 'Well of course, that's your choice. But you're a businessman and this is business.'

'What kind of business?'

Batista shook his head. 'I'm not at liberty to tell you, Marsh; I am just the messenger.'

Marsh pointed at Malik. 'So what's he doing here?'

'Why don't you ask him, Marsh? He speaks English.'

Marsh didn't have to; he knew why Malik was there. Marsh either went willingly, or he would be encouraged by Malik.

He shrugged, deciding that discretion might just be the better part of valour, providing he could let Helen know. A kind of insurance, he reasoned.

'What the hell, Julio. OK then. But give me a couple of minutes.'

Batista face broke out into a little smile as though he was relieved that force would not be necessary. 'Fine, we'll wait here,' he told Marsh.

Marsh went back inside and phoned Helen. The phone continued to ring until her answering service came on. He left a message and rang again, just in case she was away from the phone, but there was no reply; just the answering service. He put the phone down and frowned. It wasn't like Helen not to have her mobile with her, or close at hand anyway. He picked up his own mobile phone and went out to the waiting car.

Very little was said as Malik drove. Marsh was content to wait and consider the implications. He knew there was nothing to be gained by asking Batista what was going on, and any other conversation would just be small talk anyway.

Malik drove into the Lucayan Beach Hotel forecourt and swung smoothly into a vacant parking lot. They climbed out of the car and Marsh followed Batista into the lobby. Malik remained in the foyer as Marsh and Batista went straight over to the lifts.

Two minutes later, Marsh came face to face with Hakeem Khan.

Helen knew how a lot of people reacted to being burgled by saying it made them feel unclean for some reason. Now she was feeling traumatized by what she felt was almost like a physical violation, although the burglary was unlike others. Helen assumed that whoever had been in her villa were professionals and they were looking for something specific, although she had no idea what it might be. But she was determined to remain philosophical and try to get things back on an even keel. So it was for that reason that she believed she should carry on as though nothing had happened. Put it to the back of her mind. She decided to have something to eat, but she didn't feel like cooking, so a take-away meal seemed to be the answer.

Helen drove down town to a pizza restaurant that served take-away meals. She ordered a pizza and climbed back into the pick-up. There was a lot on her mind as she drove back to her villa and wasn't aware that a red Buick had been following her for a while.

She turned in to her road and swung into the driveway, bringing the pick-up to a halt beneath the carport. As she stepped out of the truck, she saw the Buick turn into the driveway. It raced up the short drive, tyres squealing and stopped.

A tall, rangy black man got out of the passenger door of the Buick and before Helen could say anything, he walked up to her, clamped his hand over her mouth and threw his arm round her waist. It was so sudden that Helen didn't take it in for a second or two. Then, as the realization of what was happening hit her, she began to struggle violently, but the man was so strong she had no effect on him.

He lifted her off the ground as the driver of the Buick got out of the car and opened the rear door. Helen was flung into the back and her captor threw himself on top of her. She tried to cry out but the force of his full weight on her just caused her to grunt, and he still had his hand clamped over her mouth. She heard the doors slam shut and felt the Buick reverse out of the drive and roar off up the road. Everything had happened so quickly that not even sixty seconds had passed.

Helen's pick-up truck still had its driver's door open and on the seat lay her handbag and the take-away pizza still warm beside it.

'Can I get you a drink, Marsh?'

Hakeem Khan had welcomed him almost like an old friend. He shook his hand warmly and guided him to a chair, then went over to a sideboard where a couple of bottles stood with glasses beside them. There was also a bucket of ice and sliced lemons and limes. Marsh refused the drink. Khan seemed unperturbed by that and left the empty glasses where they were. As he took a seat opposite Marsh, he fluttered a hand at Batista who left the room.

Marsh looked around the hotel room. It was elegant and obviously expensive, but to a man of Khan's wealth it was something he would have been quite used to.

Khan looked the epitome of a man at ease with himself. He had the complexion of someone who had spent most of his working life at sea, which added to the aura of composure. He was wearing cream slacks, a simple cotton shirt and leather, slip-on shoes. Although his hair was grey, it was well groomed and he still had plenty there. His smile revealed a full set of white teeth. On his wrist was a gold Rolex watch, and on the finger of one hand a ring of enormous size. Marsh doubted that Khan wore anything like that when he was at sea.

'Now, Marsh,' he began. 'First I must say I was appalled to hear of your partner's death, such a sad loss; not only to his wife, but to yourself and the business. And you were so lucky not to have been killed as well. Tell me, what happened?'

Marsh wondered how much of the affectation Khan would put on before they got down to the real reason for his visit.

'I remember very little about it,' Marsh lied. 'One minute we were afloat, next thing I know is I wake up on someone's boat. Even now I have a great deal of trouble recalling the moments leading up to the accident. I think we struck something submerged.' It was enough. He doubted if Khan would want to probe deeper.

'Still, it is so sad. And we are happy that you survived.' He brought the palms of his hands together in a soft, clapping motion. 'Now, the reason I have asked you here is to offer you a job. I want you to pilot the *Challenger*.'

Marsh sighed. If he was supposed to dance with joy at the prospect of piloting the submersible for what would prove to be a lucrative salary, it wasn't going to work; Khan would be disappointed.

'I told Batista that I didn't want a job.'

Khan nodded and put his hand up. 'I know, I know. But perhaps Julio did not explain to you the reason why I have asked you.'

'No, he didn't,' Marsh agreed. 'Neither did he tell me why you can't pilot the *Challenger* yourself. You've done it before.'

'That's true, but I would be risking too much. I have a serious heart condition, Marsh. I'm sure you can appreciate the dilemma I'm in. I need an experienced pilot, and there are very few available. If any,' he added

'I didn't know about your heart condition,' Marsh answered honestly. 'Perhaps the result of too many deep dives?'

Khan smiled. 'Old age, I think. But the truth is that I could not risk piloting the *Challenger* in my condition.'

'But why me? Surely there are others that can be trained?'

'Why is not important, Marsh,' Khan replied. 'You are the man I want.'

'Suppose I am already under contract?'

'You are not. If you had been, I would have bought the contract out.'

Marsh whistled softly at the breathtaking arrogance of the man. 'What else do you know?'

'I know that the *Helena* is not ready for sea. And without Walsh you cannot operate her and your company cannot function.'

Marsh shook his head. 'Helen Walsh has worked on saturation dives with me before. We could cope.'

'That is academic,' Khan interrupted. 'You need a good team on the surface. Together the three of you might have been good, but now you are only two.'

Marsh knew he was right. There would be no commissions from the oil companies or ocean survey institutes until he had recruited and trained somebody to take Greg's place. Without money to back the yard, it would be difficult for them to operate again unless he worked for Khan. But Khan was linked to the death of Greg. Even if the man did not pull the trigger, Marsh knew that there was some kind of conspiracy going on and Khan was heavily involved in it. To walk into Khan's lair could be like walking into a lion's den, and from that there would be no way out.

At that moment there was a gentle knock on the door. It opened and Malik came into the room with Batista. Marsh had noticed before that Malik was completely bald, but now it put him in mind of the eunuchs he had seen as a child in the Hollywood films of Arabian adventures.

Malik walked over to Khan, leaned close and whispered something in his ear. Khan's eyes widened in what looked like triumph to Marsh. Naturally he was curious but he could do nothing about it. Then Khan's expression changed and he returned his attention to Marsh.

'Now, what is your answer; do we have an agreement or not?'

Marsh felt uncomfortable. Khan hadn't been listening to him. He glanced at Malik and wondered just what kind of chance he had of bolting for the door. But it was an impulsive thought and he didn't really believe there was any threat in Khan's manner. He pushed the impulse from his mind and concentrated on arguing his way out.

'Khan, you know these kinds of arrangements can take time to work out. Contracts have to be drawn up by lawyers; schedules have to be arranged, contract options, timescales. It isn't simply a question of turning up at the shop and starting work.'

Khan interrupted him. 'We don't have time for that, Marsh. My word is my bond and you will be well paid, I can assure you.'

Marsh bit the bullet. 'The answer is no, I never take on a commission without a legally binding contract. I'm sorry.' He stood up. 'Now, if you'll excuse me, I have a lot to do.'

As he made a move for the door, Malik stepped forward and put his hand on Marsh's chest. Khan gestured to Batista who pulled a mobile phone from his pocket and dialled a number. Marsh looked on, bewildered. Suddenly, Batista thrust the phone at Marsh.

'Take it,' he ordered.

Marsh hesitated and Malik took the phone from Batista and handed it to Marsh. There was no need for Marsh to be told a second time. He held the phone to his ear and listened. For a while there was just a hollow silence. Then he heard the unmistakable sound of a woman's cry of anguish and suddenly she was breathing down the phone. Marsh didn't know what he was supposed to do, so he said hallo. It sounded inane.

'Who's that?' the woman gasped. 'Please, what's happening?'

Marsh felt the pain of recognition strike him like a knife. 'Helen?' His eyes opened wide, still unable to grasp the impact of what he heard.

'Helen?' he called again. 'It's Marsh.'

'Oh Marsh, Marsh,' she cried. 'Tell me what's happening, for God's sake. Why are they doing this to me?'

Her voice stopped instantly and the phone went dead.

'Helen!' Marsh shouted. 'Helen, answer me!'

Malik took the phone from Marsh's hand as easily as taking a toy from a child. Marsh looked at him with a pained expression in his face. Then he looked at Batista and finally at Khan, who was sitting quite calm and unconcerned.

'You bastard!' Marsh shouted and launched himself at Khan, but Malik's speed was so quick that he caught Marsh before he could finish the first step and swung him away from Khan bringing him crashing to his knees with a resounding slap to the side of Marsh's head. The pain roared through his body and took the strength from his legs and he went down like a bag of cement.

Khan got up from his chair and knelt beside Marsh.

'Now you understand, Marsh, what is required of you. The woman will remain our guest until it is finished.'

Marsh knew then that he really had stumbled into the lion's den and that his life was probably forfeit. The thought frightened him, but what scared him even more was that Helen's life probably was too.

CHAPTER EIGHT

Helen felt the man's hand encircle her mouth. With the other he prised the phone from her hand and put it back in its cradle. Without any thought for her comfort he dragged her into a separate room and threw her on to a bed. Then, without saying a word, he turned round and walked out, closing the door behind him. She heard the key turn in the lock.

Although Helen was afraid and bewildered, she had been able to control her fear up until the moment she had heard the sound of Marsh's voice on the telephone. It had affected her deeply, and now she was shaking badly. She squeezed her knees together and hugged them tight to her body until the shaking stopped. She knew that whatever was happening, she would not help herself by losing control.

Helen had no way of knowing who her kidnappers were, or why they had taken her. They were both black and almost certainly local Bahamians. She didn't know what they wanted because neither of them had spoken to her, but she suspected that it had something to with whoever had searched her villa.

Since his return, Marsh had been fairly withdrawn about the accident and how Greg had died. And his instant refusal at the boatyard to consider a job offer from Batista was not typical of Marsh; he would always carefully consider before turning work down. But whatever answers Helen tried to come up with, she knew that it was all conjecture. The only thing that she kept coming back to was the sinking of the *Ocean Quest*, and she was certain that Batista and the men who had snatched her were connected with it.

As she sat huddled on the bed, Helen looked around the room. It was obviously a man's room; the pictures of naked women were testament to that. There were a lot of books and magazines lying on top of a tallboy. A television at the end of the room was still on, but the sound was turned down. There was also a wardrobe with its doors half open, and Helen could see the paraphernalia associated with witchcraft hanging inside it.

Witchcraft, or obeah as it was called in the Bahamas, was a powerful voodoo medicine that was sometimes used with devastating effect among the islanders. It was a practice that was feared by most of the native people. A lot of it was more ceremonial than sorcery, but there were times when it was used as an evil tool in the hands of unscrupulous obeah priests.

There was also a window, which was shut. Not that it made any difference because the room was above ground level and Helen doubted if she would be able to open it because it was probably locked. And if she decided to smash it, her kidnappers would be on her in seconds, so she decided against it.

It was all very odd, Helen thought to herself. Kidnap victims were normally confined in cellars, remote buildings, or even holes in the ground. But this house was in a suburb, so why had she been brought here?

The thought teased her but she found no consolation in it, so she got off the bed and began pacing the room in an effort to make sense of it all. She kicked off her shoes thinking it might help her to reason more clearly. It was something she often did, but this time it didn't help. An hour later she was no further forward and had ended up lying on the bed, now very bored and getting frightened.

Despite her fear, Helen was asleep when the sound of a key turning in the lock startled her and she opened her eyes. One of her kidnappers stepped into the room. He was holding a gun which he was pointing at her. She got off the bed and stood up. The barrel of the gun followed her.

'Out!'

It was all he said.

As Helen went through the open doorway he pushed the nose of the gun barrel into the small of her back. She was taken to a garage at the back of the house. The Buick was parked there with its boot open.

'Get in the trunk,' he ordered.

Helen hesitated. 'Please, I don't have my shoes.'

'Where are they?'

'I kicked them off in the room upstairs,' she told him.

Another voice broke in. 'Leave them, let's get going.'

Again the gun was used as a pointer. 'In the trunk.'

Helen climbed nervously into the trunk of the Buick and her kidnapper slammed it shut. The crashing noise of the lid coming down made her shake violently. The tears were on her cheeks before she realized it as she gave in to her fears and began crying.

The car moved off and Helen felt every bump and turn in the road. Each jolt was a stab of pain until she thought her body could take no more. Numbness settled in and moments of cramp attacked her body as she wondered if the journey would ever end and if she would survive.

Eventually the Buick slowed to a halt and the engine died. The silence pressed in on her and her fear returned. She heard the footsteps as the men got out of the car and then the lid of the trunk was flung open. Helen remained as she was, curled up in the foetal position, terrified. It was dark outside and she could not see the faces of the two men as they dragged her out of the trunk.

She was half carried and dragged to a building, which she could barely distinguish in the darkness. It looked quite small and her own thoughts came back to her about kidnappers taking their victims to remote places. They opened a door and pushed her in. She fell on to a cold, stone floor. She wasn't hurt, but her nerves were screaming out like tautly strung wires.

The door slammed shut and she heard the key turn in the lock. Then she heard their footsteps fading away. The silence returned and she could hear the harsh sound of her own breathing. She pushed herself up and settled her back against the wall, breathing slowly in an effort to calm herself down. And, as her breathing settled and became steadier, Helen heard another noise. It was a soft sound like something moving. She couldn't figure it out at first, but as her eyes adjusted themselves to the darkness, she was vaguely aware of shapes in the room, and vaguely aware of movement.

Then something cold touched the edge of her hand where she was resting it on the floor. She snatched it away and whatever had touched her ran over her legs. She gave in to a piercing scream that bounced around the walls, and for the first time in her life, Helen knew the real meaning of terror.

Marsh found himself walking out of the Lucayan Beach Hotel like any guest would, as if it was the most natural thing in the world. He was accompanied by Batista and Malik. Apart from a few words in the hotel room, Malik had spoken very little. Marsh still wasn't sure of the man's nationality, although he looked like an Arab. Not that it mattered; the man looked tremendously fit and capable. He was also extremely quick when it came to reacting to a threat, and enormously powerful as Marsh could attest to.

They walked together to the parking lots and climbed into the car. It wasn't long before Marsh realized they were heading towards the West End. The road followed the coast for almost twenty miles passing Gold Rock Creek, which used to be the home of the American missile tracking station. It was now undergoing a $30 million transformation into a film studio and theme park.

The road crossed the peninsular towards the golf course and finally into the town of West End. Batista drove to a small bay where several boats were moored. He stopped the car. Malik got out and beckoned Marsh to follow. Batista stayed in the car. Marsh looked at him and was about to ask a question but thought better of it. He shrugged and followed Malik. Batista threw them a friendly wave and drove off.

'Where's he going?' asked Marsh.

'To the airport,' Malik answered. 'He'll be taking the helicopter back to the *Taliba*.'

'So where are we going?'

'To the *Taliba*.'

They walked along the waterfront until they came to a small cruiser; the kind favoured by many tourists for their fishing trips. Malik stepped down into the cockpit and called out. A black face appeared from inside the yacht.

'This is Romulus,' Malik told him, and disappeared into the cabin.

Marsh stepped into the cockpit, said hallo to Romulus and followed Malik into the cabin.

'You want a drink?' Malik asked him.

'I'll have a coffee. Thanks.'

Malik took a bottle of clear water from the small refrigerator for himself. He then made Marsh a coffee from the percolator set on gimbals in the small galley.

The boat's diesel engine suddenly burst into life somewhere beneath his feet and he heard Romulus break into song. He had a pleasant voice and it was a song that Marsh recognized as a local, Bahamian song. The cruiser moved slowly away from the quayside, edging its way along the waterfront until it turned and headed out to sea.

Marsh mentally charted their progress; it was not in the hope that he might learn where they were going, but more from habit. The sun was settling low on the horizon and he could just see faint shadows on the edge of the sea where it merged with the darkening sky.

Malik had said little, but Marsh had tried to make a judgement of the man from his manner and behaviour. A couple of times he had caught Malik watching him, but when challenged, Malik shrugged it off. As much as he tried, he could get nothing out of the man, so he gave up. He settled back on one of the leather chairs in the stern of the boat and tried to figure out the events of the previous week.

He tried to fit it all into a sane, logical pattern, but there was no logic because he had nothing to go on other than the fact that Hakeem Khan was involved in something unseemly, and certainly crooked; crooked enough to warrant the death of Greg Walsh and Helen's kidnap.

And it was staggering to think that Khan was quite willing, despite his international reputation and unblemished character to sanction Helen's kidnapping just to get Marsh to pilot the *Challenger*. None of it made sense.

Marsh gave up the effort of trying to work out why all this was happening. He gave up and eventually fell asleep, but he dozed more than slept. He stirred as soon as he felt the speed of the cruiser fall away and the engine note change. He stood up and looked out over the sea. They were closing in on the *Taliba*.

Romulus angled the boat in skilfully and tied up alongside the ship. Malik beckoned Marsh and they clambered aboard the *Taliba* using the short rope ladder. He heard the cruiser pull away as Romulus increased power to the diesels. He glanced over his shoulder and saw the boat moving off, gathering speed as it headed back to the mainland. He also noticed as he stood on the deck that the helicopter was on its landing pad, which meant Batista and Khan were probably now on board.

Malik took Marsh immediately to the bridge where Captain de Leon was waiting. He greeted Marsh rather formally and asked them both to follow him through to his cabin. When they were settled there, de Leon offered Marsh a drink. Marsh noticed that he had completely ignored Malik.

'Thank you for joining us, Marsh,' he said surprisingly. Marsh wondered if de Leon was fully aware of the facts, but chose not to say anything with Malik standing there. 'I know of your reputation and I am sure it means we shall see our project through to a successful conclusion.'

'What's the project?' Marsh asked him.

De Leon's face showed just a trace of sympathy. 'I'm sure Mr Khan will apprise you of everything you need to know. But with regard to the *Taliba*, you must understand that although this is Mr Khan's boat, I am the captain and you, as a member of the crew, are my responsibility. So you obey my orders. Now, unless you have any questions, Malik will show you to your quarters.'

Marsh smiled. 'Captain de Leon, I have a million questions, but I doubt if you'll answer any of them.'

De Leon became quite serious. 'Your role here is quite important, but I can only answer questions relating to the *Taliba*. Anything else you must direct to Mr Khan.'

'I understand,' Marsh acquiesced, 'believe me. But I do need some clothes and toiletries. I was obliged to leave in a hurry, you see.'

Whether de Leon saw or not, wasn't quite clear to Marsh, but the captain agreed to supply him with everything he needed.

'Malik will show you to your quarters. We'll talk another time.'

Marsh could feel the gentle throb of the *Taliba*'s engines beneath his feet as she got under way again. He put his glass down and followed Malik out of de Leon's cabin. As they walked through the small bridge, Marsh looked forward. He could see the helicopter sitting forward on the prow of the ship. And on the open deck space between the fo'c'sle head and the bridge, he could make out the shape of the *Challenger*, the sister ship to the *Helena*.

He felt a small sensation in the pit of his stomach. It was the thrill of anticipation that he would soon be piloting the submersible. He was trying to view it all with a professional detachment, allowing only those feelings to hunt around his senses, but he was aware of a strange excitement coupled with an edge of fear.

He thought about Helen and wondered if they would both have the strength and courage to see this reckless, dangerous adventure through and come out of it alive.

Inspector Bain stood in the driveway of Helen's house looking at her orange pick-up truck. There seemed to be police officers everywhere. Some were dusting the Chevrolet with fingerprint powder, others scouring the vehicle and the surrounding area, all looking for minute clues. From time to time, one of them would pick something up and drop it into a small, plastic bag. There were others inside the villa. And, as usual, there was a group of curious onlookers standing beyond the line marked out by fluttering police tape.

A witness to Helen's abduction had come forward and was talking to a police sergeant. Bain walked over to them and interrupted their conversation, smiling in a rather condescending manner.

'Mr Rackham,' he said to the witness, 'would you mind telling me again exactly what happened?'

'Of course not,' Rackham answered. 'I didn't see a great deal actually; I just happened to glance across the road when Helen, ah Mrs Walsh,' he corrected himself, 'drove in.'

'And where were you sir?' Bain asked.

Rackham pointed to a villa across the road from Helen's house. 'I was on my roof. Some work I had to do,' he explained unnecessarily. 'I saw Mrs Walsh get out of her car and then this Buick raced up the drive. They grabbed her.'

'Who grabbed her, Mr Rackham?'

'Two men. One jumped out of the Buick and grabbed her and threw her into his car while the other one held the door open. It all happened very quickly.'

'Would you recognize the two men again?'

Rackham shook his head. 'I'm not sure.'

'Were they black or white?' Rackham said they were black. 'And what about the number plate of the Buick? Did you get that?'

He shook his head. 'Sorry, no. I didn't think about that. You don't, do you?'

Bain said 'No you don't' and thanked him. 'Would you give the sergeant your personal details, please? He'll want a statement signed. You can do it at the station.'

He spun on his heels and walked over to his official car. He was furious because Rackham had failed to take the details of the car and wasn't sure if he would be able to identify the kidnappers either. How could a witness be so blind, he wondered?

But more worrying for the inspector was why Helen Walsh had been kidnapped. He was quite sure that it couldn't be for money, although that was more of an educated guess. It couldn't possibly have anything to do with her late husband's dreadful accident. And gang warfare was out of the question as were drugs. So what was it?

Bain walked down the drive and ducked beneath the police tape. He paused for a moment, imagining exactly what had happened. Then he shrugged and climbed into the back of his police car. He ordered the driver to take him back to police headquarters, and wondered if he would ever see Helen Walsh again.

CHAPTER NINE

The sun had lifted over the horizon and was flooding the Santaren Channel in a light of pure gold. The *Taliba* had left the Bahamas behind and was heading south-west towards the open waters of the Gulf. The sea lifted gently and a fine breeze swept across the water, picking up little wavelets that tossed their heads in flecks of white surf. The gulls weaved unseen patterns around the *Taliba*, waiting to pick up any scraps of food that might be thrown overboard by the crew.

When Marsh had arrived on board, the *Taliba* had remained on station for a while before heading out towards the open sea. Marsh had been quartered in crew accommodation and given assurances that he could move freely around the ship as he needed with the exception of the sea gallery where he would need to be accompanied. He was given no explanation why.

His cabin was quite small. Marsh hadn't expected anything else because space was always at a premium on board ship, particularly for the crew. He had a single bunk with drawers beneath it plus a tall, single wardrobe and a small bedside locker. There was a sink up against the bulkhead, but for his own ablutions, he would have to share the communal showers in the alleyway that ran between the crew quarters.

The bed was made up for him. He lay on top of the covers for a while, reading a magazine; one of several that had been left for his use on the table in the cabin. When he did finally succumb to drowsiness, he slept fitfully, worrying about Helen and worrying about his own predicament. He lay awake for much of the time during the night, dozing fitfully and, as dawn light began to flood into his cabin through the porthole, he decided there was little to be gained by lying in bed, so he got up and went off to find some breakfast.

One thing Marsh promised himself was to remain professional about this new turn of events. Whatever happened, it behove him to act in exactly the same way as he would if he had been working on one of his own commissions on board the *Helena*. It was vitally important that he kept this attitude to the forefront of his mind, because to let his concentration wander when diving in the submersible could cost him his life and possibly that of the divers who would be working with him.

After he had eaten and completed his morning shower, Marsh went up to the bridge. It was his intention to open up a dialogue with Captain de Leon about studying charts and way points with a view to getting himself into the right frame of mind for when he began trial dives with the *Challenger*.

He had been chatting with the captain when the sound of the bridge squawk box cut into their conversation. It was the forward lookout.

'Bridge, there's a Coast Guard cutter off the port side. It's about five miles distant, four o'clock.'

Captain de Leon walked out on to the port wing of the bridge, taking a pair of binoculars with him and scanned the sea until he could see the Coast Guard ship heading towards them.

He hurried back into the bridge and picked up the telephone that connected him directly to Khan's cabin. 'Sir, this is the bridge. There's a Coast Guard cutter off the port side. They're heading straight to us.'

Khan heard the buzz on his speakerphone and thumbed the talk switch. As soon as de Leon had finished the message, he told him to stop engines and get Malik into the sea gallery.

'Remind Malik to turn the transponder on before he lowers the device. And be sure to mark the position as we planned. Be quick,' he added.

On the bridge, de Leon ordered a crewman to get down to Malik's cabin as he rang the engine-room telegraph. Marsh watched as an obviously well-rehearsed plan swung into action. He felt the *Taliba* begin to slow as the engine room killed the power according to de Leon's telegraph signal.

Marsh turned and looked out through the windows and saw the Coast Guard cutter coming towards them. Its demeanour was one of determination and it was obvious that the *Taliba* was their quarry. It came up in an arc behind them until it was level with them on their port side. Marsh could see the name of the cutter quite clearly. It was the *Lincoln*.

Below decks, Malik had hurried down into the large room they called the sea gallery. Inside the sea gallery on the floor were two large doors. Malik closed the watertight door behind him as he stepped into the sea gallery and pushed a button situated on one of the bulkheads. Immediately a motor burst into life and the doors began to open, swinging down into the sea beneath the hull of the ship. Sea water sloughed in and ran down into the scuppers on either side of the deck.

Malik than sprinted to the end of the gallery where two nuclear bombs were stowed in a frame and locked together like a pair of conjoined twins. They were mounted on a steel pallet which was attached to a block and suspended from a running block on a gantry that spanned the open doors in the floor of the sea gallery.

Malik released the clamps holding the bombs in place and lifted the hoist controller from its stowage point. He operated the up mechanism and the steel hawser that was attached to the pallet by an open hook, shuddered into life and lifted the bombs clear of the deck.

Malik then used the traverse button to manoeuvre them out over the open space. Once it was hovering over the opening, he lowered the pallet into the sea. He let the hoist motor run for what seemed like an eternity, but was only about ten minutes, when suddenly the hawser went slack.

Once the heavy pallet was resting on the sea bed, and the weight was no longer taken up by the steel rope, the open hook swung free. Malik immediately reversed the motor and lifted the steel rope back up into the gallery. As the hook appeared above the waterline, Malik dashed over to the button that operated the doors and rammed his thumb against it. The doors closed immediately.

The sea water stopped swamping into the gallery once the doors were shut and the last residue was sucked noisily through the scuppers by the bilge pumps.

Satisfied that the job was done, Malik left the sea gallery and made his way up to the bridge.

'Coast Guard vessel, *Lincoln* to motor vessel *Taliba*! Do you read me? Over.'

Marsh's attention was drawn to the bridge speakerphone. He saw Captain de Leon pick it up and thumb the talk button.

'This is Captain de Leon on board the *Taliba*. What's your business, *Lincoln*?'

'We wish to board you, *Taliba*. Over.'

'This is *Taliba*. State your business, *Lincoln*. Over.'

'This is the United States Coast Guard working for Homeland Security in defence against drugs and terrorist activity. We are empowered to board and search any vessel operating within these waters. Over.'

'We are not terrorists, *Lincoln*, and we are not carrying drugs,' came de Leon's stern reply.

De Leon felt Khan's presence behind him. He turned round. 'They want to come aboard,' he said quietly.

Khan nodded. 'We were prepared for this eventuality, Captain. We have no choice; we have to let them board us.'

'How do you want to transfer, *Lincoln*?' de Leon called over.

'Drop a ladder over the side. We will come over in the dinghy.'

The talking was over. The two ships parted to allow a reasonable distance between them. Marsh watched the cutter lower an inflatable craft with four sailors in it. The crew of the *Taliba* dropped two rope ladders over the side. Within thirty minutes of seeing the cutter, four American Coast Guard officers were boarding the *Taliba*.

Marsh was intensely curious like anybody would be, but was not privy to whatever was unfolding below decks. Nor would he be allowed to. De Leon had escorted the Coast Guard officers, informing them before they went searching around his ship that none of them was allowed to be unescorted.

Marsh would have given almost anything to know what the Americans were up to. He even harboured a naïve wish that this was to be his and Helen's rescue, with Khan being denounced and arrested for whatever evil practice he was involved in. But it was not to be. He remained on the bridge with Khan and Malik until the Americans appeared on deck with de Leon.

It was almost an hour after boarding the *Taliba* that the Americans finally disembarked and were on their way back to the cutter. The Coast Guard captain watched the *Taliba* pull away from them as he ordered his helmsman to set a course in the opposite direction.

When the boarding party were back on board the cutter, the captain left the bridge and went down on to the deck to speak to them.

'Well?' he asked.

'Nothing, sir,' his bosun answered. 'She's as clean as a whistle.'

A few minutes after the boarding party left the captain, two other navy men appeared. They were wearing wet suits and had obviously been in the water. They saluted the captain.

'Well?' he asked. 'Anything under there?'

They both shook their heads. 'All that's on that hull are a few barnacles and not much else. There's certainly nothing hanging underneath her.'

He nodded, satisfied; job done. 'Right, you get yourself changed and I'll phone the admiral.'

Francesini sat opposite Inspector Bain having introduced himself and thanked him for seeing him at relatively short notice. As head of the Bahamian CID, Horatio Bain had a well-appointed office within the heart of the police headquarters in Freeport. Francesini could see trappings of power, but decided it was all relative; the chief of detectives in New York would probably inhabit a far superior office and hold the rank of captain, yet still do a similar job to the inspector here in Freeport.

Bain ordered tea for them both and assured him that he was happy to help the CIA in any way he could and having dispensed with the niceties asked Francesini how he could help him.

Francesini wanted to explain everything he could to the big policeman, but he felt constrained in that much of what he knew was either guesswork, intuition or a State secret. But he did his best to accommodate the inspector's questions and fill in as many gaps as he could. Francesini's emphasis was on the fact that Greg Walsh had come to him, not the Bahamian authorities, because he believed the Americans might be under a terrorist threat which was to be launched from the Grand Bahamas. It was a poor lie, but there was little else Francesini could tell him; or wanted to for that matter.

While he was talking, a young police officer brought in a tray with two cups of tea, milk and sugar on the side. Bain was not only polite and reassuringly attentive, but seemed a genuinely nice guy too. He put sugar into his own cup, splashed a little milk and lifted the cup to his lips. He sipped the first mouthful of tea and asked Francesini what he thought he could get from Marsh at this time that he had been unable to get when Marsh was in hospital in Miami.

'I did ask him to have a look through his partner's papers,' Francesini admitted.

'And did he?'

Francesini shook his head. 'I've no idea. I rang him a couple of times before I flew over here, but he's not answering his phone.'

'There's a good reason for that, I believe,' Bain said, putting his cup down with a degree of care. 'You see, Marsh has disappeared.'

Francesini sat bolt upright in his chair. 'Disappeared?'

Bain nodded and told Francesini about Helen's kidnapping and believed that Marsh's apparent disappearance was linked to it.

Francesini was used to knock-backs in his profession, but the speed of this development took him by surprise. He was quiet for a while as he tried to digest the implications of what the inspector had just revealed to him. And Francesini had to admit that everything had just got worse. The amazing turn of events had deepened his worry that Greg Walsh's fears were now taking on a life of their own and running away from him.

'Do you have any idea—?' he began, but his question was cut short because Bain was shaking his head already.

'We have a witness to Helen Walsh's kidnapping, but unfortunately he can't be relied on.'

Francesini took a cigar from a leather cigar wallet. He asked the inspector if he could smoke. Bain nodded and Francesini began the task of lighting it. Bain picked up his cup again and drank from it.

'What haven't you told me?' Bain asked him suddenly, an expression on his face that was a mixture of enquiry and threat.

Francesini nearly choked on his cigar. 'I'm sorry?'

Bain put his cup down, his action quite positive. Now he seemed to be getting down to business.

'Please do me the courtesy of not assuming that I am a little policeman on an island that has only to deal with tourists, Mr Francesini.' The expression on his face changed and Francesini could see a hardness there that belied the inspector's urbane nature. 'The CIA does not send one of their top men on a boy's errand. You must be worried about something that you haven't told me about. Whatever this threat is to your country, it must be more serious, and closer, I would think, than you are prepared to admit. And I don't believe the threat comes from this island.'

He opened a drawer in his desk and pulled out a file. Francesini watched, but said nothing. Bain laid the file on the desk in front of him and opened it.

'Does the name Mancini mean anything to you?'

Francesini was stunned. He thought he had been controlling the conversation; just feeding the inspector with a little information, just sufficient to make it appear that he was treating the inspector as an equal, but now he knew how wrong he had been: the inspector had been playing him along and allowed him to stumble into a bog of his own making.

'Should it?' he asked, still clinging grimly to a sense of some dignity.

'Mr Francesini, we can either be completely frank with each other, or we can terminate this interview here and now. It's your choice.' He opened the file and began reading.

'Harry Mancini died a few months ago. He was a retired CIA agent. His widow is a natural Bahamian; that's why they retired here. Last week, Mancini's widow brought some files into us that she didn't under-stand, but was intuitive enough to know that they could be important.'

He tossed the file across to Francesini who took it and looked through the pages, turning them slowly. Some of it was a technical report on geological survey work, obviously carried out by Greg Walsh, that was beyond Francesini's limited knowledge. But there was a summation at the end that had Walsh's signature at the bottom of the page. He knew then that this is what he had hoped his men would find when they had searched Marsh's home and that of Walsh's widow, Helen.

And he knew that it would be dynamite once it had been broken down into everyday English.

'You know what this is?' Francesini asked him tentatively.

Bain reached over and retrieved the file. 'I had somebody I know, not connected with the police department, look over it for me. He told me it was too heavy for us to deal with. He said it was dangerous.'

He laid the flat of his hand on the file and stared at Francesini for a few seconds.

'It has been on my mind for a couple of days now,' he said. 'And it has made me think a great deal about whom to pass it on to. I suppose I must have been waiting for a "trigger", you know; for something to happen that would convince me how serious this file was.'

Francesini could understand his dilemma. 'And it's happened, right?'

Bain nodded. 'It has, and I'm prepared to let you have the file, but not until we have reached a complete understanding. Do you agree?'

Just then a young officer knocked at the door and came in with a folder which he laid on Bain's desk.

'We've had some luck with the fingerprints, sir.' He glanced at Francesini for a moment and was obviously not impressed with the smoke from Francesini's cigar.

'They found a palm print and four fingerprints on the door of the pick-up truck. There were no others like it on the car. We checked the witness's statement and it's possible the prints belong to one of the kidnappers.'

'Do we have a face?' Bain asked.

'Yes, sir; Sweeting Maclean.'

Francesini thought he saw a flash of dismay cross the inspector's face. He tried not to let it bother him. Bain nodded thoughtfully, and then he looked up at the young policeman.

'I want him tailed, but not picked up yet. Keep me informed.'

'Could that be our man?' Francesini asked, when the young officer had left.

'There's every chance,' Bain answered hopefully. 'Maclean has a record as long as your arm, but he's been quiet lately. He was mixed up in a big obeah scandal a couple of years ago. That's our local witchcraft,' he explained. 'What you might call voodoo. He nearly went to prison for a very long time, but he got off on a technicality.'

'A good lawyer?' Francesini asked euphemistically.

Bain nodded. 'Bent, too.'

'What about this Maclean guy, is he a witchdoctor?'

Bain laughed. 'Maclean an obeah man? No, an obeah man would not have got himself involved in kidnapping; too many other willing hands to do the work.'

'Like Maclean,' Francesini observed.

'Exactly!' Bain replied. 'Just like Maclean.'

'So what will you do now?' he asked.

Bain almost shrugged. 'We really have to let him show his hand. Perhaps lead us to where he is hiding Mrs Walsh. If he has her, of course; we've no proof yet.'

'Will you let me know once you have something positive, Inspector?'

Bain agreed. 'Yes, as soon as we know, I'll let you know.' He picked up Francesini's business card and put it into a desk drawer.

'As soon as we can.' Then he picked up the folder he had been given by Mancini's widow and handed it to Francesini.

'Here, you'd better take this.'

Francesini took it from him. 'I'll be in touch,' he promised. He was about to leave when Bain stopped him. 'You haven't finished your tea.'

Francesini smiled a broad smile. 'Thanks, Inspector, but no thanks; I never touch the stuff.'

Bain laughed out loud and stood up. He reached over the desk and shook Francesini by the hand. For all the presumption of the American, he decided he couldn't help liking the man. He waited until Francesini had left his office and then opened the file the young policeman had brought in and began reading about Sweeting Maclean.

When Helen woke up, her mind held back reality for a brief moment and she could not remember where she was. A grey light filtered into the room and washed over the shapes, distorting them and making it difficult for her to recognize anything. Her side ached abominably where she had lain on the hard, concrete floor and she eased herself up in to a sitting position.

Then slowly, the horror of what had happened to her began drifting into her mind, filling in the edges and supplanting the vagaries of her first conscious thoughts. And, as Helen recalled those moments of the previous day and night, so she began to feel the timbre of apprehension and fear.

As a result of lying on the hard floor the aches and pains began to surface as consciousness returned. Her side was numb and elsewhere she could feel stiffness and pain. She moved to one side, turning on to her knees and then stood upright. Then she remembered that something in the room had scared the hell out of her the night before, and the awful smell that seemed to seep into every pore of her body.

She scanned the room with her eyes only, not moving her head or the rest of her body, trying to identify the shapes that were beginning to take on a life as the light brightened, seeping in through the cracks in the door and through two very small, dirty windows. There was a table and a couple of chairs in the room, some cages and small boxes. She turned round, looking behind her and saw more cages. Some were hanging precariously from the walls.

She looked round for the door and moved towards it, placing each foot carefully in front of the other, edging towards the door until she could lean her back up against it, and watched the dawn lift the grey curtain and bring light into her strange prison.

It wasn't long before Helen was able to discern some movement in the cages. There were animals in them, but she was unable to see what kind and she continued to watch with a mixture of fascination and fear. Then the truth came to her and she realized she was almost certainly in a place belonging to an obeah man.

In the normal world outside, Helen had no reason to believe in or fear the witchcraft of the islands, but she understood the mortal dread it could instil into native Bahamians. Helen was Bahamian too, but she was white and considered her European origins to be a sufficient defence against the voodoo magic. But now she was surrounded by it and felt threatened.

The light from outside was brightening through the two small windows which were set high in opposite walls. They were not barred but hanging beneath them were more cages containing rats and lizards. She could hear snuffling noises made by the rats. Helen had thought briefly about pushing the few sticks of furniture up against the wall and trying to get out through the one of the windows. But the thought of those rats and lizards made her flesh crawl.

As the light improved she could see brightly coloured masks hanging from hooks on the walls. Their distorted faces stared at her and seemed to mock her. There were chanting sticks and costumes, vicious-looking knobkerries and several animal skins. She could see dead chicken carcasses bloated with maggots and could hear the buzz of flies. One wall was splattered with blood above a wooden butcher's table and huge cockroaches scurried leisurely over the blood and dead flesh. A meat axe had been driven into the wooden top, its blade stained black with dried blood.

She looked away and saw something scurry along the wall against the floor, its black fur shining wet. She closed her eyes and felt the sting of tears. Her skin began to prickle as if a thousand needles were jabbing at her. The noise of the buzzing flies seemed to grow with an added intensity as they moved over the carcasses and the blood.

Finally the awful smell of decay and animal excreta, violence and death tore into her nostrils until she could stand it no longer. She flung herself at the door, tearing and beating at it, begging to be let out.

Sweeting Maclean could hear Helen's screams as he ambled across the yard to the hut where he had thrown her the night before. There was no hurry in his leisurely pace; he felt good and he knew he was going to make a lot of money out of this one.

He reached the door, unlocked it and pulled it open. Helen literally fell into his arms screaming and sobbing. She pushed herself away suddenly when she realized whose arms she was in. Maclean smiled and grabbed a handful of Helen's hair. He twisted it spitefully, bringing her to her knees. Then he back heeled the door shut and brought his face close to Helen's.

'You be a good girl, missy, and I won't hurt you.'

Helen's face was drawn back in pain. 'Oh please,' she cried, 'you're hurting me.'

Maclean pulled her to her feet and loosened his grip on her hair. 'We're going into the house now, missy; got to keep you clean and fed.' He pushed her forward, still holding on to her hair and led her over the rough ground to the house.

Sweeting's place, if indeed it was his, was little more than a single storey dwelling, badly in need of a coat of paint and some tender loving care. But in its location, fairly remote from what Helen could see, it was unlikely to attract more than just a cursory glance from the man who was now propelling her towards it.

Once inside, Helen was allowed to use the bathroom. Maclean told her she had thirty minutes. There was nothing inside the bathroom that Helen could have used to help her escape. As soon as she realized this, she used the time to luxuriate beneath a hot shower and wash the stench and feel of the hut from her body, and tried to forget the pain and torment she had been subjected to.

Maclean gave her breakfast after that. It was cold but Helen was starving and enjoyed every morsel. She noticed that her kidnapper kept looking at her. It troubled Helen because she knew exactly what was going through his mind. She tried, not very successfully to ignore his lustful stares and enjoy the frugal meal he had put before her.

While she ate, she kept wondering in the back of her mind where the other kidnapper was and what they planned to do with her. She decided there was nobody else in the house, so she tried talking to Maclean, but he said very little. What did bother Helen was the way in which he kept smiling at her.

When Helen had finished eating, Maclean took her into a bedroom.

'You got a choice, missy,' he said, once they were in there. 'You be good and you can stay in here. You be bad and you go back there.' He jerked a thumb over his shoulder. Helen knew where he meant; he didn't have to be specific.

'I would prefer to stay here if I have to,' she told him.

Maclean smiled and Helen felt a chill run through her. He placed his hand on the back of her neck and began rubbing it gently.

'We're gonna be together quite a while, missy,' he said softly.

Helen tried to move her head away from him but he tightened his grip. He moved his other hand up to her breast. Helen gasped as he squeezed it.

'Don't,' she pleaded. 'Please don't.'

'It's a pretty dress,' he said, and pulled her closer to him. 'Pretty little titties.' He held her tight and ran his hand down the back of her dress, popping each button until the dress fell open. Helen felt power-less in his frightening embrace. Then he relaxed and pulled the dress from her. Her breasts seemed to erupt from the material and she could see the fire burning in his eyes as he looked at her semi-naked body. His mouth opened and the saliva on his tongue moistened his lips as an atavistic urge gripped him.

Helen screamed and slashed her fingernails across his face. It stopped him but only for a few seconds. Then suddenly he picked her up and threw her on the bed. Holding her down with one hand he curled his fingers into the line of her silk briefs. He pulled them from her and Helen was powerless to stop him. She bucked wildly and Maclean seemed to become mesmerized by the sight of her open legs. The dark flash of her groin meant sensual pleasure to him and it drove him into a frenzy. He groped at the buckle of his trouser belt and fumbled madly as he straddled her and reached into the opening of his trousers. Helen fought wildly, but Maclean was too strong for her. She screamed for him to stop when suddenly a voice broke through her cries.

'Maclean!'

He stopped as the voice called a second time. He held that pose for a moment, one hand pushing down on Helen's chest, the other inside the opening of his trousers. He turned his head away and listened again as the voice came a third time. For a moment Helen thought he was too hyped up to stop and would rape her before going outside to see who was calling him.

But suddenly he relaxed and got off the bed and tidied himself up.

'Get your clothes on,' he ordered Helen, and left the room, locking the door behind him.

Helen crawled from the bed and gathered up her clothes, blinking the tears from her eyes. They ran down her cheeks and on to her naked body. The question she had asked herself earlier about the other man, the other kidnapper was answered; it was almost certainly the person who had called for Maclean.

She finished dressing and sat on the bed, trying to compose herself, but her fingers trembled violently as she tried to calm herself down. Her kidnapper had made his intentions very clear and she knew it was only a matter of time before he returned to finish what he had started. A violent shudder ran through her body and she began to feel quite unclean.

Maclean soon returned and told her to get up. He grabbed her hair again and dragged her out of the house and across the yard to the hut. He opened the door of the vile shack and pushed her in.

'I have to go away for a couple of hours, missy.' He stood in the doorway like a mountain, his chest still heaving with the tormented desire he had for her. 'When I come back I'm gonna finish what I started.'

'You can't,' Helen shouted at him. 'When they release me you'll be wanted for rape as well.'

Maclean looked at her in an odd way. 'Release?' he echoed. 'What makes you think we are gonna release you, missy? My orders are to keep you here until everything is finished. They don't want you then; you're dead meat.' He laughed. 'And while you're here, we're gonna get to know each other real well. Real well, missy.'

He kept laughing and slammed the door shut, leaving Helen staring at the door and wishing she was already dead.

CHAPTER TEN

Francesini was back in his office, his mind fixed on the problems that the death of Greg Walsh had brought to the department and quite possibly the people of America. Or was it probably? He felt he was on the edge of something so big that it was almost unbelievable. And unbelievable seemed to be the key word. Who would believe that something so outrageous and despicable was being planned by terrorists? Who would believe that such organizations were capable of such an atrocity?

The papers that Inspector Bain had passed on to him were now lying open on his desk. A report from one of the CIA's intelligence analysts, sworn to absolute secrecy, naturally, was pinned to the inside cover of the folder. A note from James Starling was attached. It read:

Don't worry about me firing you if this turns out to be an accurate assessment of Walsh's fears because I won't have a job either! Get off your backside, Remo and dig deep!!

It was signed with the Admiral's usual, indecipherable signature.

Francesini was not worried about losing his job; it was other people's lives he was concerned about. Starling's urgent diktat to dig deep was not an idle suggestion but a hint at working outside the realms of legality and going deep into the grey world of covert operations; a world which was no stranger to Francesini. The devil was, he didn't know where next to go. He already had agents working in and around Freetown, searching for Marsh and Helen Walsh. He had a security sweep in progress on Hakeem Khan and his known associates in America and across the globe. He had electronic surveillances in place wherever he could but had failed in an attempt to get listening devices installed on the *Taliba*, and all that satellite imagery turned up were some clever photographs of the ship.

He closed the folder and pushed it to one side. Beneath it were several photographs of the *Taliba* which had been taken from the Coast Guard cutter while the boarding party had been on the ship. He thumbed through them, idly speculating on what might or might not be there when he stopped and looked a little closer at one of the photographs. He then shuffled through the others but returned to the one that had caught his attention.

He pulled a magnifying glass from his desk drawer, turned on his desk light even though the sunlight was flooding through the windows, and began to study the photograph carefully.

The shot of the *Taliba* was quite good, but it was the people on the upper deck that he was interested in, not the ship. He studied one in particular, leaning on the ship's rail rather like a disinterested bystander. The image was too blurred to make a positive identification, but something had drawn Francesini's eye to it.

Two minutes later he raised his head in frustration and got up from his desk. He shovelled the photographs back into the folder and locked it in his safe with the exception of the one he had been studying, and walked out of his office.

Disappointments were not unusual in the murky world of espionage; most of the time you worked on hunches, luck and sometimes hard evidence. He had a hunch that he was right, but his limited technology in the form of a desk light and a magnifying glass needed corroboration. It was with that in mind that he was on his way to the satellite imagery department and the very clever people who worked there.

Francesini was no stranger to the graduates, analysts, scientists and eggheads who worked in the imagery department, and one in particular, Bob Cooke, had often helped him before.

Cooke was a university graduate with an honours degree in an unpronounceable subject that had something to do with computer intelligence. He also loved using fuzzy logic to solve problems that would have required the nous that old-time agents used once upon a time in problem solving.

Cooke had written a software programme, using the mathematics of fuzzy logic that had always been Greek to men like Francesini. Cooke had once explained to him that fuzzy logic was like extrapolating a point, or a position, in a logical step, to another position often before that second position was known.

'You amaze me,' Francesini had said to him when Cooke had explained the theory. 'What are you talking about?'

'Well,' Cooke said, warming to his subject, 'when you are about to make a move, like take a step in another direction or reach out for something, the movement you make will put you into an indeterminate position relative to the position you are in at the moment, unless it was a planned and purposeful move; like taking a step. Clear?'

'As mud!'

'But it may be to the left, the right, forward or back. What isn't known at the time is the reason for you making the move. But if we know the reasons, like you were about to cough, or were about to leave the room, excitement, melancholy, anything; we could feed that information into a mathematical expression and determine exactly where you are moving to, or what you are about to do.'

Cooke had gone on further to leave Francesini even more confused and thanking his lucky stars he was not as clever as young Cooke. But on reflection, he mused, perhaps if he had possessed the young man's gift of higher intelligence, he would not have been as deep into the dark as he was now.

He laid the photograph of the *Taliba* on Cooke's desk. The picture was taken from a distance of about forty metres. The *Taliba* was in close up and several of the crew could be seen on the deck.

'I need a favour,' Francesini told him.

'Fine,' he answered. 'How can I help?'

Francesini pointed to a figure in the photograph leaning on the ship's rail looking across to the Coast Guard cutter. The man's features were very grainy, which made it difficult to determine the face and the nationality.

'Can you tell me who that is?' Francesini asked.

'Sure, you got his birth certificate?'

Francesini laughed. 'Sorry, Bob, I meant can you enhance that for me. I really need to identify the guy.'

'And you haven't got a negative, have you, Remo?' he said.

Francesini shook his head. Cooke shrugged. 'Makes it difficult, but I'll give it my best shot.'

He picked up the photograph and scanned it into his computer. When the picture came up, he boxed in the figure and brought it up on screen, doing away with the rest of the imagery.

'Do you know his nationality?' Cooke asked.

'Put him down as Caucasian.'

'Height?'

And so it went on. Cooke asked Francesini as much as he could about the subject. Francesini filled him in with as much as he dared, but didn't want to presume too much, in case he was entirely wrong. Disappointments were pretty common in his game.

Cooke began enhancing the picture in small sections while feeding information into the fuzzy logic programme he was running. He talked as he put the information in. He asked if the figure was one of the crew. Was he in repose? Were the crew all of one nationality. Francesini answered as truthfully and as carefully as he could.

As the picture on the screen changed, so Francesini's excitement level rose. He could see where this was going and was glad that he had backed one of his hunches and brought the photograph to Bob Cooke.

Eventually the young man punched the print button and the printer coughed out an almost perfect print of the figure on the rail, now in glorious colour. He handed it to Francesini.

'Your man?' he asked.

Francesini breathed a sigh of relief and smiled a huge smile of relief. Bob Cooke was holding up a photograph of Harry Marsham – known as Marsh to his friends.

Marsh thought about something strange that had occurred during the evening of the previous day. Shortly after the *Taliba* had been boarded by the Coast Guard, Captain de Leon had ordered a change in course and the ship had headed back to the position, as far as Marsh could determine, where the Coast Guard had stopped them.

He had gone up on deck to see why they had stopped and also to ask the captain why the ship had turned round. He saw Khan talking pointedly to Batista who was in his diving suit. It puzzled Marsh, particularly when another diver, whom Marsh didn't recognize, joined them.

The *Taliba* dropped anchor and Batista went below with the second diver. Khan went up to the bridge and then reappeared with Captain de Leon. It was completely intriguing to Marsh and he knew something unusual was about to happen. He decided to push his luck and followed the two men when they went off in the same direction as the two divers.

It was then that he discovered they were heading for the sea gallery. He stayed with them even though he had not been specifically invited, but as nobody questioned his right to be there, he assumed they were not the least bit concerned by his presence.

He saw the two divers go into the water followed by the diving bell, which was lowered from the running block above the open doors. Its floodlights were on and, as it disappeared into the water, their luminescence began to fade as it sank lower into the depths.

Khan was also there, along with Captain de Leon who was controlling the dive. The divers had gone into the water with one tank of air each on their back, so Marsh knew it wouldn't be a long dive. Within twenty minutes Batista and the other diver were back in the sea gallery. It was then that Khan told Marsh that there was no reason now why the two of them should remain and escorted Marsh from the sea gallery.

The whole operation puzzled him intensely and he could only assume that Batista and the other diver had gone down to locate something. And whatever it was, Khan decided that he and Marsh should not be in the sea gallery when they brought it up to the ship. Perhaps for safety reasons or working on the premise that there was no need for people to be there who were not directly involved in the operation?

He had made one or two informed guesses about the strange occurrences of the night before but eventually had given up trying to figure it out. He was sure that he would learn of the reason for the dive eventually. Having still been given no idea when Khan would be asking him to begin diving with the *Challenger*, he decided it would help pass the time if he took a stroll round the upper deck of the *Taliba*.

He admired her lines with the admiration of a man who has known the sea all his life and seen all manner of ships used in oceanography. *Taliba*'s superstructure bristled with modern, marine equipment and sprouted aerials like a forest. He had no doubt that her electronics would be of the highest calibre and her navigational aids would also be sophisticated and modern.

He heard a footstep and Malik appeared on deck. He came over and acknowledged Marsh.

'Good morning, my friend. Have you breakfasted yet?'

'Yes, thank you,' Marsh answered.

Malik seemed satisfied. 'Good. In that case Mr Khan would like to see you in his cabin.' He turned on his heel and Marsh followed.

Khan's cabin was luxuriously appointed, which Marsh had expected it to be. Apart from one wall, the whole of it was given over to creature comforts of the kind one would normally find on a very expensive yacht. But here in Khan's cabin there was a subtle difference; the wall that remained unfurnished was more like a control centre than a cabin. Marsh had little time to study it except to notice that it was a curious change to the regal splendour which surrounded him.

Khan greeted Marsh and asked him to sit down. His body language told Marsh that it was to be a practical, business-like meeting rather than a cordial chat.

'Now, Marsh,' Khan began straight away. 'We are running behind schedule, but I am sure we can make up the time. I want to begin sea trials with the *Challenger* this afternoon. I cannot factor in many more delays, so will take it that you understand the urgency.'

'Urgency I can understand,' Marsh replied, 'but it might help if I know the reason for the urgency.'

Khan shook his head. 'That is not for you to know. Just understand that we are working to a tight schedule.'

Marsh didn't like it, but there was little he could do about it except try to frustrate Khan as much as possible. 'If I am piloting the submersible I need to go over the sea trials with my co-pilot. It's mandatory, as you well know.'

Again the shake of the head. 'There will be no co-pilot, Marsh. I know you will cope admirably on your own. Batista will lead the dive. He is an exemplary diver.'

Marsh couldn't argue with that. Nor could he argue with Khan because the man held all the cards. The best thing he could do in the circumstances was to act as professionally as he could, but at least he could try and unsettle Khan's plans.

'What about Helen Walsh?' he asked.

Khan's expression changed and he looked a little nonplussed. 'What about her?'

'I want to know where she is,' Marsh told him levelly. 'I will not dive unless I know where she is.'

Khan regained his composure, but Marsh's stance was a little unexpected nevertheless.

'I do not want any histrionics, Marsh,' he warned him. 'Helen Walsh is safe and well and will remain so until you have completed the dives. If you refuse to co-operate you will jeopardize not only yourself but her also.' He leaned forward. 'Do you understand that, Marsh? Do I make myself clear?'

There was something unsettling in Khan's reaction. Unless Marsh was mistaken, there was an inordinate fear in Khan's manner. Nothing he could actually put his finger on, but underneath the surface, Marsh thought he could see a man who had no way out of the dilemma he was in and would go to extremes to ensure success. Murder and kidnap were already part of Khan's world, so Marsh considered discretion was really the better part of valour in this case. But he knew he would have to keep alert and find a way of spoiling whatever plans Khan had in mind.

'Can you show me where we are diving then?' Marsh asked reluctantly. 'At least do me that courtesy.'

Khan breathed a quiet sigh of relief and got up from the desk. He looked in pain as he walked over to the control centre. There was a chart table there and he beckoned Marsh over to it.

'Here,' he said, putting his finger on the chart. 'We shall begin our first dive here in the southern channel.' He was pointing at a bearing about 150 miles south of the Florida Keys in the Santaren Channel.

'What depth will we be diving at?'

'No more than one hundred metres.'

'Have you computed the drift rate?'

'We shall remain on fixed line,' Khan told him. 'But the drift rate has been computed at about ten kilometres an hour. The dive should last no more than three hours.'

Thirty kilometres, Marsh thought to himself. Plenty of room in the channel for that. He looked up from the chart table.

'I would like to look over the *Challenger*,' he said.

'Of course,' Khan replied. He walked over to his desk. There was glass of water and a small bottle there. He shook two tablets from the bottle and swallowed them down with the water.

'Of course,' he said again, and reached for the phone. 'Captain de Leon? I shall be going forward with Marsh to inspect the *Challenger*. Have Batista there, will you? Thank you.' He put the phone down. 'Good. Let's go.'

The *Challenger* was secured across the *Taliba*'s forward deck, just below the fo'c'sle head. It was a familiar and thought-provoking sight to Marsh. She had been freshly painted and the name stood out boldly in brass lettering on the lower ballast tank.

Marsh climbed up her ladder to the topside and lowered himself through the access hatch. He could see the modifications that Khan had undertaken, but was only aware of them because they were unlike anything on his own submersible, the *Helena*. He stopped halfway down the central chamber. Batista followed him down.

'What's this chamber for?' Marsh asked him.

'Retrieval,' Batista answered, and opened the door into the decompression chamber. This was where the divers would decompress after a deep dive. Marsh realized that Batista had studiously ignored any explanation after saying, 'retrieval', but chose not to pursue it; no doubt he would learn more as time went on.

Marsh looked around the chamber. It was cramped and there was barely sufficient room for two divers, but there was enough. There was a control console with some basic controls on it from where the *Challenger* could be operated in an emergency. There was also a couple of television monitors. Although Marsh had never known of a submersible being operated from the decompression chamber, it was an exercise he and Greg had conducted with Helen and other divers in the past.

There was sufficient space for two divers to sleep and relax while decompressing plus an assortment of charts, lockers, small drawers and an outdated calendar.

He climbed out of the *Challenger*, going up through the central chamber and back on to the deck of the *Taliba* then made his way forward to the cockpit. It was a round bubble of acrylic co-polymer plastic, 170 millimetres thick, designed to withstand a pressure of 2000 pounds per square inch up to a depth of 1500 metres.

Inside the cockpit, the pilot worked at normal atmospheric pressure. Everything needed to control the submersible, including the remote arms and external monitoring cameras was within easy reach.

Marsh opened the door of the cockpit and climbed in, settling himself comfortably in the pilot's seat. There was another seat beside him for a second crew member, whether pilot, engineer or simply an observer.

He looked at the controls in front of him. The instruments were lifeless except one, which showed that the submersible was connected to an external power source; in this case the *Taliba*. He reached forward and flicked the master switch. The panels and screens flickered into life and the instrument readouts flashed on in a glow of colours and digits. He scanned from left to right: battery power, air-conditioning, oxygen and carbon dioxide content, forward sonar display, gyro compass, scanning sonar, explosive collar arming switch, GPS navigation system, television monitors, trim monitor, repeater and depth gauges.

Marsh unwittingly enjoyed the unashamed luxury of settling into a world where he was the master. He was like a child with a new toy. All thoughts of the reasons why he was here had vanished, tucked into the recesses of his mind; locked away.

Marsh was home, comfortable; like a foetus in a womb.

Francesini lifted his head at the sound of someone rapping knuckles on his office door. He called whoever it was to come in and Cooke, from the satellite imagery department, poked his head round the door. Francesini was surprised to see him.

'Hallo, sir, have you got a moment?'

Francesini put his pen down and leaned back in his chair. He signalled Cooke to sit down. 'What can I do for you, Bob?' he asked.

Cooke put some photographs on the desk. 'Well sir, you know we've been looking out for those nukes?' Francesini said he did. Cooke continued, 'Well, I've been looking at the images we recorded at the time they disappeared, and I think I might have come up with something.'

Francesini leaned forward. There were various satellite images showing dates, times, satellite identification, etcetera. He could see trace lines over the images like the fine, gossamer threads of a spider's web. 'Go on,' he said, and wondered if there was to be more talk of fuzzy logic. But whatever the young man had to tell him, Francesini knew he would not be wasting his time.

'It's like this: there's a lot of shipping spilling out of the Gulf into the Indian Ocean, right? Looking at the tracks, most of it travels in much the same direction whether it's west, east or south. It's all impossible to track really. But the further away from the Gulf and major continents, the thinner the tracks become until we can begin to identify the individual ships more easily. If we want to, that is.'

This began to sound extremely interesting to Francesini. 'Have you identified something then, Bob?' he asked.

Cooke shook his head. 'Well, not really; it's just a theory. Possibly,' he added pointedly. Francesini thought about Einstein. He let the youngster go on.

'There are two ships heading for South Africa, right? Nothing unusual in that. But these two haven't stopped; they've sailed round the Cape and are now heading north-west towards the mid-Atlantic. That's the long way round, you know.'

'I know,' Francesini agreed.

'Why didn't they go through the Suez? Much quicker.'

'What are you getting at?'

'It's just a hunch. It's like the second ship is riding shotgun. If you've got something really valuable on you, why let anyone know? So you avoid docking at any port. And it always helps to have a little security along for the ride. It's just a gut feeling I've got, sir.'

'Rather like your fuzzy logic, eh, Bob?' He couldn't resist that.

'Nothing to do with it sir,' Cooke replied with a self-conscious, almost apologetic, chuckle. 'It's like I said; just a hunch.'

Francesini liked the young man. He trusted him, too. And if Cooke's hunches were anything like his ability to interpret obscure imagery and apply mind-blowing logic to problems, Francesini knew he would probably be on good ground by going along with him. And if Cooke was right; they might even know where the nukes were.

But like the man told him, it was just a hunch, and Starling would have his balls if he relied on hunches when something as serious as missing nukes was concerned; so he had to let it go, reluctantly.

He settled back in his chair. 'You know, Cookie, I could start a major diplomatic incident if I went along with this; to say nothing of losing my job.' He shook his head gently, wrestling with his own conscience and took a cigar from a humidor on his desk. He lit the half corona and let the smoke drift from his mouth.

'Damn it Cookie, why couldn't you give me facts?' He wasn't angry, just frustrated. 'You're probably right, but I can't put this in front of the admiral; he'd throw it out.' He put his hand on the photos. 'Leave them with me anyway, and thanks again.' He winked at Cooke. 'I'll buy you and your lovely wife dinner at the restaurant of your choice if you're right. OK?'

Cooke grinned. 'No sir, it's not OK,' he answered. 'It will have to be my wife's choice.' He laughed and left Francesini sitting at his desk with a rueful expression on his face.

They launched the *Challenger* shortly after noon. Marsh had switched from external power supply to the submersible's own power plant and unplugged the umbilical chord that brought power in from the ship's generators. The sea was reasonably calm although there was a fairly stiff breeze blowing. The *Challenger* settled into the water and Marsh ran a few checks before securing the entry door to the cockpit. This was just a precautionary measure.

Batista entered the water and clambered on to the submersible's starboard ballast tank. His job was to connect the ship-to-sub communication line to a watertight port on the *Challenger*'s pressure hull. Normally this would not be used; transmission was usually by a sonar device, but because this was a practice dive, it was decided to use a hardwire link.

Marsh was wearing espadrille shoes, loose fitting denim trousers and a T-shirt. He had also taken with him a woollen jersey and a canvas jacket. Although the cockpit was heated he knew that the temperatures at depth could drop dramatically. The extra clothing was a precaution. He swung the clear, transparent door shut and wound the lock in, then strapped himself in using a simple lap strap. He then began his pre-dive checks.

Above and behind his head were the lithium hydroxide panels used to filter the air he breathed. Below them were the oxygen bottles used to replace the spent oxygen if the carbon dioxide content shown on the instrument gauge rose above two per cent. The pressure inside the cockpit was carefully monitored because of the risk of over pressurizing should the bottles bleed too much oxygen into the air.

Marsh set the internal cabin temperature to 20° Celsius, checked communications with the *Taliba*'s bridge and began opening the air valves on the ballast tanks to allow the sea water to flood in.

When he had completed his immediate checks, he looked round for Batista. The diver was still in the motor dinghy forward of the *Challenger*. Marsh put a thumb up and Batista acknowledged. This signal told Marsh there were no divers in the vicinity and it was safe to run the propulsion motors. He powered them up one at a time, checking their power levels. When submerged he would only be running them at twenty per cent of their full power.

When Marsh was finally satisfied that it was safe to dive, he informed the *Taliba*.

'*Challenger* clear to dive. Have Batista stand by. Lowering to ten metres.'

He watched as the water lapped over the curved surface of the cockpit. It was a sensational effect, one that Marsh never tired of. The *Challenger* stopped and Marsh looked up. The sun's rays poured through the surface of the water like threads of gossamer and above him the sea burst into a million tiny bubbles as Batista plunged in.

Marsh checked the depth reading. It had just moved off the zero mark and would probably not register accurately until he had dived another ten metres or so. He switched on the submersible's interior monitor, giving him a wide angle view of the decompression chamber. Warning lights in front of him on the control panel told him which water tight doors were open and which were not.

The upper access hatch was open and its warning light was flashing red. It stopped and remained permanently lit as Batista entered the submersible. Once he had secured the hatch, the light changed to green. Although Batista had entered the diving chamber, closed and secured the hatch, the chamber was still full of water.

Marsh thumbed a panel switch. There was a gentle vibration as compressed air forced the water out of the chamber. A green light came on which meant Batista could now open the door to the decompression chamber safely.

Marsh watched the monitor. Batista appeared on the screen and gave him a 'thumbs up' signal. Another light came up on the panel telling Marsh that the decompression chamber door was now locked and secured and they could begin the dive.

For the next hour, Marsh and Batista conducted exercises which involved Batista leaving and entering the submersible, practising hand-signal manoeuvres, diving to depths in stages and holding there, and generally testing themselves and the men watching everything on the bridge of the *Challenger*.

It was just before the dive commenced that another diver joined them. He came down by way of *Taliba*'s diving bell, known as a *Galeazzi Tower*. Marsh was to learn later that his name was Zienkovitch. He was a safety diver, which was a requirement under diving legislation.

Marsh settled into the routine of piloting the submersible quite happily. It was as if he had been doing it all his life. He manipulated her so that she performed with the grace of a sea creature, following Batista and Zienkovitch in complete circles under the powerful on-board spotlights. A ballet of man and machine; 200 pounds of flesh and blood against 50,000 pounds, over 20 tons, of sophisticated technology, floating in a marine universe.

The only limit to their stay beneath the surface was physical. The divers were breathing a mixture of helium and oxygen which was absolutely essential to guard against nitrogen narcosis; the euphoric state some unfortunate divers get into which usually leads to death.

That was the reason the *Galeazzi Tower* was being used. It was suspended from the *Taliba* at a depth of thirty metres. Inside were two other divers. If an accident occurred where Batista or Zienkovitch were overcome, they could be taken up to the diving bell by the two safety divers and returned to the surface.

At the end of their planned dive, Batista and Zienkovitch returned to the submersible's decompression chamber. When Marsh was satisfied they were both in the first chamber, he expelled the water and brought the air pressure up to that at which they had been diving. Then they opened the door of the decompression chamber and acknowledged Marsh on the monitors. Marsh noted the time and logged it. He knew Batista would do the same. They would now remain in the decompression chamber for an hour or more to allow them to decompress safely.

Marsh signalled to the *Taliba* that the dive had ended and he was now about to bring the *Challenger* to the surface. He blew the sea water out of the ballast tanks, filling them with compressed air. He felt good; it has been a successful dive. Slowly and gently the *Challenger* rose to the surface.

CHAPTER ELEVEN

The police picked up Sweeting Maclean about midday; bounced him on a traffic violation and suspicion of a crime committed the previous day. The officers claimed he fitted the description given by a witness and was required for an identity parade.

It was easy picking up Maclean because men of his character break the rules as regularly as drawing breath. He protested vigorously when they told him they wanted him down at police headquarters for the identity parade, but all his protestations about human rights, being allowed to contact his lawyer, arrest warrants, and claims that they couldn't do this to him simply fell on deaf ears and he ended up at police HQ.

Inspector Bain knew they had no real grounds to hold the man, but they were buying time and needed him out of the way while they searched his house during the process of recording his traffic violation and putting him into a line-up of five, off-duty policemen.

There was nothing grand about the place Maclean lived in. It was situated in the poorer district of Freeport, but men like Maclean had no use for grandeur; their money was usually spent on drink, women, drugs and fast cars.

The police searched Maclean's place thoroughly. It didn't take long and they made sure that everything they touched was returned to its proper place. The two men searching noticed that the bed appeared to have been slept on, rather than slept in; as though somebody had lain there. The room itself was typically male but there was a pair of ladies shoes that looked as though they had been tossed carelessly on to the floor. One of the men picked them up.

'Look at these,' he said to his colleague. 'And the bed.'

The other policeman was puzzled. 'What am I supposed to see?' he asked.

'Girl's shoes. If Maclean had a woman here last night, the bed would have been in one helluva mess. But the bed's made. If a woman had made the bed before she left this room, it would have been tidy, and she wouldn't have left her shoes behind.'

The other man nodded. 'I see what you mean; the girl's been here and gone.'

His companion put the shoes down and shrugged. 'Might as well get back to the station; tell the inspector what we've seen.'

They let Maclean go, not because they had nothing on which to hold or charge him, but because they needed him back out on the street; he was their only lead to Helen Walsh.

He left the building with the air of someone who had cocked a snook at the police, but beneath the veneer, Maclean was angry. He was like a disturbed wildcat. He climbed into his car. It wasn't the Buick; that was now a pile of scrap, and pulled away from the parking lot. He drove back to his house, parked the car on the roadway outside and let himself in through the front door.

The moment he stepped inside he could sense there was something wrong. He could almost feel it. Just inside the door was a tallboy drawer unit. He opened the top drawer and took out a small .22 calibre Beretta pistol, a ladies gun, but useful if needed. He walked from room to room with a growing feeling that somebody had been there. Although Maclean was not a particularly tidy man, he was a man of habit and knew where things were.

But everything seemed a little too precise. Everything was in its place, but they had another spirit on them. His obeah instincts manifested themselves in a growing belief that his house had been searched while he had been held by the police. And now he knew the reason they had picked him up, because they a suspicion he was involved in the woman's kidnap and wanted him away from his house while they searched it. He knew now that he would have to be very careful.

When he walked into his bedroom, he saw Helen's shoes. They were placed neatly at the foot of the bed. He knew they had not been like that when he took the girl away. He picked up the shoes and held them for a while. Then he smiled and lifted his finger in silent rebuke.

'Oh, Mr policeman,' he intoned. 'You have made a big mistake.'

He knew then what the police were up to; they wanted him back on the street to lead them to Helen Walsh. He gave up looking round the house and went to the windows, looking from each one until he saw the car with two men in it, sitting there waiting. He wondered if the police were being deliberately stupid.

So be it, he thought, let's give them something to follow. He would not go back to Helen Walsh for some time. Instead he would stay in Freeport.

He thought about the shoes and how absent-minded someone had been to put them back so neatly. He laughed.

'Oh yes, Mr policeman; a very big mistake.'

After the dive, Marsh asked Khan to tell him exactly why he wanted him to pilot the *Challenger* and what for. He was in Khan's cabin with the captain and Malik. Malik always seemed to be around. Marsh wondered if it was protection for Khan. He noticed also that Khan's face had taken on a very pallid colour and he wondered just how ill the man really was.

'Very well, Marsh, I suppose you are entitled to know what it is we want you to do and why we need your skill and experience.' Khan was sitting in a comfortable chair. Marsh was leaning against the desk, facing him.

'The *Challenger*,' Khan began, 'will dive on to a capped well-head. It is a dry well. The cap of the well-head is designed to allow the submersible to anchor on to it using the skirt that is attached to the underside of the *Challenger*. Batista and Zienkovitch will take care of that procedure. Your job is to guide the *Challenger* on to the well-head following precise instructions from either of the divers.' He coughed and reached for a glass of water, his face mirroring the discomfort he felt in his chest. When he had drunk a little of the water, he continued.

'There is sufficient room for one diver to work inside the skirt. Zienkovitch will do that while Batista remains in the central chamber to prepare the device for lowering into the well.'

'What device?' Marsh asked.

Khan held up his hand. 'Later. The device will be lowered into the well-head to a depth of five hundred metres. Once it is secure in the well, Zienkovitch will recap the well-head and you will all return to the surface.'

'What's the device?' Marsh asked again. 'Was that what you were lifting when you asked me to leave the sea gallery?'

Khan then breathed in deeply and looked like he had come to a decision. He struggled to his feet, pausing as he stood to regain his breath. 'Very well,' he said tiredly, 'we shall go below; then all your questions will be answered.'

They filed out of Khan's cabin and into a wind that seemed to be getting stronger and Khan, more than the others had to lean into it to make headway. Malik shadowed him all the way. They reached a door just beneath the fo'c'sle head and went down the companionway to the sea gallery.

Marsh recalled his brief visit there before. He took in all that he could see, which included a pallet on top of which was a tarpaulin cover. Malik immediately went towards the pallet and removed this cover, dropping it on to the deck and beckoned Marsh forward.

The pallet was quite small, but on it were two cylinders. At first Marsh assumed they were small oil drums, but saw quite clearly that they were nothing as simple as that. What he saw were two cylinders strapped together.

Marsh looked at them beneath the light from the bulkhead lamps. Malik watched him with a curious expression on his face, like someone who was about to reveal something remarkable. The others, Khan and de Leon all seemed to look at it with a kind of reverence. The cylinders had been highly polished and had markings on their sides which he was unable to decipher. The others continued to watch him as he peered closer. On top of each cylinder was a lifting ring. He saw lettering on the far side of one of the cylinders. He was quite sure it was Russian. There was also a series of numbers there which meant nothing to him.

Then he saw something which did: three black segments within a yellow circle – the international sign for radiation.

Marsh straightened and looked directly at Khan, whose face was washed in the poor light.

'They're nuclear bombs,' Marsh whispered, as though the sound of his voice might trigger the thing.

He looked back at the cylinders, strangely fascinated by them, by their incongruity. Then it struck him that the Coast Guard had failed to find them. He was also surprised at how small they were. Although he had never seen a nuclear bomb before, he had always assumed they were quite large. But he had also heard of battlefield devices which could be carried in the trunk of a medium-size car. He decided these were probably typical of such bombs.

'But the Coast Guard, why didn't they find them?'

Khan smiled. 'They weren't here when the Americans searched our ship.'

Marsh realized now exactly what had happened when he saw Batista diving and the *Galeazzi Tower* being lowered. They were retrieving the bombs from their hiding place on the sea bed where they had been dropped when the Coast Guard appeared. The tower had only been used as a source of lighting because Batista had finished the dive within twenty minutes or so.

Marsh shook his head in dismay. 'You're an evil bastard, Khan. I don't know what it is you are up to, but that's why Greg died, wasn't it? Because he knew about the bombs and was trying to stop you.'

Khan shook his head. 'Walsh was in the wrong place at the wrong time. And it was the providence of Allah that you were spared, so that you could complete the work against the great Satan, America.'

With that he signalled that the demonstration was over and walked out of the sea gallery leaving Marsh standing there with Malik.

Sweeting Maclean spent the day moving from one place to another, trying to make himself look busy and give the police something to watch. He made a couple of phone calls from a public telephone box in the early part of the afternoon, and continually checked to make sure the police were still following him.

He called into a Pizza Hut and spent some time there, later moving on to a beach bar where he had a drink with some of his other acquaintances. He spent a couple of hours on the beach before returning home where he took a shower and watched some TV.

As evening drew near, he made another phone call. Maclean's plan depended a great deal on the answers he received. But being the kind of man he was, the answers were favourable, and he came out of the phone booth feeling quite confident. And because the sky was darkening nicely, he felt pretty good about the whole thing.

He drove down to the quayside and parked his car in a parking lot while keeping an eye on the car tailing him. He got out of the car and walked along the quayside a little, past the shops and bars and the bobbing boats and cruisers that lined the boardwalks, and found the bar he was looking for. He went inside.

One of the policemen following Maclean got out of his car and went into the bar. He saw Maclean ordering a drink at the bar and making small talk with a girl. They walked over to an empty table and sat down. It wasn't long before Maclean was nibbling at the ear of the girl. Soon some others joined them and more drinks were ordered. It seemed so normal that the policeman went back to his car and the other officer to wait.

Maclean finished his drink, slipped a few dollars to the girl and went to the back of the bar, through the kitchen and out through the back door. He walked quickly and as quietly as he could along the boardwalk until he could see the boat he wanted among the line of boats tied up there.

He stepped on to the boat, slipped the ropes fore and aft, and then pushed the boat away from the boardwalk. He dropped into the cockpit and found the ignition key which had been taped beneath the driver's seat. The diesel engine coughed and rumbled into a low throated roar and he piloted the boat out of the marina and into the open sea.

In the waiting, unmarked police car, one of the watching men saw the boat and realized what had happened. He climbed out of the car and went into the bar. A minute later he was back.

'That was Maclean,' he said to his companion. 'The bastard's conned us.'

Sweeting Maclean was laughing as he opened the throttles once he was out into open water. The wind was up and the boat began to rise and fall in the swell. He turned the boat on to a northerly heading, reckoning that he would reach the swashland beneath the safe-house before dawn.

One of the phone calls he had made confirmed his suspicions that the police were on to him. In the same way that the police had informers, so to did Sweeting Maclean. But he also got word off the street that the police might know where the safe-house was. Maclean's only advantage lay in the fact that the house was up on the northern shore and he could get to it by sailing inland through the mangrove swamps. He knew that the police could not tail him, but if they did learn of the whereabouts of the safe-house, it would be a close run thing.

He looked up at the clear, bright moon, checked that the fuel tank was full and set the boat on autopilot. Then he dived into the cabin for the food he knew had been left for him.

As he ate, Maclean studied the charts. He had asked for a full tank because his intended journey was going to be lengthy. Picking up the girl was only going to be part of it. He finished a can of Budweiser and went back up on deck clutching more sandwiches. He had a jacket on which had also been left for him.

He disengaged the autopilot and took control. Apart from the strengthening wind, Maclean knew his course would be fairly straightforward, but once he had closed in on the swamps, it would take a certain science, and a bit of luck, to locate the creek that would lead him up to the safe-house.

He felt pretty good. He had the girl and he began forming a little plan that might make him a few dollars. Perhaps even plenty of dollars. He would take the girl for himself too, he decided. Yes, he felt pretty good, he mused, and there was nothing to prevent him from coming out of this a good deal richer. And once he had used the girl, he would dispose of her.

Inspector Bain's eyes snapped open when the phone rang. He had been watching the news on television and had fallen asleep. The shrill ringing of the phone slashed into his brain like the savage assault of a wild animal and he sat upright immediately, his heart thumping in his chest. The television sound had been muted, and he knew that his wife had been into the room to do that while he had been asleep in the chair.

He reached for the phone. 'Bain here.'

'Sir,' the voice said, 'we've lost Maclean.' Bain was instantly awake and sat bolt upright. The voice went on, 'He duped the boys tailing him and took off in a boat. He's heading north and we think we know where he's going.'

'Where?'

'He has a place up in the north swashland. We're going now, sir. Do you want us to pick you up?'

Bain frowned. 'How long have we known that he has a place up in the swashland?' he asked.

'I know what you're thinking, sir, but we only learned about it fifteen minutes ago. We had to lean on the owner of the bar; threatened him with closure. He put us on to one of Maclean's associates. We had something on him,' he said unnecessarily.

'I'll be out front,' Bain told him and put the phone down.

Maclean throttled the engine back until the boat had lost most of its forward motion. The wind rocked the boat and the sea splashed against the sides, sending the occasional wavelet into the boards. He studied the shoreline, picking out salient features in the moonlight. He had been cruising at a near walking pace for thirty minutes, searching for the creek he wanted.

Suddenly he saw it and edged the throttle forward, guiding the boat gently towards the open mouth of the creek. It was about fifteen metres wide where it spilled out into the open sea. He kept the boat in mid channel, using the moonlight to guide him.

The creek split into two and he took the left fork. The gnarled mangrove roots closed in on him, bumping against the hull. He followed this narrow inlet for about a mile. From time to time he would close the throttle right down and listen very carefully for any unusual sounds, allowing the boat to drift under its own inertia.

He looked up at the moon and then at the low skyline. There were no hills to mark and no man-made features, just an endless miasma of pine and mangrove. But Maclean knew exactly where he was.

A light flickered in the corner of his eye. At first he thought it was a light from a cabin; there were several doted around the swashland area he was in, but it was very early in the morning and he hadn't expected any sign of life.

The light appeared again; a flicker behind the trees. It came from a road in the distance, Maclean was sure of that. It had to be a car. Then he saw another light and frowned; there was more than one car, which probably meant trouble. He moved the throttle forward, pushing the boat faster through the narrowing creek. He figured he had about another mile to go before the creek split into several meandering streams.

It had to be the police, he decided. And if it was, they would have to stay on that road for a further ten miles or so before it swung north-east. Then they would be on little more than a track, which meant slow progress. Twenty minutes perhaps. No more.

The hull of the boat bumped into submerged roots, throwing Maclean forward. He fell into the cockpit and struggled to get back up. Then he reversed the boat away from the obstruction and inched forward again.

He encountered more obstacles, which he would normally have avoided, but the situation was fraught and it was not the best time to try and negotiate these narrow creeks. And because he believed the police might be in those cars up on the headland, he could not use the boat's powerful searchlight for fear of drawing attention to himself.

When he finally reached the landing stage, no bigger than a table, he knew he had taken much longer than he wished. The creek was too narrow to turn the boat round so he had no choice but to tie her up facing inland.

He jumped ashore and carefully negotiated the rough path through the mangroves to the safe-house. It was in total darkness. He waited on the edge of the clearing and listened. Faintly, but without any doubts in his mind, he could hear the cars in the distance. He knew they were coming this way.

He sprinted across to the house; a ramshackle affair, weathered and needing paint. The stiff breeze was rattling some of the timbers on the roof and threatening to rip them off. When he reached the house he went in through the back door, but did not switch on any lights. He dragged the kitchen table across the floor until it was beneath a ceiling hatch. He clambered on to the table, reached up and pushed the small door up out of the way, then put his hand in the opening and began feeling around.

His hand touched the cold metal of an Uzi machine-gun. Beside it were two magazines taped together in such a way that either could be snapped into the gun. He jumped down from the table, checked the magazines. Both were full; a total of sixty-four rounds. He opened a cupboard door in the kitchen, still without light and pulled out a box of cartridges, stuffing them into his jacket pocket. Then he grabbed a flashlight and went out of the house at a run.

Helen was asleep inside the shack. Her sleep was a sleep of total exhaustion. She hadn't eaten for twenty-four hours and had been in fear of her life and her sanity. All her attempts at escape had simply reduced her to a hysterical wreck. Several cages had been knocked over. One had burst open and the rats inside had scattered, leaving Helen living on the edge of her nerves.

The first she knew of Maclean's presence was when the door burst open and he stood framed in the moonlight. The light from his torch stabbed through the darkness.

Helen didn't scream because she knew instinctively it was Maclean. She shrank away from him in terror, shielding her eyes against the glare of the flashlight. He kicked the door shut and flicked the torch beam around the shack until he saw a length of chord hanging from a hook on the wall. He pulled it down and stood over Helen.

'What are you going to do?' she cried in alarm.

'We're going away, missy; you and me.' He passed the chord around her waist and knotted it tight. Then he tied a loop round his own waist and dragged her to her feet. He paused at the open door, taking care not to leave the torch switched on and looked out. Then he turned to Helen and pulled her through the door. As they stepped out into the yard, a loud, hollow voice boomed out.

'Maclean, this is the police. Give yourself up!'

Maclean pulled Helen in front of him, lifted the Uzi machine-gun and fired a scything arc at the shadows. Helen screamed in mortal fear. Maclean grabbed her hair and started to run.

The voice boomed after him, 'Maclean, leave the girl. Maclean!'

Maclean raked the shadows again, peppering the darkness with bright flashes from the breech. Someone cried out and Maclean laughed. Helen was still screaming as he dragged her down towards the boat.

Each time Helen fell, he just lifted her bodily to her feet. He wasted no time, clutching her like a sack and urging her to keep up with him. They reached the boat and he pushed her on board. He slipped the painter, started the diesel and whipped the gear stick into reverse.

Not afraid now to use the powerful spotlight, Maclean turned it on and swivelled the beam along the creek. He could hear the police crashing through the trees in their desperation to get to him, but he was in his element now; in control.

He changed the magazine on the Uzi and hammered the mangroves until the last round of ammunition was gone. Then he swung the boat round and opened up the throttle and headed out towards the open sea.

'Missy,' he cried elatedly, 'now we're going away where they'll never find us.'

CHAPTER TWELVE

Marsh sat comfortably inside the cockpit bubble on board the *Challenger* and worked his way through a comprehensive check list that would ensure that all systems on board were satisfactory and he could proceed. It was barely dawn and the sea was almost like a mill pond. The *Challenger* was a little south-west of the Santaren Channel. There was little or no breeze to stir the air and the sun had lifted its head above the horizon to wash everything in a beautiful, golden glow. The earlier weather reports of a potential hurricane developing south-east of the Caribbean out in the Atlantic Ocean had given them food for thought, and the rising wind of the previous day had only seemed to confirm what the meteorologists were saying. But now, for a while at least, they could enjoy a peaceful calm.

Marsh reckoned fortune was smiling on them, but if the burgeoning wind force developed, continued to grow and tracked north-west, they would soon begin to feel the peripheral winds. Any dives that Khan had planned would have to be postponed, and the ship would have to sail into relatively calmer and safer waters. Not a bad thing, thought Marsh, as he completed his checks.

The internal speaker behind Marsh's head crackled into life, and a metallic voice broke the stillness.

'We are lifting now, *Challenger*. Acknowledge through the sonar phone at thirty metres. Batista will detach the umbilical.'

Marsh said nothing but gave a hand signal to the men up on the deck of the *Taliba*. He felt *Challenger* judder slightly. Then it lifted suddenly as the deck winch hoisted it up and over the side of the ship. Marsh looked anxiously through the polymer walls of the cockpit, but transfer to the ocean was steady, and once the submersible was settled in the water, one of the divers removed the four lifting hooks.

There were four divers on station altogether: Batista and Zienkovitch, who were actually in the decompression chamber behind him, and two other divers who would be going down in the *Galeazzi Tower*. They would be breathing air with aqualungs and would remain with the tower at a depth of thirty metres. Batista and Zienkovitch were breathing a mixture of helium and oxygen.

Once Marsh had received the all clear from the *Taliba*, he began flooding the ballast tanks. He watched the readout on the instrument panel for each tank as their internal pressures began to rise so that he could monitor the ingress of sea water and maintain an accurate stability and sink rate. This would allow the *Challenger* to settle slowly into the water without pitching and rolling excessively.

At thirty metres he closed the air valves and the submersible settled. He waited for the instruments to stabilize then pulled the sonar phone from its cradle and put it to his ear.

'*Challenger* at thirty metres. Please acknowledge.'

'*Taliba*. Acknowledged *Challenger*. Please call out depth during descent.'

'*Challenger* acknowledged.' Marsh opened the air valves to flood the tanks and the *Challenger* began her silent descent to the bottom.

Francesini was in a deep sleep when an alarm bell began sounding off in the distance. The dream dissolved and he was suddenly aware of where he was as the telephone rang again beside his bed. His wife, sleeping beside him, stirred and rolled over muttering something unintelligible. She reached out and patted his back with the palm of her hand. Francesini sat up and pulled back the covers. He swung his legs over the edge of the bed and glanced at the clock. It was 4.15 in the morning. He picked up the phone and turned on the small, bedside light.

'Francesini here,' he mumbled. 'I hope this is important.'

'Good morning, sir,' the voice on the other end of the line began. 'I'm sorry to call you this early in the morning. This is Sergeant Donaldson of the Bahamian Police Department. We've had a development here in the Walsh kidnapping that Inspector Bain thinks you should know about.'

'Go on,' Francesini told him. He was wider awake now but not wanting to hear what was likely to come next. It couldn't possibly be good news at this time of the morning, he thought.

'We located the place where Sweeting Maclean was holding the woman, Helen Walsh. It was up on the northern swashland. We raided it just a couple of hours ago, but I'm afraid he gave us the slip; took the girl with him as well.'

Francesini closed his eyes and uttered a silent curse. The word 'incompetents' slipped into his mind apart from others. 'Go on,' he said again.

'Well, sir, Inspector Bain has been shot. He's in hospital, sir. I'm afraid we lost another officer. Terrible thing, sir.'

Francesini wondered if the Bahamian police had ever been involved in gun battles, but he thought it wise to revise his earlier thoughts.

'How bad is the inspector?' he asked, genuinely concerned.

'He's OK; he'll live, sir. He took a bullet in the arm. I'm afraid we didn't stand a chance really against Maclean; he seemed to have plenty of firepower. I'm sure the inspector will explain, sir.'

'Do you know where Maclean is now?' he asked hopefully.

'No, sir; he slipped out through the mangrove swamps. He had a boat and headed out into the open sea. There was no way we could follow, seeing as we'd come by road.'

Francesini ran his fingers through his hair and looked at his wife who was already fast asleep. He was going to have to wake her and tell her he would be away for a while. Not that it made a great deal of difference telling her; she was always complaining that he should get a proper job, but she loved him and knew that he loved her and his job. He'd leave a note; she would understand. She always did.

'I'll be over. Have someone meet me at the airport.' He put the phone down before the sergeant had a chance to reply.

Had they been diving during the day, Marsh would have been able to see the golden fingers of sunlight penetrating the depths and lighting the world of marlin, barracuda, sting rays, manta rays and a whole host of beautiful fish that lived in the watery, twilight world of the sea. But the dawn light offered no such spectacle and Marsh concentrated on bringing *Challenger* down gently towards the sea bed.

To counter the effects of any drift that was unwanted, a small turbine no bigger than a beer can rotated in the current. By measuring the rate at which it spun, the on-board computer powered *Challenger*'s thrust motors at a sufficient speed to keep the submersible on station. It was a standard servo system cleverly adapted for accurate work in oil exploration and using a global positioning satellite that tracked the submersible to within five metres of its reference point.

As *Challenger* descended, Marsh trimmed her out by transferring water from the aft tanks to the forward tanks and *vice versa* as the situation demanded. It was a delicate operation and could also be done by the on-board computer system, but Marsh preferred the hands-on approach knowing that in an emergency, his piloting skills would be better by having control of the submersible as often as possible.

And so the *Challenger* descended gracefully. It was like going down in a slow-moving lift. The deeper they went, so external vision deteriorated, because less light penetrated the clear waters. Marsh switched on the submersible's powerful floodlights.

To slow up the rate of descent and hold the *Challenger* steady so that she would neither rise nor fall, Marsh used static balancing as opposed to the dynamic balancing he had used on the way down. Quite simply, *Challenger* had 300 kilos of lead shot on either side of the hull which could be dumped slowly by metering it out from the small holding tanks in which the shot was stored. As the lead shot was dumped, so the weight of the *Challenger* decreased along with the sink rate.

He began dumping the lead ballast as *Challenger* approached the planned operating depth and Marsh could see the sea bed lit by the *Challenger*'s powerful arc lamps. Inside the decompression chamber, Batista and Zienkovitch would know from the instrument read out that it was time to begin their part of the operation.

Marsh flicked a switch on the panel and ordered them into the central chamber. Batista and Zienkovitch pulled on the huge, yellow bottles containing helium and oxygen. Because the air pressure inside the chamber was changing automatically to equal the pressure at the depth they had reached, there would be no inconvenience to the divers as they were already breathing the same mixture of gases.

They stepped into the central chamber, closed the watertight door to separate them from the decompression chamber behind them and waited. They would wait until Marsh had flooded the central chamber before opening the upper and lower hatches.

They were standing just half a metre from the nuclear bomb.

Marsh held *Challenger* steady for the next phase of the dive as Zienkovitch swam out of the central chamber once it had been flooded. His exit was through an opening in the metal skirt. The skirt was rather like a large, overturned bowl, beneath the submersible.

Batista remained inside the central chamber. Above him the bomb was held rigid by three pressure pads extending from the side of the chamber. He floated upwards until he was looking down at the bomb, then he hooked up the cylinder to a lifting arm which was attached to the chamber wall.

When he was satisfied that everything was secure, he opened a small panel and operated a winch which tensioned the nylon rope now attached to the lifting eye of the bomb and released the pressure pads so there was a small clearance between them and the smooth sides of the cylinder. Then he pressed the lift button until the bomb was at the top of the chamber which gave him a clear working space beneath it. Satisfied with what he had done, Batista patted the side of the bomb and swam out of the chamber.

Marsh had been so engrossed in maintaining the trim that he was surprised to see Batista and Zienkovitch so soon. He acknowledged them both and let water into the ballast tanks and *Challenger* began descending the last few metres to the bottom.

One old-fashioned method used to tell a submersible pilot when he is near the bottom is by way of a weighted rope hanging free beneath the craft. As it touches bottom, the rope slackens and allows a switch to operate, signalling to the pilot that he has the length of the rope to go.

Marsh was already slowing when the signal lamp flashed on and a small buzzer sounded. He immediately dumped ballast and *Challenger* settled as he trimmed her out. Batista and Zienkovitch then guided Marsh on to the capped well-head which was barely five metres from him. Marsh could speak to both divers through the sonar link but it was only Batista to whom he spoke to avoid mistakes. By following Batista's one word commands, he successfully brought the submersible immediately over the well-head.

On the outer rim of the well cap were three bullet-shaped spigots which located into three holes on the rim of the *Challenger*'s skirt. Marsh felt her twitch as she settled on the spigots. Immediately

Batista and Zienkovitch closed a set of spring clamps which were also attached to the skirt rim.

Marsh thought back to that moment when Khan had showed him the nuclear bomb. If only the Coast Guard had found the bomb when they searched the *Taliba*, he thought to himself bitterly.

Suddenly Batista's dismembered voice broke into Marsh's thoughts.

'You can relax now, Marsh,' he said. 'The cuckoo is on the nest.'

Francesini heard the sound of his wife's soft footfall behind him. He was in the kitchen fixing a cup of coffee and a bowl of cereal. He turned towards her as she came through the door. She looked a little sleepy still, her hair tousled and untidy. She walked over to him and kissed him gently on the cheek. He loved her as much now as he did when they married, probably even more. He welcomed the show of affection, even at such an ungodly hour.

'Coffee?' he asked.

She shook her head, pulling her dressing gown round her body unconsciously, accentuating the curves of her body. He never tired of looking at her, whether she was dressed for a dinner party or for bed. It mattered not to him.

'Go sit down,' she ordered. 'I'll fix this.'

He put his arm round her. 'Laura, I'm sorry about this. I—'

'Remo,' she interrupted, 'we've been through this before, so don't beat yourself up about it. I knew what I was letting myself in for when I married you.'

He did as he was told and sat down at the breakfast bar. He remembered the day they married, in New York, just a week after he had graduated from the Farm – the CIA Academy. It had rained, but they were happy. And yes, she did know what she was letting herself in for. She had courted him when he was working the beat, on shifts with the NYPD, knowing in her heart what he really wanted to do, and that was to join the CIA. He had studied law in the evenings at night school when he was able and graduated with a good degree. Some thought he would stay with the police force, but the CIA was his calling.

'When are you leaving?' she asked. 'And where are you going? Or am I not permitted to ask?'

He smiled. He could never tell her where he would be because he might not know or, perhaps worse, he might have to lie. But this time he knew and this time he wouldn't lie.

'There's a car on the way,' he told her. 'Should be here soon.' He looked at his watch. 'Then I'm off to the Grand Bahamas. Freeport.'

'Jimmy Starling going with you?'

She always called James Starling by that name, but never to his face. It was her way of reducing the admiral's heavy reputation to one of more manageable proportions. But behind that she quite liked her husband's boss. He was a pussycat really, she often told her husband, but she never told Jimmy Starling.

'Not yet.'

She put the coffee and cereal in front of him. 'This going to be the last job?' she asked, tongue in cheek.

He held a spoonful of cereal in front of his mouth. 'As ever,' he lied.

She reached down and kissed him again. 'Don't let anybody shoot you,' she warned him. 'I get used to having you around. Sometimes!'

'I'll give you a call,' he said, when he had finished eating the mouthful of cereal, but she was already through the door and on her way back to bed.

Perhaps this should be the last one, he thought to himself. He got up and put his empty cereal bowl into the sink and drained his coffee cup.

But if that bastard Khan has three nuclear bombs to detonate, he thought to himself, it could be the last one for a lot of people.

On board the *Taliba*, Hakeem Khan breathed out heavily and settled back in his softly upholstered swivel chair. His face was ashen and a small pain had been gathering force inside his chest. He had been sitting at the control console in his cabin, monitoring the dive. Malik was with him. Neither had spoken as *Challenger* had descended to the well-head. For a long while all that penetrated the silence in the cabin was the sound of the strengthening wind hurrying along the superstructure of the ship, and the occasional depth calls and simple commands from the submersible and the bridge of the *Taliba*. It was ethereal and unreal; the other world beneath the sea intruding into the real world of his well-appointed cabin.

Normally, Khan would have been on the bridge with Captain de Leon, but he had been persuaded to remain in his cabin because the captain was concerned for his condition. Khan realized that his own health could jeopardize the entire mission should he collapse with heart failure. It would have disastrous consequences to their mission and all would be lost. He had no choice but to heed his own counselling and that of de Leon.

During the dive, Khan had followed each move in his mind as though he was piloting the *Challenger*. He resisted the impulse to move his hands in mimicry of the moves Marsh would be making as he guided the submersible on to the well-head. His spine had stiffened gradually as Marsh descended with the *Challenger* until he heard Batista guide Marsh on to the spigots. And, as the *Challenger* locked on to the well cap, he felt his strength leave him.

He reached for the bottle containing the white tablets. He took two and washed them down with a glass of water. Malik looked concerned.

And it still wasn't over!

Batista entered the central chamber by swimming through the open gap in the side of the skirt. Once inside he floated to the top of the chamber. Zienkovitch entered the skirt to release the cap over the well-head. He used a compressed air gun already attached to the underside of the submersible. Placing this on the hub of a wheel on top of the cap, he pulled the trigger of the gun and released millions of tiny air bubbles into the water around the cap as the wheel spun free.

Zienkovitch switched off the gun and pulled the well cap open. It pivoted on its counter weight revealing a black hole which descended over 500 metres to a blind end.

Batista waited until his colleague was clear of the skirt and lowered the bomb until it was low enough for him to complete the next stage. He pulled out a small metal object from his wet suit. It was attached to a silver chain which was looped around his neck. He then unlocked a small panel that was on the outside of the bomb casing. Inside this panel was a plate on which was etched a rectangular shadow beside an unlit window.

He placed the metal block, which was hanging from his neck on its safety cord, on top of the rectangular shadow. There was a click and suddenly the unlit window burst into a dazzling row of illuminated numbers which had been initiated by a proximity magnet inside the block.

Batista watched the numbers spin until they settled from left to right into a predetermined number. Hanging on the same cord as the metal block was a Castell key. This was a like a small cup, no more than two centimetres wide in which was engraved a letter. He inserted the key into a recess beside the panel which contained the same engraved letter, recessed and reversed, which located snugly into the matching Castell key.

Then he pushed the key firmly into the casing and turned it in a clockwise direction. He heard the sound of a lock engaging and he released the pressure on the key which sprang back under spring pressure. He then turned the key counter clockwise and removed it, letting it hang from the cord.

He glanced up. '*Taliba*, Trinity One is primed.' Then he removed the block, snapped the panel door shut and put the magnet and Castell key back inside his wet suit.

The next part of the procedure was simple. All Batista had to do then was to lower the bomb into the well. He reached across the chamber to a button set into the wall and pressed it. An electric motor hummed quietly and the rope attached to the bomb began to pay out as the bomb began to drop slowly into the well.

A strain gauge, calibrated in metres, showed Batista how far the bomb was travelling. Batista knew the depth of the well and concentrated on the depth gauge.

In his cabin, Khan breathed a deep sigh, carefully letting his lungs settle gently as beads of sweat touched and formed a patina over his face. He listened as Batista called out the descent of the bomb in metres, his voice distorted by the helium gas.

Marsh listened too, impotent, unable to stop this terror. He scanned the instrument panel and watched the numbers rolling over as the bomb descended. Around him the sea was almost totally black save for the glare of the arc lamps which diffused and scattered through the sea. Small life-forms drifted by, then a school of fish. The beginning of creation he thought, and now possibly the end.

300 ... 350 ... 400. It went on, counting the bomb into its last resting place, deep beneath the sea bed. Into the crust of the earth.

'Five hundred, mark!'

'Secure the rope!' Khan ordered involuntarily. No one could hear him.

Batista secured the wire rope on to a clamp welded on to the wall of the chamber, leaving about two metres free, so that it wouldn't drop into the well, cut the rope and attached a ferrule to the end that was still connected to the bomb. He then clamped this to a watertight antenna that was secured to the inside of the well cap. Satisfied that he had completed the correct sequence of events, and satisfied that everything was in order, Zienkovitch then lowered and secured the well cap.

Once the job was complete, the two divers exchanged hand signals and swam out from beneath the *Challenger*, and round to the cockpit. Batista showed two thumbs to Marsh: job complete!

The signal from Batista was not a self-congratulatory message to Marsh, but to let him know that it was time to take on 150 kilos of water into the ballast tanks to compensate for the weight of the bomb. This would enable the two divers to spring the clamps on the skirt. Without the weight of the bomb, the submersible would be exerting a stronger, upward force on the clamps and make release that much more difficult and dangerous.

Once the ballast tanks had been flooded and the *Challenger* was now at its previous weight, Batista and Zienkovitch were able to release the clamps in safety. They then swam into the central chamber, closed both the upper and lower watertight doors and signalled Marsh to purge the chamber of water. Once Marsh had completed this, they were able to enter the decompression chamber and allow Marsh to begin the ascent.

Challenger surfaced twenty minutes later about fifty metres from the *Taliba*. Marsh used the thrust motors to keep station until recovery could begin. Batista and Zienkovitch were in the decompression chamber on the *Challenger* and would remain so for a couple of hours to decompress safely.

Once the submersible was secure on the deck of the ship, Marsh opened a small valve beside him to let a small amount of compressed air into the cockpit bubble. Normally it was impossible to open the door after a deep dive because such a tremendous pressure had been exerted on it at depth. Allowing just a small amount of compressed air in allowed the door to pop. Marsh closed the valve and opened the door.

Power switched to the *Taliba*'s system informed the two divers they were now under de Leon's control so he climbed out of the cockpit. From the point of view of a professional, Marsh could be satisfied by a job well done. But from the point of view of a man whose life was forfeit and that of the woman he loved, it was an unmitigated disaster.

Khan was on deck when Marsh climbed out of the *Challenger*. He shook Marsh's hand, taking him completely by surprise.

'Congratulations, Marsh, a fine job.'

Marsh was not interested in Khan's gratuitous praise and wanted nothing other than to get the job finished and get back to a normal life; if that would ever be possible. He was about to say something when a member of the crew came up to Khan and told him that Captain de Leon wanted to see him urgently on the bridge. Khan acknowledged the crewman and turned to Marsh.

'We'll debrief when Batista and Zienkovitch are ready,' he said to Marsh and walked away.

CHAPTER THIRTEEN

De Leon was in his day cabin behind the bridge when Khan walked in. The ship's captain had a concerned look on his face. Khan looked a little ruffled from his exertions walking from his cabin up on to the bridge against the wind which was freshening.

'We have just received a call from Romulus,' he told Khan. 'The police are on to that fool Maclean; the safe-house where he had the woman has been raided.'

Khan's dark eyebrows lifted and he tilted his head slightly, a questioning look on his face. 'What about the woman?'

De Leon nodded. 'Well, thankfully Maclean still has her. He managed to escape; took her with him.'

Khan sat down and sighed deeply; he could have done without this new development. He looked up at de Leon, deep disappointment and anger clouding his face. 'Where are they?'

De Leon shook his head and held his hands out in an empty gesture. 'We don't know,' he said with a shrug. 'Romulus doesn't know where they've gone.'

Khan hissed through closed teeth and thumped his hand gently on the table in a tapping rhythm. 'Why do we suffer such fools?'

It wasn't a question that needed answering. De Leon knew that their operation depended upon loyalty, efficiency, dedication and security. With any one of these jeopardized, the whole plan could collapse, taking them all with it. Unfortunately it was sometimes necessary to enlist the help of people who were, to put it bluntly, mercenaries; loyal only to themselves and the money they were receiving. Sweeting Maclean fell easily into this category.

Suddenly Khan stirred as though he had come to a decision. 'Nothing changes,' he declared. 'Marsh still believes we have the girl, which I assume we do, so he'll still co-operate. We'll send Malik; he can dispose of Maclean and bring the girl back here.' He stood up. 'Contact Romulus, find out where they are and let Malik know.'

He turned as if he was about to leave the bridge, then stopped.

'By the way, it was a successful dive. Thank you, Captain.' With that he walked out of the cabin and left Captain de Leon with the task of arranging the demise of one Sweeting Maclean.

Francesini stared at the clock in his office; it was four o'clock in the morning. Less than an hour earlier he had called James Starling and told him about the recent turn of events. Starling was not too pleased at being woken at such an early hour to be told that their operation was going belly-up. He told Francesini to meet him at headquarters before flying out to Freeport.

He was smoking a cigar; something he rarely did at such an early hour in the morning, but he had given in to a degree of fatalism, and broke one of his own rules. It was something he usually abhorred in his agents, or anyone who worked for his department – giving in to maudlin self-pity. The curl of blue smoke drifted up from the cigar without a sign of tremor, which pleased Francesini because there were times when he thought he was going to break out in a cold sweat over the prospect of conceding defeat in this case.

What bugged Francesini most was that he wasn't in complete control of all the elements involved in the kidnapping of Helen Walsh, Marsh's disappearance and the unfathomable actions of Hakeem Khan. Much of his investigation relied on what he considered to be provincial policing in the form of the Freeport Constabulary.

There was a sharp knock on the door and Admiral Starling walked in. There was no preamble. He shut the door and sat down opposite Francesini.

'OK, Remo, what do you have for me?'

Francesini began as best he could by outlining the events following the kidnapping, despite Admiral Starling knowing most of them anyway, and brought him up to date with the local police department tailing and losing Sweeting Maclean, and then the subsequent discovery that Maclean had access to a safe house. It beggared belief in Francesini's opinion, that the Bahamian authorities had no knowledge of this bolthole.

'Inspector Bain had planned to lay siege to the safe house until he could negotiate something with this Maclean guy,' he told Starling. 'Then all hell broke loose and Inspector Bain gets wounded and another of his officers gets killed.' He put the cigar to his mouth and drew in a lungful of smoke. Blowing it out steadily, he looked across the desk at Starling. 'This Maclean guy sounds dangerous.'

'Anybody with a machine-gun can be dangerous, Remo,' Starling reminded him. 'But it takes brains to be really dangerous and that's the domain of the man at the top.'

'Khan?'

Starling shrugged. 'If we could positively link him with Maclean, then, yes. But why are they holding Greg Walsh's widow?'

'It must be leverage,' Francesini suggested. 'They have Marsh on board the *Taliba* so perhaps they need something from him.'

'Like what?' Starling asked. 'He's not a nuclear scientist, he's an engineer; engineers they do not need.'

'He's an underwater specialist; an oceanographer,' Francesini replied lightly. 'That's what Khan is involved in; has been all his working life. Like Marsh, in fact. Perhaps Marsh is working for Khan. And perhaps he really was involved in Walsh's murder.'

Starling's eyebrows collapsed into an unbroken line. 'I think you're being frivolous now, Remo.'

Francesini accepted the put down from his boss. 'I'm sorry sir; I guess I'm getting apprehensive. There are too many unanswered questions to which I don't have the answers.'

Starling chuckled. 'No, you get apprehensive when the President makes it quite clear he hasn't forgotten the meeting we had the other day. He wants a personal update from me before the Secretary of State flies out to Dubai for a Middle East conference.'

'When is that?' Francesini coughed and cleared his throat. He lifted up his cup and took a mouthful of the coffee which was now quite cold.

'Day after tomorrow.'

Francesini put the cup down. It was contrived to look like the act of a condemned man. 'You want my resignation now, sir?'

Starling's hand came down on the desk like a ton of bricks, startling Francesini.

'I've told you once already not to be so damned frivolous!' he bellowed.

'But what the hell, sir,' Francesini flung back at him, 'these damn politicians go pussyfooting round each other's conference tables promising *détente* and all the other crap, glad handing and acting like the best of pals when truth to tell they are dealing with a bunch of mavericks and crooks most of the time and haven't the guts to tell them.'

'Calm down.'

Francesini calmed down. 'I'm sorry, sir.'

Starling leaned forward. 'That's the second time you've apologized in less than a minute, Remo. When you have to do that to an admiral it could be your career on the line.' Then he leaned back into his leather chair. 'But I've got more respect for you and I'm not about to take any notice of your outburst because I agree with you anyway. So what we've got to do is come up with some ideas about what we intend to do about Mr Khan and find some way of stopping him. We need facts and balls. You get off to Freeport and come up with the facts. Let me know what you have and I'll come up with the balls to make the decisions.'

Francesini knew what his boss meant. An illegal strike at Khan would reap all kinds of repercussions spinning down on them from the White House. But if it meant stopping the madman, Starling was willing to do it. All Francesini had to do was load the gun: Starling would pull the trigger.

Marsh sat through the debriefing with as much professional interest as he could muster but managed to feel completely wooden about the whole business. He answered Khan's questions, responded to Batista's suggestions and generally behaved as though he was co-operating willingly, and in a professional manner, but there was little he could add to the meeting. One small distraction he had was a germ of an idea that was growing in him, and he flirted with it in the likelihood that it might at least bring some hope and a little encouragement into his current predicament.

He let the mechanics of the debriefing drone on and thought also about Khan's plans, convinced now that he knew what the madman was up to. The picture of Greg Walsh's body being peppered with bullets came into his mind, and then the realization at the time that Khan was part of some murderous scheme. He could now make educated guesses at Walsh's involvement in it and wondered why his partner had never shared the secret with him. Perhaps, in some perverse way, it was to protect him and Helen. But despite the reasons for Walsh's secrecy, the whole aspect of what had gone before and what was likely to come filled him with horror.

He thought about the idea that had germinated in his mind to raise the odds a little. If he could persuade Khan to bring Helen to the *Taliba*, he believed it might give the police at Freeport a chance to pick up the trail, providing they were actually aware of her kidnap. He was sure that Mac, the technician at the boatyard, would have reported Helen's disappearance by now and the police would be searching for her. It was a long shot but he was willing to try it. Besides, he desperately wanted to see Helen again.

'How many more dives?' he asked suddenly.

Khan was talking to Batista. He stopped and looked at Marsh. 'Two. Why?'

'When is the next dive?'

Khan appeared irritated. He glanced at de Leon. 'I presume the freighter captain is aware of the change of schedule?'

De Leon concurred. 'We should rendezvous with her tomorrow evening.'

'Seventy-two hours perhaps,' Khan told Marsh, 'weather permitting. Why do you ask?'

Marsh bit the bullet; he had nothing to lose. He stood up slowly, making them all wait. Khan's eyes followed him, his expression folding into one of deep curiosity.

'Before I dive,' Marsh told Khan, 'I want to see Helen Walsh.'

Khan bridled and seemed to grow a few centimetres. 'That is impossible, Marsh. And impractical! I can assure you Helen Walsh is in good health and being well looked after.'

Marsh walked over to the cabin door. Pausing at the door, he turned and looked directly at Khan. It was dramatic, but he wanted Khan to know that he was serious.

'Khan, your word is not good enough. If there are any assurances to be made, I will be the one to make them. If Helen Walsh and I do not meet before the next scheduled dive, I promise you I will not pilot the *Challenger*.' Marsh knew instinctively that he held the whip hand for the moment. 'You can threaten me if you wish, or threaten Helen, but it will have no effect on my decision. Unless I see her alive, I will not pilot the *Challenger*.'

He walked out of Khan's cabin without waiting for a reply. If it was possible to feel like a million dollars at that moment, Marsh did. He took a few, good deep breaths of the cool, ocean air and went aft to his cabin.

The presence of Francesini at the police headquarters in Freeport left them with no doubt now just how serious the Americans viewed the degree of escalation in the Helen Walsh kidnapping, and the presence of Police Commissioner Henry Cleve gave credence to that realization. Any officers who might have assumed otherwise were now in no doubt that however serious a crime one considered kidnap to be, there was something else that put this one at the top of the pile.

Henry Cleve, the Police Commissioner, was a large, rotund man; Bahamian by birth, black with grey, tight curly hair. He was well over six feet tall and dominated everyone and everything around him. Even Inspector Bain managed to lose stature alongside him. With his arm in a sling from the gunshot wound inflicted on him by Sweeting Maclean, Bain had paled into the position of an interested onlooker.

Cleve's voice boomed out, 'Admiral Starling and I have spoken at length on this,' he was telling Francesini, 'and we both understand how difficult it is to do anything about Mr Khan and the *Taliba* unless he steams into Bahamian territory. To date he has committed no crime, none that we can prove anyway, and your Coast Guard failed to find anything incriminating on him or his ship. And we have nothing to link him with Helen Walsh.'

Francesini knew the business of protocol, international relations and all that ensued, and the difficulty of a CIA operation working smoothly without the knowledge of the local police force, but there were times when it was necessary to involve the local security forces even when he was extremely reluctant to do so. He also understood how corrupt some minor police forces could be and their lack of internal security could jeopardize a complete operation. But for Francesini it was *force majeure* and he had no choice but to ask the help of the Police Commissioner and to feed him as much information as he dared.

'I understand, sir, but we consider your co-operation to be of the highest priority. It's vitally important that we find Helen Walsh and the man who kidnapped her. That way we might be able to link him directly to Hakeem Khan and give us the evidence we need to arrest him.'

Commissioner Cleve turned his attention to Bain who was sitting alongside him. 'Inspector Bain is aware of the high priority you have placed on this and he has expressed his wish to continue as officer in charge of this investigation.' He looked back at Francesini, the condescending look barely leaving his face. 'And I am quite happy he should do that,' he went on, 'but it is appropriate, I think, that he should be informed of all the relevant facts.' He made the point of emphasizing the last sentence.

'I'm sure he will be, sir,' Francesini answered lamely.

'Admiral Starling has left this to your own judgement, I believe. But I can tell you that I will be favourably disposed to your request for our continuing assistance only if you show good judgement. You do understand, don't you?'

Touché! Francesini admired the commissioner's style. Diplomatic gobbledegook and framed in such a way that left Francesini in no doubt who was in charge and that he expected to know as much as the CIA.

With that, Commissioner Cleve stood up and took his leave.

One hour later, Francesini was sitting in Inspector Bain's office enjoying a coffee and a cigar. He had spoken at length with Starling on the phone to confirm that he would be taking the police inspector into his complete confidence and assured his boss that he would keep him informed of developments.

'How secure is your intelligence network?' Francesini asked the inspector.

'What we have is reasonable, but we are usually dealing with drug smugglers.' He considered the importance of the question for a while. 'In normal circumstances I could rely on our security, but I cannot regard this as normal.'

Francesini drew heavily on the cigar and drank another mouthful of coffee. Bain had offered him tea before remembering his last attempt at getting the American to drink his own favourite brew.

'We need to know where Maclean disappeared to after your last contact,' Francesini told him. He didn't want to refer to it as a *débâcle*, but in his opinion it was nothing short of a bloody catastrophe, particularly considering the loss of a police officer.

Bain nodded and opened a file that lay on the desk in front of him. 'We do know that the boat Sweeting Maclean used belonged to Romulus Swain. We've sent a sergeant down to the marina, but Swain may be out on charter work. He does a lot of fishing trips for the tourists,' he added unnecessarily. 'I'll check, see if he's back.'

He picked up the phone and asked for Sergeant Deakin. Francesini watched him speak in short, stabbing sentences to someone.

'Tell him I would like to see him now,' he said, and put the phone down.

A couple of minutes later, the sergeant was in his office.

'I spoke to Swain,' Deakin said, when asked about the man, 'but he wasn't very co-operative. He said he charters boats out all the time. He'd have to check. He said that often he has clients who just turn up, hand over the cash and take the boat out, no questions asked.'

Francesini curled up inside at the lackadaisical attitude of the police sergeant. But this was the Bahamas and being laid back was almost an act of faith here.

'So what did you do then?' Bain asked.

'Well, sir, we left a couple of men there on surveillance. This afternoon two men turned up and took a hired a boat from Swain.'

'And?'

'My men figured they weren't the usual tourists. Swain went with them. It was late this afternoon and most tourists want their boats early morning. Spot of fishing,' he added unnecessarily.

Francesini wondered if the sergeant was not as dumb as he first thought. 'Were your men able to tail them?'

Deakin turned towards him with a surprised look on his face. 'They were in a patrol car, so there was no chance. But they contacted Inspector Eustace; he's the captain of our Freeport gunboat, and asked him to follow Swain, see if he could make contact. They gave the inspector an estimate of Swain's heading.' He shrugged and turned back to Bain. 'That's it I'm afraid, sir.'

Bain thanked him and dismissed him. 'I'll contact Inspector Eustace and ask him to get in touch with me immediately he has anything,' he told Francesini.

In the circumstances, it was all they could do, apart from continuing to scour the countryside for Sweeting Maclean and Helen Walsh.

Maclean heard the boat before he saw it. He was sitting in the cockpit of the boat he had hired from Swain giving a lot of thought to how best he could turn the present situation to his own advantage. He knew that the woman was valuable to whoever his employers were, but being a man who always had his eye on the chance to improve his situation financially, he could see no reason why he shouldn't assume control of the whole operation. Maclean's biggest problem, not that he realized it, was that he was contemplating suicide.

He lifted his head and picked up the Uzi machine-gun in one movement, peering over the side of the boat. Seeing nothing yet, he stood up and clambered over the side, jumping on to the makeshift landing stage. He kept his shoulders hunched and ran through the undergrowth with his head bowed until he reached a vantage point. From there he could see across the small creek that flowed into the sea.

As the boat came into view he could see Swain at the wheel. The sight of his friend immediately made him relax and he straightened up. He then sauntered down to the jetty and waited for the boat to nose its way up the creek. He had no idea why Swain had come out to the island, but he had no reason to be concerned. He stood there quite casually, the Uzi hanging comfortably in his hand.

As it drew closer, he could see two other men on board. He frowned and automatically tightened his grip on the gun. One of the men was a colossus of a man. He wore a shirt that almost didn't fit him and three-quarter length boat pants. He dwarfed Swain and the other man with them. Maclean recognized neither of them.

Swain put up his hand in a natural gesture and Maclean could see the grin on his face, his white teeth showing clearly in the evening light. He caught the rope that Swain threw over to him and, with his free hand, looped it over a wooden stump. He held it fast as Swain jumped ashore with the aft painter.

When the boat was secure, the two strangers stepped ashore. Swain introduced them to Maclean as Mr Malik and Mr Batista.

'You come to see the girl?' he asked the smaller of the two men who looked to be the spokesman although he had said nothing yet.

But it was Malik who answered. 'How is she?' He had seen the machine-gun in Maclean's hand and his stance was not that of a man who was simply carrying it about as an accessory. Malik decided to show caution. 'May we see her?'

Maclean glanced at Swain as if to seek an answer to his unasked question, but whatever it was, he thought better of it and pointed the barrel of the Uzi towards a small path.

'This way,' he said, and turned round, letting them go by.

Swain took the lead followed by Batista and Malik. Maclean brought up the rear, his senses still on alert. Eventually the path brought them to a small hut in a clearing, another one of the many retreats that dotted the archipelago; each small island as secluded as the next.

Swain paused by the door, ready to open it. Malik and Batista came up behind him and all of them turned to Maclean. He stood away from them, guardedly, and nodded to Swain who opened the door. The sun was low in the evening sky and shadows were beginning to lengthen. They chose not to walk in but to peer inside instead. It was Batista who recoiled in horror. Malik merely turned away with a look of disgust on his face.

Helen was sitting on the dirt floor with her back to the wall. She was covered in grime and dried blood from a patchwork of scratches and bruises that could be seen clearly on her exposed skin. There was a dog bowl on the floor beside her which had the remains of something in it. There was no sign of water. Against the far wall of the hut was a bed frame but no mattress on which to sleep. The hut was windowless and, although the evening air was cooling, it was still hot and stifling inside. Helen looked up from where she was sitting, but didn't seem to be aware of them, probably because she could only see Swain, and his presence was unlikely to bring her hope of release. She turned her head away and her chin dropped to her chest.

A smile hovered on Malik's lips, but in his heart he wanted to tear Maclean apart with his bare hands.

'She is still alive,' he said. 'That is good.' He stepped away from the hut and beckoned Maclean to follow. When Maclean drew a little closer to Malik, the big man brought his head closer and dropped his voice into a conspiratorial whisper.

'She has been good sport for you?' he asked, feigning interest.

Maclean shrugged dismissively. 'She's no good for me. She's woman of obeah man.'

Malik arched his eyebrows. 'You mean she will tell her man. But she is here, what can she say?'

Maclean tapped his head. 'They talk with their minds. They know.'

'But she is a white girl,' Malik pointed out.

Maclean shook his head. 'She is Bahamian. That is enough.'

As he said it, Maclean looked in the direction of the hut. It was the moment that Malik had been waiting for. He drove his fist into the side of Maclean's ribs with such a force that the big black man's breath locked in his throat as his rib cage literally folded in on him. He dropped to his knees and the Uzi fell from his grasp.

Malik scooped up the machine-gun, pointed the barrel at Maclean's head and pulled the trigger. Maclean's head burst open like an exploding melon and he pitched forward without a sound.

Swain came running from the hut the moment he heard the crackling burst of machine-gun fire. Malik lifted the barrel and aimed it towards him. The bullets flew from the snout of the stuttering gun and tore his chest away. The force of the blast flung him back against the flimsy wooden shack. It collapsed inwards beneath his dead weight and long fingers of rotting roof thatch slipped down and covered his twisted, bloody body.

Malik waited for Batista to bring Helen out. As soon as he appeared with her, they took off down the path to where the boat was tied up. Malik lifted Helen on board and Batista helped her down into the small cabin amidships.

Before slipping the painters and moving off, Malik aimed the Uzi at the diesel tank of Maclean's boat, emptying the magazine into it. Then he tossed the machine-gun into the water.

Twenty minutes later, on board the Freeport gunboat, Inspector Eustace looked through his binoculars in the fading light and saw a spiral of smoke curling upwards from one of the small islands. It bent its head in the evening breeze and drifted out towards the setting sun.

CHAPTER FOURTEEN

The knock on Marsh's cabin door was short and perfunctory. Marsh was lying on his bunk reading a yachting magazine, although his mind was not wholly absorbed by what he was reading but more on what he had threatened at the debrief. He wondered if he really had the courage to carry out his threat. Marsh was not by choice a brave, fearless fighter of a man, although his unquestionable courage in working beneath the ocean surface was undeniable, but he was wise enough to see the folly of standing up to someone like Malik in a physical confrontation, which is surely what he believed this whole thing could lead to.

The *Taliba* was sailing on a course that took them in a south-easterly direction, away from the site of their first dive. Naturally Marsh was not privy to Khan's plans, but the ship had turned on to the new heading immediately after they had surfaced. About the same time, Batista and Malik had left in the helicopter. That had been twenty-four hours ago. Now the helicopter had returned. He wondered idly why the two men had left the ship for that short time. Not that it mattered; it was none of his business.

He began to think about their new heading and, from the feel of the wind buffeting the ship, it seemed that they were heading towards the growing hurricane. He wondered if this was the change in schedule Khan had referred to when he asked de Leon about the freighter. The strengthening wind was beginning to affect the smooth passage of the ship as it moved across the growing wave tops.

He put the magazine to one side and swung his legs off the bed and went to open the door. He was not surprised to see Malik standing there because he was usually the errand boy.

'Mr Khan wants to see you on the bridge,' he told Marsh.

On the bridge, Khan waited a little impatiently, not because of the deteriorating weather, but because of the recent turn of events. They had not been of his choosing and the elimination of the two men guarding Helen Walsh could only add to the preponderance of police now looking increasingly closer at any link he might have with their murders. On the brighter side though, he hoped the turn of events would lead to a lessening of Marsh's truculence.

Khan turned as he heard Malik open the door and step on to the bridge with Marsh.

'We have something for you,' he said sharply to Marsh, and pointed to Captain de Leon's cabin behind the bridge.

Marsh hesitated at first, but then he walked over to the cabin and opened the door. At first he saw nothing, so he stepped inside. Helen was sitting on a chair, her head bowed. She looked up and turned towards him. As her eyes fell on Marsh she stood up quickly, her hand flying up to her mouth in a gasp. Marsh just stared for a moment, then closed the door behind him and went over to her. He barely had time to clear the threshold and she was in his arms.

They said nothing, just held each other tight, blotting out the memory of what had been and what might come. Their circumstances were not of the best, but they both needed the warmth and pleasure of each other's contact. Marsh held her so tightly he wondered if she would cry out in pain. Soon he had to release her, push her back gently and look into her eyes.

He could see pain there, but not from him. The pain had been inflicted deep within her, in her soul. Her face looked drawn and frightened. He could see the extensive scratches and bruising on her exposed flesh as he held her at arm's length.

'In God's name, what did they do to you?' he asked softly.

'The man who did this is dead.' She shivered. 'Oh Marsh, it was horrible.' She buried her head in her hands and began sobbing fitfully. He pulled her in close again and held her tight until her tears stopped.

Suddenly the cabin door opened and Khan stepped into the room with Malik. Marsh turned towards him.

'Was there any need for this, Khan?'

'No,' Khan agreed. 'But the man responsible has paid for it. As you can see, I've kept my word; your woman is safe now, which means we can continue with our work and you will make the dive.' He turned to Malik. 'Take them aft.' Then he turned and walked away without another word.

Francesini had been weighing up all the pros and cons until his head was bursting open and had only managed to doze off when the phone rang. He opened his eyes, slightly disorientated because of his strange surroundings. He reached for the phone and plucked it from its cradle, held it to his ear and sank back on to his pillow.

'Sir? This is Cooke.'

At first he didn't recognize the voice at the other end of the line, but that was probably because he hadn't expected to hear from him.

'Cooke? Oh, Bob. Hi!' It was the young man who worked in the photographic intelligence section at CIA headquarters. 'What can I do for you?'

'Is this a secure line, sir?' Cooke asked.

Francesini smiled and shrugged, looking round the hotel room. Not exactly five stars he thought to himself.

'Didn't know I was coming here myself until a couple of hours ago. You can say what you like, so long as it isn't a State secret.'

'Thank you, sir. Well, it's like this. You know the ship we've been keeping an eye on?' Francesini was pleased he hadn't mentioned the *Taliba* by name. Cooke carried on before waiting for a response. 'Well, the helicopter left the ship yesterday with two men on board. It returned today with three people; one of them a woman. I enhanced the image and she looked to be in some distress. Does this mean anything sir?'

Francesini sat up immediately. Helen Walsh; it had to be Helen Walsh!

'Mean anything?' he repeated. 'Cookie, if we get through this unscathed, I'm going to recommend you for a medal. Do me a favour and fax me the photo to this hotel. Do it now, will you?' He searched round for the hotel information booklet and found the hotel's fax number. He read it out to him and put the phone down. Then he got dressed and went down to the hotel reception to wait for the photograph to come through.

Marsh leaned on the aft rail with Helen. The *Taliba* was in open water. The Bahamian Islands had long since disappeared into the distance behind them and could no longer be seen. It was now early morning and the Atlantic Ocean looked unwelcoming and threatening. But for the two of them it seemed to offer a haven of tranquillity; an escape from the events that had happened to them. The wind that Marsh had been concerned about had all but disappeared, although he knew from questioning the captain that the wind was approaching from a southerly direction and they had sailed through the rim of a low pressure system.

The night before, the two of them had talked long into the night. They had talked of what had happened to Helen, what had happened to Marsh. They had talked of their fears and their futures, if they had one. Helen had told Marsh how she convinced Sweeting Maclean that she was the wife of an obeah man. Marsh had commented that it was 'powerful medicine'.

'And he fell for it,' Marsh had said.

'I'm not sure if he really did fall for it,' Helen had replied. 'But I had sown the seed of doubt. It was enough; it seemed to work anyway. He's dead now, poor man.'

'Poor man?' echoed Marsh. 'He tried to rape you.'

'Nobody deserves to die like that,' she reflected, 'with the back of his head blown off.'

Marsh stood up from the rail and breathed in a lungful of the sea air. 'You told me last night that Malik also killed another man.'

'Yes,' Helen agreed.

'I think that must have been Romulus Swain, poor bastard,' he added. 'They mean business then.'

Helen thought she detected a note of resolution in his voice. 'They mean to kill us, don't they, Marsh?'

The previous evening he had avoided coming to that conclusion for Helen's sake. Although he knew it was pointless trying to hide it from her, he tried, and came up with an indirect answer.

'We've got two more dives.'

'And then?'

He stared into the Atlantic. 'Nothing has been decided.'

She touched his arm, closing her fingers round it tenderly. 'Marsh, I do understand, but we must find a way of getting out.'

He closed his hand over hers. 'If there is a way,' he said ruefully, 'it's going to take a lot of finding.'

'We have found Sweeting Mclean,' Inspector Bain informed Francesini solemnly, 'with the back of his head blown off. Swain was there too; dead, I'm afraid.'

'What about Helen Walsh?' Francesini asked, even though he knew where she was.

Bain shook his head. 'Gone.'

'Any idea where?' Francesini asked.

'No.' It was final.

Inspector Bain had phoned Francesini at the hotel. His voice sounded disappointedly dull. Francesini knew immediately that it wasn't good news. He was already dressed because of his early morning phone call from Bob Cooke, so within five minutes he was driving his rented car over to Freeport Police headquarters.

After the preliminary discussion about the events of the previous evening, plus Francesini's concern that he hadn't been informed earlier, he tossed a manila envelope on to the desk in front of Bain.

'What's this?' Bain asked.

'Open it,' Francesini told him.

Bain did as he was asked with a little difficulty because of his injured arm and studied the enhanced satellite photograph of three people walking away from the helicopter on board the *Taliba*. After a while he looked over the desk at Francesini without lifting his head, staring over the top of his glasses. He jabbed his finger at the picture.

'Helen Walsh?'

Francesini nodded. 'She was taken on board the *Taliba* early last evening.'

Bain settled back in his chair and let the photograph drop on to his desk. He didn't look too pleased.

'Why have you waited until now to inform us?' he demanded to know. 'We could have boarded the *Taliba* and brought this whole episode to a conclusion.'

'It's not that easy, Inspector,' Francesini told him. 'I didn't receive this until about two o'clock this morning. By the time we'd organized a boarding party, the *Taliba* would have been long gone.'

Bain's eyebrows met in a deep frown. 'What do you mean, long gone?'

'It looks like Khan has gone. By now the *Taliba* will be about two hundred miles away. At this very moment she is heading out into the Atlantic Ocean, and goodness knows where she's going, but with luck, she won't return.'

But as much as Francesini wished it were true, he doubted that was the end of Hakeem Khan and the *Taliba*.

It was night and the *Taliba* moved slowly through the water, the thrust of her engines almost gone, but with just enough power to keep her on station. The ship lifted with each wave that passed beneath its belly, but fate was being kind and the gentle swell was giving no trouble to those on board. There were no lights showing and she rode the waves like a ghostly chariot; a silent phantom on unlawful occasions.

Marsh peered through the porthole of his cabin. He had no lights because all electrical power to the accommodation section had been turned off. Helen stood beside him, her arm round his waist. Malik had warned them not to venture outside their cabins until morning for reasons of safety. He wouldn't explain quite what he meant by that, but Marsh saw no reason to antagonize the man.

Marsh was soon aware of the arrival of two ships. From his vantage point he saw one of the ships slide alongside the *Taliba* while the other disappeared from his view, but its speed suggested it had taken up station on the other side. He could hear shouted commands in a language he did not understand, but soon he realized that a cargo was being transferred from the ship that was now alongside the *Taliba*.

His mind went back to the night Greg Walsh had been killed, and in his mind's eye he could see the loading operation taking place. So deep was the nightmare burned into his brain that he could see the two ships locked in a graceful embrace while one transferred the seed in its belly into the care of the other.

The whole operation lasted less than an hour, and soon the water boiled beneath the freighter in luminous phosphorescence as she edged away. Moments later she was gone, fading into the darkness like a wraith, and only Marsh's sanity kept him from believing that it had never happened at all. He felt the *Taliba*'s engines power up and soon they were under way. He wasn't sure of the heading but he guessed they were travelling back to the Gulf to plant another demonic seed.

As dawn broke over the Atlantic, Marsh woke and could feel the rollers lifting the ship with more power than previously. The *Taliba* was a sturdy vessel and could handle almost anything the sea could throw at it. He felt there was very little to concern him so he went up on deck with the intention of spending ten minutes there before having breakfast. He decided not to wake Helen who was now in her own cabin.

As Marsh came out on to the after deck and turned towards the bridge superstructure, his eyes gaped in amazement. The *Taliba* had taken on a different outline! He shook his head and looked again, but it was there as clear as day. He walked forward slowly, looking at other changes he could see. Around the superstructure he noticed that canvas awnings had been erected at strategic points, changing the outline of the ship. He ventured further forward and saw that the *Challenger* was hidden beneath a canvas awning stretched right across the deck. Parts of the deck and the bridge had been painted to give a subtle change to the appearance of the ship's lines. He couldn't believe it, but there was no mistake; under close scrutiny, certainly from overhead observation and even from a passing ship, the *Taliba* had ceased to exist.

As evil as Khan's intentions were, he knew that the game had now entered its most dangerous phase. Marsh returned to his cabin with the absorbing and frightening thought that his own time was limited and there was very little he could do about it.

For the remainder of the day, Marsh and Helen were confined to their quarters. No reason asked; no reason given. They used the time to hatch various escape plans and to immediately discard them until the game became useless and an admission of defeat was all they could muster. Marsh knew he could refuse to pilot the submersible, but he also knew that Khan could take over, even if his heart was suspect. Khan would probably survive the dives; his own fanaticism would push him beyond his own limits. Marsh understood that.

But Marsh also understood that he would not be allowed to live beyond a refusal to co-operate, and they had no way of knowing what would happen to Helen; probably the same fate. No, Marsh decided that while he was still in some kind of control, with some part to play in Khan's evil scheme, he might have a small bargaining counter that could guarantee his and Helen's freedom. But in his heart, he knew he was kidding himself.

Francesini arrived back at his office with a degree of pessimism clouding his day. Such was the urgency now of Francesini's mission, he had flown from Freeport direct to Langley Air Force Base, and was picked up by a staff car. It had been a demanding flight, not from the point of being tiring, but he had so many unanswered questions floating about in his mind and no one to bounce them off that he had almost succumbed to melancholia.

It didn't help when Admiral Starling had admitted to him that he, too, was under pressure from the President's National Security Adviser; he wanted results. This meant that the President's man was under pressure from the President himself. And this meant that the pressure rolled all the way down to the man at the front – Francesini. The buck may stop at the Oval Office, Francesini had told the admiral, but it was certainly uncomfortable from where he was standing.

He thought about the child's song he would sometimes chant when he was at junior school. 'Big fleas have little fleas on their backs to bite 'em. Little fleas have littler fleas and so *ad infinitum.*'

Did we sing that? He wondered as he sat down at his desk. There was a yellow Post-it note on his desk. The message was scrawled in almost unintelligible writing.

'*Your phone is off. Ring me please.*'

It was signed by Cooke. Francesini frowned and pulled his mobile phone from his pocket. Sure enough it was switched off. He shook his head and turned the phone on. He remembered switching it off during the flight. He reached for the desk phone and dialled Cooke's number.

'Hallo, Bob, Francesini here. What can I do for you?'

'We've lost the *Taliba*, sir. It's gone!'

Francesini sat bolt upright. 'What?'

'It's gone, sir; disappeared during the night. We tracked her image into the Atlantic. Her signature was pretty strong for a while, but when I came in to work this morning ...' He paused there. Francesini could hear him breathing. He sounded nervous. 'Well, sir, it's like I said; she's gone.'

'Have you checked all the images?' Francesini asked. He knew it was unnecessary.

'All of them, sir. She just faded away.'

Francesini felt the 'fleas' on his back. 'I'm coming down to your office. Have the images ready for me, will you?'

'Yes, sir.'

He put the phone down, the song running through his head: '... little fleas have littler fleas and so *ad infinitum.*'

Marsh thought the *Challenger* was beautiful. To others she was ugly and ungainly, which she certainly was. But Marsh looked at her from an engineer's point of view, from an oceanographer's perspective. Everything on that submersible was designed with a distinct purpose in mind; there was nothing surplus. She might not have had an aesthetic appeal, Marsh realized that, but he was still fascinated by her.

He clambered up the short ladder to check the umbilical was securely attached and while he was on top of the submersible, he checked the security of all the lifting rings. He then dropped down the far side and continued his checks along the whole length of the submersible. When he was satisfied that everything was in order, he opened the door of the cockpit bubble and climbed in.

The *Taliba* had maintained a good speed to get back on station below the Florida Keys. The dive had been planned for early dawn about twenty-four hours after being alongside the freighter. A grey light was beginning to seep over the horizon but it was still dark as Marsh began his internal checks. When he had completed those he thumbed the speech button.

'*Taliba*, this is *Challenger*. How do you read? Over.'

'Loud and clear, Marsh,' Khan's voice came back to him. 'Dive should commence in thirty minutes.'

Before Khan could close the communication link, Marsh heard a voice in the background. 'It's the rig, sir.'

A moment later Khan came back to him. '*Challenger*, we shall be on station in fifteen minutes. Computed drift rate four knots, twenty degrees north, north-east, surface wind, force five.'

'*Challenger* acknowledged, roger and out.'

A fresh breeze, thought Marsh. The rim of the hurricane was

drawing closer. It was a good thing it didn't blow under water, he mused, although it could still cause a lot of problems.

Batista appeared at the front of the *Challenger* and motioned to Marsh that the lift was about to begin. Marsh acknowledged him and waited. Suddenly the submersible moved and slipped sideways about three or four inches as the deck winch took the weight of the *Challenger* and lifted just clear of the deck.

The four hooks attached to each lifting eye spun momentarily and then stabilized. All eyes were on the lift as they swung the submersible over the side of the *Taliba*, looking curiously odd in her hastily renewed superstructure. Marsh wondered if the dummy rigging on the ship would survive the strengthening winds, but he was sure Khan would have allowed for that and for time being on his side.

As *Challenger* rotated slightly on the lifting ropes, Marsh thought he saw another ship off *Taliba*'s beam, but the light was too bad to discern any real shape. And whatever it was, it was soon hidden from view. He ignored it and concentrated on getting the submersible settled on to the surface.

Once the *Challenger* was on the water, the lifting sling, with its four wire ropes was quickly detached. Marsh waited for an all clear signal from the *Taliba* and allowed the *Challenger* to slip beneath the waves, calling out the depth as it sank slowly towards the sea bed.

When the submersible was ten metres from the bottom, Marsh trimmed her out and held her there. Batista and Zienkovitch left the chamber. At that moment Khan's voice crackled inside the bubble.

'Marsh, we estimate the well-head is one hundred metres off your port beam.'

Marsh frowned. It was not like Khan to make such an error and miss the well-head by such a margin.

'One hundred metres off port beam,' he repeated. 'Still holding at seventy metres depth and turning left.'

Marsh piloted the submersible almost blindly, relying on the *Taliba* to call out his position. He could have navigated using the global positioning system on board, but it was much easier to let Khan guide him on.

The two divers followed him as he brought *Challenger* over the well-head. He reduced power to the thrust motors and settled the submersible above its station, keeping an eye on the hand signals from both divers. Ten minutes later the *Challenger* was attached to the well-head by its skirt and Marsh sat alone in the bubble. He felt detached in the underwater world that surrounded him.

Francesini put the tip of his finger on the grainy, satellite photograph. He could see the *Taliba* clearly. At least, that's what Cooke had told him. But the subsequent photographs showed a fainter, less clear image. Weather conditions had done much to obscure the ship, plus the time: two o'clock in the morning. The final print showed nothing, simply a computed position of where the ship would probably be, given that she had stayed on the same heading and not changed course.

'The weather didn't help sir,' Cooke offered. 'But we have these.'

He pulled up a picture on his computer screen that showed several erratic traces. Closer inspection showed that there were actually three distinct traces layered one above the other.

'This top trace,' Cooke was saying, pointing at the screen, 'is the *Taliba*'s signature. The other two are unknown.' The screen changed as Cooke punched a finger at the keyboard. 'Here the three signatures merge. Almost as if three ships are about to collide,' he added. '*Taliba*'s computed direction brings her into this contact with the others. And in the next shot,' he said, pulling up another image, 'they all merge into one, indistinguishable blob.'

Francesini straightened. 'These signatures are through the cloud, right?' Cooke nodded. 'And you think the *Taliba* has made a rendezvous with two other ships?' Cooke nodded again. 'So how come you couldn't pick up *Taliba*'s trace once the ships had parted company?'

'The satellite was ordered to lock on to the three signatures. But for some reason, it only locked on to two. Neither of them was the *Taliba*.'

Peering through the gloom, Marsh thought he saw something. Whatever it was lay just on the edge of the arc spread by *Challenger*'s powerful lamps. He leaned forward instinctively, hoping to get a clearer view, but it didn't help. He wondered if it was a natural feature of the sea bed; a small outcropping of rock perhaps. He put the submersible's radar scanning head on and looked at the image on the radar monitor. It was unclear and, as far as Marsh was concerned it was unimportant, but he had little to do except wait until he received instructions from either the divers or the *Taliba*.

He looked up from the screen and peered out again through the cockpit, but the longer Marsh stared at it, the more bewildering it became. It began to dance and change shape and become distracting, so he gave up looking at it. The important thing was to think more about Batista and Zienkovitch and to keep *Challenger* functioning, not concern himself with some illusory object of no importance.

Soon the operation was complete and another bomb had been lowered into Mother Earth. Marsh flooded the ballast tanks to compensate for the weight of the bomb and trimmed the submersible to rise a few feet once he had received the signal from the surface.

Khan's voice crackled through. 'We have a small problem, *Challenger*.'

Marsh's heart skipped a few beats. 'Say again, *Taliba*.'

'A problem, Marsh, but don't worry. A squall has appeared on radar. We had hoped it would pass us by, but judging from its present course, it will pass through us. It will make recovery difficult.'

'I'll remain on station, *Taliba*.'

'Negative, *Challenger*, drift with the stream for a while. It should take you clear. Say three miles.'

'Acknowledged, *Taliba*,' Marsh replied. 'Three miles, drifting now.'

There was nothing wrong with this type of manoeuvre and the *Taliba* had all the necessary sonar and GPS tracking gear to keep station almost immediately above him, so Marsh was not concerned. And he realized it was simple expediency to move away from the path of the squall to recover a few miles distant.

In the event, the recovery operation was completely successful and the *Challenger* was on board the *Taliba* and hooked into the ship's generators in less than two hours. Marsh clambered down from the cockpit in a sombre mood. Two bombs were now in position, one left to be planted. The more he thought about it, the more his own fears grew, and the more probable and realistic they became.

If Marsh was right, and he had figured out exactly what Khan was up to, then only a terrible catastrophe could result. The line was right, the depth was right. One more bomb, one more chance to do something, but no hope in hell of getting away and telling the world.

CHAPTER FIFTEEN

The phone on Starling's desk jangled at him. He lifted it from its cradle without looking at it and continued writing.

'Starling,' he growled.

'Sir, this is Jennifer.'

He stopped writing and grunted an apology; he wasn't allowed to growl at his secretary. 'Sorry, Jennifer. What is it?'

'I have Commander Spade on the line, Admiral. From the US submarine *Oregon*.'

Starling frowned. The *Oregon* was a Benjamin Franklin Class submarine, converted from a former Fleet Ballistic Missile Submarine, an SSBN, but no longer part of America's nuclear fleet. So what on earth could Commander Spade want, he wondered?

'Digger? Well, well. Put him on, please, Jennifer.'

He heard a click and Commander Spade came on the line. Spade and Starling were old friends going way back. They had both been commissioned as young naval officers during the Vietnam War. Their careers had run along similar paths and they usually managed to meet up with each other every two or three years. Spade had been known as 'Digger' and had chosen a career in submarines, whereas Starling known as 'Birdy', opted for a career as a navy pilot. Neither of them had used their nicknames for years.

'Jim Starling?'

Starling smiled at the sound of his old friend's voice and recalled many fond memories. 'Hallo, Digger, how are you? Long time no see.'

'Hallo, Birdy, pressure of work I'm afraid,' Spade answered. 'How are you these days?'

'Mustn't grumble. Although my secretary says I often do. How can I help you?'

'Is your line secure?'

'Secure?' He laughed. 'This is the headquarters of the CIA,' Starling reminded him.

'Oh, in that case perhaps I should use a call box,' Spade joked.

Starling laughed again. It felt good. 'So why are you calling?'

'I believe you're interested in the *Taliba*?'

Commander Spade's immediate mention of Khan's ship took Starling by surprise. 'Damn right I am,' Starling answered. 'But I'm told we've lost her.'

'Well, we've found her. We picked up her signature on sonar an hour ago.'

For a moment Starling didn't quite know what to say. So he asked the obvious.

'Where?'

'At the moment she is steering a course towards Cuba. We are keeping a discreet distance from her, but we're on station.'

Starling couldn't understand it. 'How come you're involved in this?'

'We had a request about twenty-four hours ago. We were given a bearing and asked to do a search. We're on a shakedown cruise at the moment, so it gave us a little time to play. We're "off book". Been transferred OPCON.'

In the world of military games and necessarily expedient decision making, it was sometimes useful to have a vessel transferred from its Command HQ to another agency so that it remained temporarily 'off book'. The transfer was always OPCON; operational control.

Starling's face screwed up into a frown. 'Who requested your involvement?' he asked.

'Don't know, man, but it had to go through NorthCom [Northern Command]. Almost certainly originated from your department.'

Starling thought about Remo Francesini and his own order to dig deep.

'I see,' Starling responded, non-comittally. 'I see. You know we lost her on satellite?'

'So I believe, Birdy. But when it comes to satellite tracking, you can't beat the submariners.'

They both laughed. 'I'll give you that, Digger. Well then, seeing as you're on the case, there's something I'd like you to do for me.'

'Certainly, as long as my admiral approves. What is it?'

'I won't tell you over the phone, Digger; I'll send a signal within the hour. Just don't lose that boat.'

They finished the conversation in pleasantries then Starling set about putting a plan into operation that would involve the US Navy Seals. He was also beginning to feel a little better about the whole thing because the latest developments had handed him an element of control.

Four hours after James Starling had spoken to his old friend; a Hercules transport plane flew over Commander Spade's submarine, the USS *Oregon* as twilight began to wash over the approaches to the Bahamian Island chain. There was a slight swell, but the submarine managed to cope with that despite being on the surface.

The rear doors of the Hercules opened. Inside the aircraft, standing by the doors but attached to a safety line was the loadmaster. Beside him were two men dressed completely in black and wearing parachutes. As the Hercules approached the drop zone, the voice of the pilot could be heard by the loadmaster through his headset. Suddenly the two red warning lights above the door went out and two greens came on in their place.

'DZ! DZ! Go!'

As the loadmaster shouted and waved the men off, the two figures dropped from the rear door of the Hercules and slipped away swiftly in the slipstream until their fall was checked by the unfurling of their parawing chutes. As they deployed in the darkness they glided gently down towards the sea and the USS *Oregon* until they both landed on the surface within fifty metres of *Oregon*'s inflatable rescue boat. Within thirty minutes of leaving the aircraft, the two members of the US Seals were standing in front of Commander Spade inside the submarine's control room.

The *Taliba* lay at anchor off the island of Cuba. Although the lights from the shore were clearly visible, the ship was anchored well away from the shoreline. It was past midnight and nobody stirred on deck except the two men on watch; one forward, the other aft. It was a warm night and music could be heard very faintly drifting over the calm sea from other craft anchored offshore. The lights of the distant port shimmered above their reflections in the water, their colours fused into the mirror blackness. The riding lights of the other boats swayed gently.

The cocktail of distant lights and faint music drew the attention of the two men on watch, each in his own private world, each one wishing that he could be ashore, enjoying the seductive pleasures on offer. Behind those two men, each separated by the length of the *Taliba*, the black ocean swept out into the vast emptiness of the night, offering nothing of interest other than an occasional passing ship.

And in that vast emptiness, two heads bobbed above the surface without a sound, just thirty metres from them.

The two US Navy Seals were wearing wet suits. Their faces were blackened and although one of them was of West Indian origin, his face was blackened to keep it to a matte appearance. They both had rubber caps covering their heads and were virtually invisible to anyone on board the *Taliba*.

After several minutes studying the ship, they swam beneath the water towards her, surfacing alongside the hull. Then, carefully, they moved to the stern of the vessel where they knew they would find the boarding platform common with ships using divers. The platform was hoisted vertically into its stowage position, but that presented no obstacle for the two Seals.

They climbed aboard the aft deck and slipped out of sight behind the base of a lifting winch. One of them pointed to the crewman on watch, barely ten metres from them and made a gesture to his companion. Then he edged forward.

The crewman continued leaning on the ship's rail, blissfully unaware that he now had company. The Navy Seal stood up behind him without a sound, whipped an arm around his neck and pressed two fingers into the side of his neck beneath the ear. He held him like that for a while until he felt the crewman relax. To avoid letting the man slump to the deck, he positioned him in such a fashion that the unconscious man's bodyweight kept him propped up against the rail. To casual observation, it looked as though he was staring absently into the sea below.

He quickly turned to his colleague who sprinted from his hiding place to a locker fixed horizontally along the ship's inboard bulkhead. It was alongside the one that faced the shore. Inside were mainly lifejackets and ropes. Satisfied it would serve his purpose, he unzipped his wetsuit and pulled a plastic bag from inside, opened it, and sprinkled the contents into the locker. Pulling a lighter from his pocket and shielding the flame with a cupped hand, he lit a piece of saturated gun cotton and dropped it into the locker, closing the lid.

The other Seal waited until he could see smoke billowing from the locker, then he ran across the deck to the crewman who was still unconscious and shook him vigorously. He shouted '*Fuego! Fuego!*' well into the man's ear and ran for cover on to the opposite side of the ship.

The crewman shook himself and began rubbing his neck, thinking he had fallen asleep. Suddenly he straightened and turned round, his expression turning from one of puzzlement to shock. He began shouting and ran for a fire extinguisher. The crewman on forward watch heard the shouting and ran down to join him. On the way he pushed an alarm button fixed to a bulkhead and suddenly all hell was let loose. Alarm bells burst into life; someone dashed from a door and ran up the steps to the bridge. Others began falling out of doorways, half asleep, all of them heading towards the pall of smoke that billowed out from the rope locker.

The two Navy Seals waited until most of the activity was on the far side of the ship from where they were concealed. Then they ran towards the door leading to the accommodation deck. They took the steps two at a time and pushed open another door. One of them pulled the door back on himself so that he was partially concealed while the other Seal went along the companionway trying each door. As he suspected, none of them was locked because their occupants had all gone to their emergency stations. Except two. One would be Helen Walsh and the other Harry Marsham.

At the first locked door he came to, he called out Marsham's name.

Inside the cabin, Marsh was awake. He had heard the commotion but had made no attempt to leave his cabin because he and Helen were locked in at night. When he heard his name being called out, he assumed for a moment that it was Malik. But the voice was different; it was deliberately quiet and hurried. Whoever it was called his name again.

'Marsham! Are you in there?'

Marsh nodded. 'Yes!' he answered.

The voice told him to wait for a moment. Marsh could then hear an unfamiliar sound at the keyhole of his door. Suddenly the door flew open and Marsh reeled back in shock.

Standing in front of him was a giant of a black man wearing a wetsuit. He had his finger pressed to his lips, urging Marsh not to say anything. He stepped into the cabin and closed the door behind him.

'Harry Marsham?'

Marsh nodded. 'Yes. And who are you?'

'Lieutenant Santos, sir, United States Navy. Now will you please tell me what the hell is going on?'

The door of Francesini's office swung open and Starling burst in like a bear with its backside on fire. The expression on his face left Francesini under no illusion that this was anything but a friendly visit.

'Read this,' he said, and flung a file on Francesini's desk.

Francesini picked up the file, opened it and began to read. Starling poured himself a coffee and sat in the chair beside the desk. His eyes never left Francesini's face. He was smouldering.

'Well?' he asked, when he saw Francesini look up. 'There's little doubt now, is there?'

Francesini shrugged, still erring on the side of caution. 'It's still supposition and theory, sir. We need expert advice on this. And I don't mean a bunch of gung-ho generals leading the way. If it's purposeful and genuine oil exploration using new techniques and we go in with all guns blazing, there'll be hell to pay.'

'There will be hell to pay if we don't,' Starling countered.

'I understand that, sir, but I need twenty-four hours before I can recommend what you're asking.'

'And what will you do if I agree to wait that long?' Starling would only concede this because he trusted Francesini's judgement completely, and valued it.

'I'll go to Massachusetts, sir; to the Woods Hole Institute.'

'What's up with our own specialists?' Starling asked. 'I know they're clever buggers at the institute, but can we trust them?'

'It isn't a question of trust, Admiral. If we hand this to our own specialists we could be in danger of having this taken out of our hands. I know it may not seem reasonable to go outside of the CIA, but in this case I am prepared to back my own judgement.'

There was a profound logic in Francesini's argument. The admiral often found himself fighting his own corner because of internecine warfare breaking out between departments at Langley. And there always seemed to be wounding security leaks between heads of departments. By going to the specialists in the Woods Hole Institute, they could swear them to secrecy under the dire threat of draconian measures if they dared pass on anything the department had released to them.

Starling acquiesced. 'OK, Remo, twenty-four hours. Meanwhile I'll get an assault team on standby.' He stood up. 'Incidentally, was that your idea to get the US Submarine *Oregon* on Khan's tail?'

Francesini shook his head. 'No, sir, that was Cooke's. He told me that satellite imagery is fine if the weather's OK, but the submarine's a better bet. If you can get one!'

Starling chuckled. 'We ought to promote that boy. Good, sound thinking. And with the *Oregon* on station—'

Francesini interrupted his boss, holding his hand up. 'Ah, no such luck I'm afraid. Operational priority has taken *Oregon* off the case. She'll be miles away by now.'

Starling's eyebrows knitted together in an instant frown. 'So who's keeping an eye on the *Taliba* now?'

Francesini didn't want to tell him, but he had to. 'I'm afraid we're back with the satellite.'

'You're still not convinced?' Captain de Leon asked Khan.

They were in Khan's cabin and had been discussing the sudden outbreak of fire in the rope locker.

'That fire was no accident, I'm sure of it.' Khan insisted. 'But Allah is still with us.' He reached for the familiar bottle of tablets. A glass of water was beside him. The pain was more advanced now. He swallowed the tablets and gulped the water down. De Leon could see the pain in Khan's face and almost feel it himself.

'You should be in hospital,' he told him.

Khan reacted angrily. 'No! In two days the trinity will be complete. I will live to see it. I must live.' He kept striking the top of his desk lightly with a clenched fist as he spoke. 'Two days, Captain. Two days.'

'*Inshalla*,' the captain said.

Khan looked up at de Leon through hooded eyes and nodded gently. 'You think like an Arab, too. It is good.'

'You are paying me a lot of money.'

'Ah,' Khan said lightly. 'And would you sell to a higher bidder?'

De Leon shook his head. 'Not my soul, but my mother? Maybe.'

Khan laughed softly. 'Then I am glad I am not your mother.'

The ship rocked suddenly as a gust of wind slammed into the hull. Khan looked over to the cabin window. Outside the sky was overcast and he could see the storm clouds moving quickly.

'How long do we have, Captain?' he asked.

'Forty-eight hours at the most,' de Leon told him. 'The wind is strengthening from the south east. At the moment we are safe, but if the winds strengthen any more, we can expect a hurricane, here in the Gulf, within two days.'

'What about the rig?' Khan asked.

De Leon shrugged. 'The direction of the storm is unpredictable, but we have to assume the rig will be hit. To think otherwise would be neither logical nor sensible.'

Khan gave this some thought, and then shrugged. 'No matter; once we have Marsh and *Challenger* under water, the third bomb will be in place and the trinity will be complete. Then the hurricane can do what it likes.' He stood up from his desk with some effort. A thought crossed his mind. 'Incidentally, have you arranged for the freighter?'

De Leon nodded. 'As you asked, sir. It's offshore about fifteen miles. We'll call it in after nightfall.'

Khan was satisfied. 'Good. Then I'll leave everything to you, Captain.'

De Leon gave a perfunctory nod. 'Anything else, sir?'

'No, nothing else. Thank you, Captain.'

De Leon thought that Khan might have mentioned the fire again, and was relieved that he hadn't. Heart attacks he could handle; paranoia he couldn't. He threw up a gratuitous salute and left the cabin.

Khan glanced out of the window and offered up a prayer. His heart trembled and a sudden fear flashed through his mind. He reached for the water bottle and his tablets.

Two days, he thought; just two more days. *Inshalla!*

*

As the light of a grey day filtered through the windows of his office at the Woods Hole Oceanographic Institute in Massachusetts, Professor Alan Schofeld grappled with the desperate thoughts running through his mind, fervently wishing that his conclusions were wrong.

But they were not; of that he was absolutely convinced.

He turned away from the window, his expression as grey as the overcast sky outside, and picked up the report from his desk that he had received that morning. It had been delivered by hand, by two senior officers in the CIA who had considered it important enough to bring it in person.

Schofeld had decided that it was his own natural and professional scepticism that had persuaded him to ask them for time. His initial reaction was perhaps a trifle condescending, but now, having had time to consider the impact of what he had read, he realized just how shamefully patronizing he had been.

The two men from the CIA had introduced themselves as James Starling and Remo Francesini. They had agreed to leave the report with him but had sworn him to absolute secrecy. Schofeld had reluctantly agreed to their request, wondering what all the fuss was about. Now it all seemed so preposterous and churlish of him. What he had concluded after studying the document and researching the facts was quite frightening, and he wished he had never seen it or the two men who had brought it to him. He had used several computer programmes to convince himself of his own diagnosis. He had used computer modelling to try and break down his own argument, based on the information he had before him, but finally he had come to the inevitable conclusion that the two men from the CIA had every right to swear him to secrecy.

He leaned back on his desk, the report still in his hand and wondered if Starling and Francesini already knew just how big and dangerous a threat it contained. And now he knew he had been invited to sup at the Devil's table and he didn't like it at all; it frightened the life out of him.

He twisted round and pushed the button on his desk intercom and asked his secretary to contact the two CIA officers and ask them to come to the office.

Schofeld was still struggling with the incredible possibilities of the report as he poured coffee for Starling and Francesini. He pushed their cups towards them. His face was like stone.

'Gentlemen,' he began. 'I suspect that some of what I am about to tell you, you will already know, but it will be necessary for me to recount the facts in order to persuade ourselves that my deductions are sound and my conclusions honest. Although I wish to God they were wrong.'

He picked up the report and they could almost see his nose wrinkling at the prospect of what it contained.

'I was sceptical at first, I must admit,' he told them, 'but I know Harry Marsham quite well. I've worked with him on several occasions and trust his professional and personal judgment completely. Everything he has suggested accords with my own view.' He cleared his throat. 'Unfortunately. Anyway, let us begin.'

He switched on a projector that immediately showed an oceanographer's map of the Atlantic Ocean stretching from the east coast of the United States and Canada to the western approaches to northern Europe.

'During the winters in our northern hemisphere, a high-pressure system develops over Siberia and Central Asia which brings the coldest temperatures on earth outside of the Polar ice caps. It means that a great many of the northern countries like Latvia, northern Russia, etcetera, are frozen over for almost six months of the year. The average temperature in those areas can be as low as minus eighteen degrees Celsius; about minus sixty degrees Fahrenheit. It wouldn't happen, of course, if it wasn't for the fact that the Himalayas buttress the warm air of the Indian Ocean, preventing it from flowing up into Central Asia.'

He paused as if to consider his next point. 'So, the only tempering influence on the upper reaches of the northern hemisphere comes from the Gulf of Mexico by way of the Atlantic Ocean.'

'The Gulf Stream,' Francesini said. Starling nodded and continued to study the professor's face.

'Quite,' the professor continued. 'Now, global warming seems to be coming to the aid of these frozen parts, but quite slowly, and, of course, not for a good many years yet. Those countries will still continue to struggle under these extreme conditions, probably for much of what's left of this century, maybe longer.'

Starling and Francesini nodded, neither of them sure just where this was leading. Schofeld carried on.

'Now, let's consider the Gulf Stream for a moment. As you both know, I'm sure; it is born in the Gulf of Mexico, jets through the Florida Narrows between Miami and the Grand Bahamas, and flows up the eastern seaboard of America as far as Cape Hatteras. From there it swings right across the Atlantic Ocean, passes by the British Isles, continues up to Norway and then on to Russia. By which time it doesn't do the Russians much good at all.'

Francesini and Starling allowed themselves a little victorious smile.

'There are two important considerations here: the Gulf Stream has a direct effect on the Sargasso Sea. That's the large, almost motionless area in the centre of the Atlantic. It holds it in check. If the Sargasso Sea was able to drift and circulate a few degrees north, it would provide a warmer climate for the whole of Scandinavia.'

He paused, letting it sink in. But for the two men listening, there was nothing yet that worried them. They both wondered when the professor would get to the point.

'The other important consideration, gentlemen, is the Irminger Current. This is a small finger of warm water that leads away from the Gulf Stream. It flows up to the western coast of Greenland and helps to prevent that coastline from freezing. If it were not for the upward flow of the Irminger Current, then the Labrador Current, sometimes known as the Ogden Pump, would flow down through Newfoundland as far as Cape Hatteras, and the eastern seaboard of America would freeze over in the winter. It would mean extreme conditions all along the eastern territories of the United States during the winter months and perhaps longer.'

Schofeld stopped then and lifted his cup from the desk. He looked over the top of his cup at the two men, waiting for them to either say something or let him continue. They said nothing.

'If it was possible,' he went on, after finishing his coffee, 'to alter the direction of the Gulf Stream by a couple of degrees, or indeed even stop it, the following things would happen.'

He began ticking them off on his fingers.

'The Sargasso Sea would tighten and warm up. The prevailing westerly winds would absorb much of this heat and bring a more temperate climate to parts of Scandinavia. Good for them, no doubt.

'The Irminger Current would almost certainly disappear, and the effect would be to bring the Labrador Current sweeping down the eastern seaboard of America. This would change the climate of the north-eastern states drastically, and they would be like Siberia for much of the year.'

He picked up the report which had been drawn up by Francesini, using the information obtained from Marsh by the Navy Seal Lieutenant Santos.

'Marsh says there are three bombs. To alter the topography of the sea bed between Florida and the Grand Bahamas in order to achieve a two degree shift of the Gulf Stream and possibly stopping it altogether, would result in a rise in sea level of about two feet along the eastern side. This would almost certainly flood the entire Bahamian Archipelago. Everything would disappear.

'When the bombs explode, the resultant tidal wave, a tsunami, would overrun the whole of the State of Florida as far south as the Keys. It would engulf most of the Gulf of Mexico seaboard, Central America; places like Guatemala, Belize, eastern Mexico. Coastlines and low-lying countries like Cuba, Puerto Rico and all of the West Indies would be devastated. The tsunami that struck Indonesia and killed two hundred and thirty thousand people in 2004 would be small fry in comparison.

'The energy pulse from the three bombs would silence all communication, cell phones, air-traffic control systems, public transport, computer highways, the internet, everything. Anything that relied on telecommunications would cease to work within a two hundred mile radius. Everything!'

He dropped the report on to his desk. The two men remained silent. Schofield continued.

'Khan is attacking the soft underbelly of America. There are nearly four thousand oil and gas rigs in the Gulf of Mexico supplying almost thirty per cent of our domestic oil and gas. Our economy could be wrecked. The knock-on effect for the other Western economies would be disastrous. The death toll in the Gulf alone would reach well over a million; to say nothing of the total devastation and havoc brought down on the survivors.'

He paused, letting it sink in. Starling and Francesini sat there impassively; their expressions almost wooden.

'Gentlemen,' the professor said gravely. 'You must stop this madman. If you do not, you are looking at a scenario of apocalyptic proportions.'

CHAPTER SIXTEEN

The lines on Francesini's face looked as though they had been painted on with an artist's brush. They were deeply etched into his expression and showed the considerable pressure he was under. Since his meeting with Professor Schofeld at the Woods Hole Institute, he had been subjected to a very uncomfortable meeting with the President's National Security Adviser who had wasted no time in trying to reduce him to a nervous wreck by an attack on his character, his department, his appalling efforts to stop the madman, Hakeem Khan, and anything else he could lay his political tongue too.

James Starling had allowed himself a wry smile after the disastrous meeting and offered the opinion that he was glad to have men like Francesini in his department who could take the flak from career politicians. He also told Francesini that he would still be in a job even after the National Security Adviser had joined the ranks of ex-senators and become part of the after-dinner speaking circuit, albeit earning large sums of money.

Starling's levity did little to alter Francesini's demeanour because his own worries were genuine; he really feared for the safety of the millions who lived within the killing zone of those three bombs. And the devil of it was, he now knew exactly what Khan was up to but, ludicrous as it was to even consider, he felt it might be too late to stop him.

He was now standing in a room at the Guantanamo Naval Base set aside for him by the commanding officer of the base. He had flown down with James Starling immediately after the meeting with the National Security Adviser. Although there was no change in the time zones, both of them were feeling distinctly jet-lagged.

In the room, in two rows facing Francesini and the admiral, were eight men. In the front row was Lieutenant Santos, the Navy Seal who had boarded the *Taliba*. Francesini stood up. On the wall behind him, pinned to a white board, were several photographs. None of them had an identifying label. He pushed his own thoughts of Armageddon to the back of his mind and addressed his audience.

'Gentlemen, your brief is straightforward and one which I am sure you have all been asked to do before, but unlike some of your missions, we cannot contemplate failure on this. I will not go into details why, although I know Lieutenant Santos is aware of the reasons. His urgent desire to go on this mission should convey sufficiently to you all just how vitally important success is.'

He did not really believe that these men, all experts in their field of covert operations should need convincing, but he laid it on the line for them more for his own sake than theirs. He turned to the photographs and touched one.

'This is the oceanographic survey vessel *Taliba*. At the moment we understand she is sheltering in Cuban waters. Anywhere else and this meeting would not have been necessary. We are pursuing diplomatic channels, of course, and have asked the Cuban Government to impound the ship, but, as you all know, President Castro is no friend of the Americans.'

He moved to the next photograph. 'This is Hakeem Khan, the vessel's owner. He was never considered an extremist, quite the opposite in fact; however, we now suspect that he is a member of al-Qaeda, the extreme Islamic terrorist organization.'

He moved to the next photograph. 'This is Abdul Malik, Khan's bodyguard. He is a killer, nothing more, nothing less.' He left the rest unsaid. The men in that room were also killers, but only out of expediency.

Lieutenant Santos nodded to himself softly, not because he had seen Malik when he boarded the *Taliba*, but because he hoped he would meet Malik face to face.

'This photograph,' Francesini continued, 'is of Doctor Harry Marsham, to give him his full title. He is known as Marsh to all his friends. If you speak to him, call him by that name. He's probably forgotten his real one by now.'

A chuckle spread through the men. Even Starling allowed himself a smile.

'And this woman,' he said finally, 'is Helen Walsh. What this young woman has been through you wouldn't wish upon your worst enemy. Handle her very carefully, gentlemen; she could be at breaking point.'

He turned and looked at the admiral who nodded. He sat down and James Starling took over.

'Your brief, gentlemen,' Starling began, 'is to board *Taliba* the moment she leaves Cuban waters. We want Hakeem Khan alive. We also want Marsh and the woman, Helen Walsh. Malik is to be eliminated. Charges are to be placed below the water-line and the *Taliba* sunk *immediately*.

'If there is armed resistance to the point where the mission could be jeopardized, Khan *must* be snatched and the *Taliba* sunk. All others on board are forfeit. I repeat: "all others". There are details of the vessel for you to peruse, courtesy of the Naval Architects Department in the CIA.

'At the moment the weather, as you can tell just by looking out of the windows, is against us. We expect *Taliba* to leave Cuban waters soon. We have been unable to track her successfully by satellite because of the unusually deep cloud cover and the fact that we believe she has had some temporary structural alterations to confuse our satellites. There is a hurricane moving into the Caribbean, although we don't expect it to track too closely to *Taliba*'s position. But, in any event, whether the hurricane changes course or not, we do not have time on our side. We have land-based agents in place and they will inform us as soon as *Taliba* puts to sea. If there are no questions gentlemen, I wish you all good hunting.'

Marsh had been ordered forward to *Challenger*. It was barely midnight and the order puzzled him, but he had learned not to ask questions. The directive had been very clear: *Challenger* was to be made ready for a dive.

He found the task unrewarding. Working at night seemed to demand stealth where in fact it was quite unnecessary. Strangely though, he was aware that the rest of the crew were moving about on deck with an almost tangible feeling of anticipation, accompanied by a worrying silence.

This feeling edged its way into his mind and he knew that something extraordinary was going to happen; something to which he was not privy. It troubled Marsh because he knew this was to be the last dive, the last chance to do something. He felt hopeless and helpless, and tried losing himself in the task of readying the submersible, but found even that could not dispel the gnawing fear that was burning away inside him.

Suddenly an order came down from the bridge to extinguish all lights. Marsh climbed out of *Challenger's* open cockpit door and dropped down on to the deck. There was no moon or starlight because of the cloud cover and the order to extinguish all lights did not make sense. He knew they were anchored in Cuban waters, but none of the crew had been allowed ashore.

Malik appeared almost ghostlike beside Marsh and put his finger to his lips. Marsh frowned at the gesture, although he understood clearly what Malik was saying; the warning was pure and menacing. Malik then pointed towards the side of *Taliba* and Marsh became aware of the shape of a cargo ship looming up on their starboard side.

He glanced up at *Taliba's* bridge as the red and green navigation lights went out. There was a sudden grumbling noise as the anchor chain was pulled up, and the deck trembled slightly beneath his feet. The engines were starting.

As the freighter slipped alongside, Marsh could feel the screws thrashing the water, and *Taliba* began to move slowly. The freighter was now almost stationary. Marsh knew then that *Taliba* was under way: Khan was slipping out under the cover of the freighter.

The crew were all, metaphorically, holding their breath, and Marsh realized then that they had all been warned of what was about to happen. He also knew that Khan must be playing a very dangerous game now and wondered if he suspected that the Navy Seals had paid him a visit twenty-four hours earlier. But he dismissed the notion as soon as it entered his head; there was no way Kahn could even suspect that the United States Navy had actually been on board.

He looked at Malik. 'Why the subterfuge?' he whispered, ignoring Malik's earlier warning. 'Why are we leaving like thieves in the night?'

Malik's look of surprise was not apparent in the darkness.

'Thieves in the night?' he repeated. Then he pointed towards the aft end as a smile spread across his face. 'Look.'

Marsh followed his direction. *Taliba* was beginning to turn away from the freighter. Just aft he could see another ship. It was about the same size as *Taliba*. He could not see the superstructure too clearly, but she appeared to have moved up in the shadow of the cargo ship. She was coming alongside the freighter.

And then it came to him: Khan had pulled a switch! The ship behind them had taken up position exactly where the *Taliba* had been anchored. Marsh realized then that Khan was deliberately trying to confuse any observer on the Cuban shore. And it would be dawn at the earliest before the switch was noticed. By then the third bomb would be in place and Khan would have won. Marsh felt a spill of fear trickle through his veins and he wanted to vomit.

He turned to Malik and let out a burst of uncontrollable anger at him.

'You miserable bastards,' he snarled. 'If you think I'm going to plant your evil bomb, you're badly mistaken.' He turned swiftly and went to walk away from Malik, but before he could take two steps, Malik had him by the neck and almost twisted his head from his shoulders.

'The woman still has a chance, Marsh,' Malik whispered angrily in his ear. 'But if you refuse to take *Challenger* down, I will kill her, I promise.' He gave Marsh's neck a painful twist. 'Do you hear me, Marsh?'

'Yes, I hear you. Now let me go,' he pleaded.

'But do you understand? If you do not co-operate, your woman will die in front of you.'

Marsh knew Malik was the kind of man who carried out his promises and this would be no exception. He had no choice, as weak as he felt and as abysmal as he felt, Helen's life was of paramount importance to him.

'Yes Malik, I understand. I will take *Challenger* down,' he assured him. 'Now let me go.'

As Malik let him go, he noticed that the freighter was turning too. And then he understood that the two ships, the freighter and *Taliba* would sail alongside each other to avoid detection from radar. And he understood the cunning and the sheer bravado of the man they were up against.

The two ships sailed together for three hours until they eventually separated. Within minutes, the freighter was lost in the darkness and

Taliba was alone. The task of keeping the two ships separated in the badly deteriorating weather had called for a high class of seamanship, and Marsh knew that Captain de Leon possessed that in spades.

The wind had freshened to twenty knots, normally too high to launch the submersible. This added to Marsh's fears, but was small beer compared to the fear he had for his own life. He knew that the high wind speed would not stop Khan from launching *Challenger*, but it could seriously jeopardize recovery. At the rate the wind was freshening, it could reach moderate to gale force by the time the dive was over.

And the devil of it was he knew they were sailing into the edge of a hurricane.

Working in almost total darkness was dangerous and stressful, particularly when the load going into the submersible was a nuclear bomb. Marsh found it difficult to maintain a level conversation with Batista and Zienkovitch; their responses often seemed careful and guarded. He had expected to see Khan but the man did not even venture down to oversee the loading operation. In fact, everyone was on edge.

The one, bright moment during the lengthy night was Helen's appearance. She told Marsh that she had insisted on seeing him. Had he not seen her before the dive, it would have added to the inexplicable feeling of being a condemned man.

With barely minutes to go before he was due to shut himself in *Challenger*'s cockpit, Helen put her arms around him and drew him in close.

'I love you, Marsh' she whispered. 'Remember; to have faith and hope is to survive.'

He held her tight for a moment, and then kissed her passionately on her lips. They were soft and yielding, like tender pillows to cushion his anxiety.

'I love you too, Helen.'

He pulled away and looked over at Malik who, as ever, was never far away. He walked over to him and stood in such a way that Helen would not be able to see his face. Summoning as much strength and appeal in his voice as he could, he spoke to Malik through gritted teeth.

'Don't let anything happen to her, Malik. Make me that promise.'

Malik nodded slowly. 'You have my word.'

Satisfied, Marsh turned away and climbed into the cockpit.

The young signals officer hovered beside James Starling; afraid to deliver the message that he was sure would bring down the world of Hades on his vulnerable young shoulders. The admiral was sitting in an upright chair in the base commander's office. He was talking earnestly to Francesini and was unaware of the young signals officer.

The young man coughed. 'Excuse me, sir.'

Starling stopped talking to Francesini and looked up at the officer. 'Yes, what is it?'

'I'm afraid we've lost the *Taliba*.'

Starling said nothing for a few seconds. His expression darkened. 'What did you say?'

'It's the *Taliba*, sir; I'm afraid we've lost her.'

'Lost her?' Starling sprang to his feet. His chair toppled over behind him and crashed to the floor. Francesini couldn't believe it. The might of the American security services had lost the *Taliba* again. He bent down and picked up the fallen chair.

'Lost her? What the hell do you mean?' Starling asked angrily.

'Simply that, sir,' the signals officer replied nervously. 'Our observers have reported that the *Taliba* slipped out under the cover of darkness.'

'Well dammit, man,' Starling bellowed. 'We knew she would. That's why we've been watching her.'

'Yes, sir,' the young man agreed meekly. 'But it would appear that the *Taliba* managed to leave a decoy ship in her place. That's why the disappearance wasn't noticed until first light this morning.'

Starling continued to stare at the young officer. 'What about the F-16s we have on patrol?'

'We contacted Homestead Base, sir. There are no reports of any changes to the situation. They were not aware of the *Taliba*'s disappearance until we advised them.'

Homestead was base to the National Air Reserve in Florida, the most southerly of America's bases.

Starling hissed through closed teeth and nodded his head resignedly. 'Damn you, Khan. Damn you and all your kind to Hell.'

His massive shoulders heaved and he looked at the signals officer from beneath his dark eyebrows. Looking at his watch he began to compute times and distances in his mind.

'The observers noticed the switch at first light; about six o'clock. We have to assume the switch was made at midnight. Six hours.'

He turned his attention to Francesini knowing he would be automatically computing the figures with him. 'If she makes twenty knots and is still under way, she could be one hundred and thirty miles out by now.'

Francesini cut in, 'But with the weather conditions deteriorating, we might have to assume half that speed and distance; seventy miles.'

Starling swung back to the signals officer. 'Contact Colonel Riddell at Homeland Base and ask him to scramble four F-16s. I want them on a quartering search, one hundred and fifty miles north of Havana. As soon as contact is made, I want to know.'

The signals officer thought that there might be more, but there wasn't. Starling glared at him.

'Now, sonny, now!'

The young man ran from the room and Starling shook his head and gazed into thin air.

'Where are you, Khan? Where are you and your insidious crew?'

Francesini stood beside him. His face seemed to be carved from stone as he let the awful truth sink in.

Once inside the cockpit bubble, the outside world was shut away. Marsh was cocooned like an embryo in his own, silent world, feeding off the warm belly of the *Challenger*, but he was the beating heart of the submersible.

He went through his checks, automatically, throwing switches, checking pressures, reading gauges. He checked the television monitor, peering unseen into the decompression chamber like an Orwellian overlord. He nodded his satisfaction.

He reached forward towards the communication panel and hesitated, as though that single act would presage an unstoppable chain of events more terrible than he could ever imagine. He cursed his own weakness and flicked the switch. The click intruded sharply into the silence.

'*Taliba*, how do you read?'

Khan's hollow voice washed over him. 'Loud and clear, *Challenger*. Please transfer power.'

'Transferring now.' He fingered the button that would energize a solenoid to operate a heavy-duty contactor, switching power from *Taliba*'s generators to the *Challenger*'s on-board power system. The gauges flickered momentarily, and then held rock steady.

'Transfer complete.'

The cables hanging slack from the ship's crane went taut and sang in the high wind as it lifted *Challenger* clear of the deck. Although it was still dark, Marsh could see spindrift whipping off the tops of the waves. They were like thousands of white handkerchiefs, mirroring his cowardice.

The *Challenger* began to swing. Gently at first, but soon the arc increased until Marsh feared the lines would snap and hurl him to an uncomfortable dive into the fierce sea.

Despite their care, *Challenger* hit the water hard and wallowed in the pitching waves. Marsh was helpless because the submersible was still attached to the lifting frame, and would remain so for a while due to the inclement conditions. It took some considerable time, and nerve, for the divers to release the four hooks that attached the frame to *Challenger*'s superstructure.

Once he had received the all clear from the bridge, Marsh immediately flooded the diving tanks. All he wanted to do now was to get beneath the waves into a calmer, safer environment.

He trimmed out at fifteen metres and went through a series of checks with Batista and Zienkovitch. He paused for a moment, not knowing why, and thought of Helen. To have faith and hope is to survive, she had said. Then why the hell was he so frightened? Probably because of some evil portent sitting invisibly beside him in that cockpit – invisible, intangible, but there!

'… whenever you are, Marsh.'

Marsh blinked. 'Say again, *Taliba*.'

'It's not the ship, Marsh, it's Batista. We are ready whenever you are.'

Marsh admonished himself the unprofessional slip and began flooding the tanks. Slowly *Challenger* began to sink. He called out the depth mechanically as though he was utterly alone, speaking to no one but his own soul.

A warning light blinked, as the rope hanging beneath the submersible touched bottom. He dumped ballast and trimmed her out. Then he switched on the powerful arc lamps and called Batista.

'Go plant your devil's egg,' he said. 'And may whichever god you worship damn you all for eternity.'

The F-16 rolled over at 15,000 feet and dived towards the sea, its starboard wing squeezing water vapour out of the air in a spiralling trail of white mist. The young navy pilot pulled the stick over to check the roll and eased it back gently to bring the nose up. He had seen the *Taliba* and was turning to confirm the sighting.

He levelled out at 1000 feet and set his course to parallel the ship, switching the range on his radar scanning head to fifteen miles. He had deliberately overshot *Taliba* in order not to arouse the suspicion of anyone on board, and had turned back only when he knew he would be out of sight.

Taliba came up on the radar screen allowing the pilot a thin smile. There were other signals imaging on the screen, but *Taliba*'s seemed to shine like a beacon. He had her, like a hound on the scent. The trail was hot and he would report it to the rest of the pack.

The two divers worked swiftly guiding Marsh over the well-head until the submersible was firmly clamped by her skirt. There was nothing for Marsh to do now except monitor the systems on the submersible and wait. And keep checking his instruments. And worry about the weather up top and the hobgoblin sitting beside him in the cockpit.

His attention was drawn upwards and he was surprised by the appearance of a very faint yellow light. He focused on it, wondering what on earth it could be. The light grew in size until it broke up into several lights. There were six, forming a circle, slowly descending towards him.

His expression changed from one of curiosity to one of concern. He turned one of the arc lamps up towards the light and could now see the object clearly.

They were lowering the *Galeazzi Tower*.

He looked at the depth: eighty metres, about 250 feet. Normally the tower would not be lowered to that depth, unless it was an emergency.

So what the hell was Khan playing at?

He called them up. '*Taliba*, Marsh here. Why are you lowering the tower?'

There was no response.

'*Taliba*, I say again, *Challenger* here. Why are you lowering the tower?'

He waited a little longer but there was still no answer.

'*Taliba*!' he called again, a note of urgency creeping into his voice. 'Answer me, damn you!'

What Marsh saw next was beyond his comprehension and silenced him completely: Batista and Zienkovitch had emerged from beneath the hull and were swimming up towards the tower. As they swam upwards, both caught in the glare from the *Challenger*'s arc light, neither of them looked in Marsh's direction.

Marsh found his voice again. '*Taliba*, what the hell is going on? Why are the divers using the tower?' He could feel himself sweating. '*Taliba*!'

The response came so unexpectedly, it startled him.

'Marsh, this is Khan. The third bomb is in place. The trinity is complete; our work is done.'

'What's happening, Khan?' he demanded to know. 'Why have Batista and Zienkovitch gone up to the tower?'

'How else would they get back to the *Taliba*?'

'Don't play games with me, Khan. This is not part of the brief. They should be returning with me!'

'You are not returning.'

As a statement it was simple, but so stunning that Marsh was unable to say anything for a moment. It was surreal. It wasn't happening.

'Khan, for God's sake, what are you doing?'

'Nothing, Marsh,' came the laconic reply. 'As far as you're concerned, our work is complete. Goodbye, Marsh.' The communication link went quiet. Marsh heard the click as Khan closed the speaker switch on the bridge.

Marsh felt beads of sweat begin to break out on his forehead. His mind froze itself to the realization of what Khan had planned for him. Strangely though, he couldn't believe that Khan was willing to leave *Challenger* beneath the surface. Abandon it? Although he had never really believed that Khan would kill him, the reality of it hit him with shocking force: Khan had planned this moment all along. He cursed himself for his own stupidity and weakness.

He tried to think rationally. Fear was impeding his thought processes and he was on the verge of blind panic, but he knew that those emotions would never get him out of the awful nightmare he was in.

He breathed in slowly in an attempt to calm himself, trying to reduce the rate at which his heart was now pounding in his chest. He had to think. Think!

He started dumping ballast. He dumped the lot. As he did, thousands upon thousands of particles of lead shot tumbled from the submersible and turned the sea bed into little spiralling columns of sand that drifted upwards in a cloud to envelop him.

He felt the *Challenger* strain, but she didn't move. He knew then that Batista and Zienkovitch had not released the clamps on the skirt.

Marsh slumped back in his seat. He was devastated. He could not believe that the two divers would be willing accomplices in this deadly game. But it was no game: it was murder.

He then thought of the explosive collar, but something told him it would not work. But he had to try. He leaned forward and opened the firing panel. There were two buttons and two lights. He pressed and held the green button which, he hoped, would charge the firing capacitors. He expected to see the red light glow that would signal that the explosive collar was armed and ready to fire. But nothing happened.

He tried again, holding the charging button longer than the mandatory five seconds. But still nothing happened; there was still no light. Desperate now he flipped the cover of the firing button open and pushed the button all the way home.

Five seconds and the explosive collar would fire.

He counted.

'... four, five, six, seven.' Nothing. 'Come on, come on!' he shouted in desperation. 'Fire, damn you, fire!'

But there was nothing. He hammered the firing button, but still nothing happened; the explosive collar remained dormant.

He looked up at the tiny speaker mounted just above his head and screamed abuse at Khan. He hurled every blasphemy he could lay his tongue to and screamed insensibly. But there was nothing except his own voice in that bubble; bouncing off the smooth interior, assaulting his ears and fading into a sob; the deep despair of a frightened man.

And outside the cockpit, the arc lights peered into the emptiness of the pervasive darkness. Now there was nothing but silence, and a thousand demons laid their hands on him and waited for him to die.

CHAPTER SEVENTEEN

H elen could hear the wind; its whining threnody changing pitch as the *Taliba* dipped its prow and then lifted above the restless waves. She sensed that the motion of the ship had changed in a subtle way, as if shorn of a burdensome yoke.

By now, Helen would have expected Marsh to have returned to his cabin. He would usually have knocked on her door to let her know the dive was finished. The fear that he had attempted to conceal from her before the dive now drove itself into her and she felt impatient to be with him.

For some reason, unknown to her, Helen's cabin door had been locked from the outside, which only added to her blossoming fear. She banged on the door for a few moments and called out, but there was no response. She pummelled the door again with her closed fists and called out Malik's name, but still there was silence.

Her fear was turning to anger and she began beating ferociously on the door and picking up loose objects from her cabin and hurling them at the barrier between her and the corridor outside the cabin.

It was some time before Helen heard a cautioning voice and a key turning in the lock. Her hands began to tremble and she had to clasp them together to stop them from shaking. The door opened and Helen reached forward, pulling it open. She knew now, instinctively, that something was terribly wrong. Ignoring the crewman who had opened her door, Helen pushed past him and rushed out, flew up the stairs two steps at a time and fetched up on the open deck.

The wind struck Helen with such savagery that she almost toppled over. It took her breath away and she had to clutch at the handrail for support. She suddenly felt very cold; the temperature had dropped remarkably and there were dull, thunder clouds scudding overhead like massive anvils that obscured the sun.

The sea around her was grey and the waves burst open upon each other in fingers of angry surf which the wind picked up and flung at the *Taliba*. Helen gasped at the cold and winced as the driving spray lashed at her clothing. She put her head down and lunged forward awkwardly, grasping the handrail with each step, hand over hand.

She reached Khan's stateroom just beneath the bridge and clutched at the handle of the door. Just before she made an attempt to open the door, she glanced forward and froze in terror: *Challenger* was no longer there!

Helen held that pose, staring with disbelief at the forlorn, empty space where the submersible was always stowed. For a moment she was oblivious to the cold spray and punishing wind. All that occupied her thoughts then was that something terrible had happened and Marsh would be with the *Challenger*.

That moment of realization numbed her so intensely that she no longer felt any fear. She reached for the cabin door and wrenched it open.

The Navy Seals were assembled in the briefing room at the United States Base at Guantanamo Bay on the Island of Cuba. Lieutenant Santos had briefed his men and they now waited the word to go. Outside the operations building, on the pad was a Sea Stallion Helicopter, crewed up and waiting for the Seals to board once they had received the final brief from James Starling. Remo Francesini was standing nervously beside his boss silently praying that everything would go smoothly and they would be in time to prevent an awesomely, devastating terror. And he prayed that the weather would not be against them.

In the Ops room, the commanding officer was conferring with his met officer about the risks of sending the Sea Stallion into the storm that was fast approaching. The phone bleeped and the met officer picked it up.

'Ops.'

He listened for a moment and held the phone out for the captain. 'It's Lieutenant Santos, sir.'

The CO took the phone and listened, then gave an affirmative. 'We go now.'

In the briefing room, Lieutenant Santos replaced the phone and gave a nod to his men. Silently they all stood up, gathered up their equipment and followed a deck officer, who had been assigned to them out to the waiting helicopter. Francesini, who had been given permission to ride with the Seals, followed them out; his nerves bubbled inside him like a boiling cauldron of water, and he prayed fervently that these men would be able to stop Khan and his murderous plans. As he boarded the Sea Stallion, Lieutenant Santos turned and helped him up.

'We're in God's hands now, sir,' he said, and pulled the door shut behind him.

Khan looked up from his desk as the door flew open. Helen stood there, framed in the doorway. Her hair was wet and much of it lay across her face in waspish strands. Her dress clung to her body accentuating the curve of her breasts and the provocative bulge between her hips. Had he not known why she was there; Khan could not have failed to be aroused by her ingenuous display of overt sexuality.

'Where's Marsh?' she asked with a biting edge to her voice. The sound of the wind almost whipped her words away.

'We had to leave him,' Khan answered levelly, without a trace of emotion in his voice. 'The weather was too bad for recovery.'

His voice rattled suddenly in his chest and he coughed as Helen stepped into the cabin.

'I don't believe you,' she screamed at him. 'You've murdered him!'

Her eyes were blazing with an intensity that made them sparkle like precious stones. Khan thought it looked like controlled insanity. Although Helen had not closed the door there was a great deal of warmth in the cabin, and her cheeks began to glow fiery red. Khan found the whole effect quite disarming.

He got up from his desk and walked past her to the cabin door which he closed. The noise of the wind abated and a semblance of peace descended.

'*Challenger* was unable to surface because of the storm,' he told her tritely.

Helen's teeth flashed as she spat out her words.

'You're lying, Khan. Marsh has sat through worse storms than this. He is a very skilful pilot. He would know what to do.'

Khan shrugged. 'We did all we could, but Marsh understands. We have marked the area. Recovery will begin as soon as the weather conditions permit.'

Khan's manner was so offhand it was offensive. Helen swung her hand out and slapped him with a tremendous blow to the head. Khan rocked back immediately as blood began to seep from the marks left by Helen's slashing fingernails.

'Then why are we underway?' she shouted at him. 'We should be keeping station over the *Challenger* until the weather calms down.'

He put a hand to his face and pulled it away. He looked at the blood on his hand and then at Helen.

'You bitch,' he snapped back at her, ignoring her question. 'You will pay for that.'

His breathing began to sound quite laboured.

'You've murdered Marsh,' she screamed at him. 'You're nothing but an evil, murdering bastard.' She flung herself at him and started punching him about the head.

For a moment, Khan was too surprised to react to the torrent of blows that Helen rained down on him. Then suddenly he thrust his arms upwards and brought a single, punishing blow with the back of his hand that caught her on the jaw bone.

Helen rocked back and staggered towards his desk, falling against it. The blow jarred her spine and the pain seemed to rocket through her body. She cried out and clung to the desk for support as her legs weakened and threatened to buckle beneath her.

The fight was gone from her; drained in that one awful blow from Khan. She knew that she would be no match for this man's strength and would achieve nothing but pain if she tried to attack him again.

Khan walked past her and slumped in the chair. He looked up at her and suddenly smiled.

'I admire you for your pluck, but it serves no purpose. Marsh is not here and you now have to think of your own safety.'

'I can think of nothing but Marsh,' she cried. 'Why did you have to kill him? He did what you asked.'

'No,' Khan said sternly. 'Marsh did what I told him to do. If he had agreed to do what I had asked, you would not have been involved and you would have both been free to live your lives as you both saw fit. Marsh has brought this upon himself.'

She studied him for a while. There was an eerie silence, intruded upon only by the sound of the winds outside. He looked expressionless; absolved by his own warped ethics of complicity in Marsh's death.

'What are you planning to do that is so important that you quite willingly took the life of a perfectly innocent man?' She asked quietly.

Instead of answering immediately, Khan got up from the desk and walked over to a control console from where he could listen to, and if necessary, supervise the dives. Above the console was a small door set into the bulkhead. He unlocked it with a key from his pocket and swung the door open. He turned then and looked at Helen like a man who was about to reveal a masterpiece, a hidden treasure.

Helen could see a series of illuminated digits on a screen. Below these was a combination wheel, similar to those found on safes. Beside the wheel was a red button.

'The bombs that Marsh placed beneath the sea for us are the frontline of our war against the unbelievers, the Great Satan of America and the heretics who persecute Islam and the prophet, Muhammad.'

His eyes glazed over and Helen realized he was switching mentally from his Western, democratized character to that of his terrorist masters in their Middle East hideouts. It was a sudden metamorphosis that Helen found both intriguing and appalling.

'When I key in the correct figures,' he went on, pointing to the panel, 'a lock is released. This will allow me to arm the bombs and commence a countdown to their firing. But to arm them, a satellite has to be in position above us. The computer behind this panel transmits a command to the satellite which will then arm all three bombs simultaneously by digital signal. It is vitally important that the bombs are all armed at precisely the same moment. Once the arming has been completed, I can then begin the countdown sequence by pressing this red button.' He reached up and touched the red button.

Suddenly he felt a pain ring itself around his heart and he fell forward, clutching his chest. Helen instinctively made a move towards him, but stopped herself. Khan straightened and turned away from the console.

'Once that button had been pressed,' he muttered breathlessly, 'there is nothing on this earth that can stop the countdown. Victory will be ours.'

Helen felt herself weaken and she began to shake uncontrollably. She was in the company of one of the most evil men on earth and she felt powerless to stop him. She leaned against the desk for support before she collapsed and felt something bulky press against her side. She glanced down at it and saw it was a heavy, paperweight cast in bronze.

It was the *Challenger*.

In that moment an uncountable number of things tumbled through Helen's mind with such speed that she was unable to find time for cogent argument. She picked up the paperweight and hurled it with all her might towards the screen.

Khan ducked instinctively and put his hands up, crying out as he did so. The paperweight flew past his head and impacted on the glass. The screen immediately disintegrated with an implosive 'plop', and a fine, grey dust billowed out from the scarred and jagged gap.

Khan's face fell apart. He couldn't believe what had just happened. He kept looking at the smashed monitor and then at Helen, an uncomprehending expression on his face.

Suddenly, Helen felt very afraid, expecting him to hurl himself at her and beat her savagely in his blind fury. But unexpectedly, Khan's expression changed. He seemed to relax and stood up straight. He reached up to the door, pushed it shut and locked it.

'You know, my dear. We men still have a lot to learn.' He walked toward her. 'I'm afraid my ego got the better of me. But not to worry, it's only a monitor. It can be replaced.'

He saw the look of dismay on Helen's face. 'And we also have a back-up,' he said. 'It would be insane not to.'

He took her arm and led her towards the cabin door. Pulling open the door he looked at her.

'Now, go back to your cabin and stay there. If you become too much of a trial, I will have Malik deal with you. Do you understand?'

He pushed her out and closed the door. Then he leaned back against it as the pain began to assail his chest. He staggered towards the desk where his tablets were and prayed to Allah that he would live to complete his glorious *intifada* against the great Satan, America.

Helen found herself out on the windswept deck wondering if it had indeed really happened. The surf lifted itself above the handrails and drove into her. She felt cold and miserable as the ship heaved beneath her.

'To have faith and hope is to survive,' she had told Marsh. And now it was all in vain.

She looked at the grey, beckoning sea and pushed the thought from her mind.

Marsh sat slumped in his seat, the agony of despair and hopelessness weighing on him like a physical burden. He stared at the instrument panel without seeing it. The images in his mind were not those in front of him, but dark, coalescing images of revenge and despair. He wanted to reach up and tear the black heart from Hakeem Khan, from Malik, from Batista, from them all. But he could not; he had no hope. Even while his heart beat strongly within him, he knew this would be the end. He lifted his head and breathed in a sigh of deep despair and closed his eyes. Now there was only blackness where there should have been light.

Beneath the dark waters he imagined the warmth of the sun; its caress like the touch of a woman. He rolled his head back and imagined the fragrance of flowers, of new-mown grass, all offering a pleasure as tangible and apposite as the fear now crawling round in his belly.

He blinked and shut the hallucinatory images from his mind, bringing it to bear on the dreadful predicament he was in. He knew there was no way out of his prison and he knew that there was no way Khan would return to rescue him from his misery. He was cocooned in an environment that was designed to support life yet ironically; it was holding him in a deadly embrace and eventually he would die.

Marsh wondered what death would be like. Would he succumb to insanity before death took him? Would he grow weary and eventually suffocate in his own, exhaled carbon dioxide? Would he just fall asleep and not wake? Would he be given the last, immeasurable pleasure of being with Helen, even if only in a dream?

He shook his head vigorously and snapped out of it and began to apply his mind to the problem again. He knew that to give up so soon was to accept the inevitability of death. He checked the power meters; the instruments that told him how much longer *Challenger*'s own batteries would last and how much oxygen was left in the cockpit.

He knew that if the oxygen content fell below a dangerously low level, the automatic valves of the oxygen bottles would bleed a steady amount of life-giving gas into the bubble's atmosphere so that life could be sustained until an orderly recovery or rescue could be carried out. But if the submersible's power became low and unstable, there was a risk that the bottles could eventually pressurize the cockpit and kill him.

He began to shut down various systems that were no longer needed, to conserve battery power. He extinguished the low grade cockpit lighting, relying instead on the glow from the instrument panel.

After about two minutes of technical distraction, he found himself devoid of ideas and things to do. He knew there was no hope of anyone finding him on the sea bed, so his last hours would be painfully slow and would probably end in insanity.

'Damn you, Khan!' he shouted suddenly. 'Why didn't you just put a bullet in me?'

His shoulders sagged and he slumped back in his seat. That was the first sign of the loss of control. How long would it be, he wondered, before he was clawing at the smooth walls of the bubble in a manic, pitiful attempt to escape? He let his mind drift again, peering out into the deep, mindful yet mindless.

How long Marsh sat in torpid despair, he didn't know, but suddenly he sat up straight. The diving tanks! God in heaven, why hadn't he thought of it?

Marsh kicked himself for not thinking of it earlier but put that down to his state of mind. He forced himself to think clearer now because he believed this would be his best chance of getting out of this alive. By blowing the water from the diving tanks and the decompression chamber, he would lighten the load and greatly increase lift, and the upward thrust of the air, less the weight of the water, should overcome the force of the clamps.

He began switching *Challenger* back on to full power. He knew he was taking a chance because of the drain on the batteries, but it was his only hope. Once the computer signalled that all systems were operational. Marsh keyed in the commands that would open the air valves. He listened to the rush of compressed air leaving their cylinders and flowing into the diving tanks and the decompression chamber.

All at once the sea boiled around him as the *Challenger* purged herself of the surplus sea water, and something moved beneath him as the enormous thrust of air fought to break the power of the clamps.

'Come on, damn you,' he mumbled through clenched teeth. 'Come on!'

He could feel *Challenger* straining at every limb to break free of the deadly grip of the clamps.

'Come on,' he urged again. 'Get up, get up!'

He moved his body, pounding the seat with his own weight as if to add impetus to the mighty struggle going on beneath him.

'For God's sake, *Challenger*, break free, damn you! Break free!'

The noise of the rushing air reached a crescendo and then began to subside until finally the pressure in the tanks and the decompression chamber reached that of the air cylinders.

'No, don't stop now!' he beseeched her. 'Not now! Please, not now!'

Challenger seemed to give one last desperate heave and then succumbed to the awesome strength of the clamps.

She didn't move.

'No. Oh God, no.' Marsh looked around him imploringly. 'Please, *Challenger*, please. Don't let me down. Please.'

But *Challenger* had lost the battle, surrendering herself to the deadly embrace of the clamps.

Marsh stopped shouting and cursing. His mouth fell open as tears streamed down his face. He could taste the salt on his lips and he kept blinking the wetness from his eyes. His head fell forward into his hands and he kept asking 'Why?'

He cried alone in his tiny world; a ball of encircling light, holding life like a baby in the womb, suspended in dark waters. He cried until there were no tears left to cry and soon his mind closed down and he drifted off into the merciful world of sleep.

Marsh woke in a sleepy haze, his mind unable to focus at first on his surroundings. Sleep had robbed him for a moment of the ability to recognize or be aware of anything. But quite soon, recognition dawned on him and the awful truth of his dilemma swung down on him like the sword of Damocles.

He was aware of condensation building up on the inside of the smooth polymer. It gathered in small droplets, like pearls in a polymer oyster. He glanced at the power meters and saw there was little left in *Challenger* now. Soon the valves on the oxygen bottles would open. He reached up and closed the valves, prepared now to suffocate in his own exhaled air as the oxygen fell below the danger level. Once the carbon dioxide was concentrated enough inside the bubble, he would drift off in to an eternal sleep.

Marsh thought of pleasant things, but mainly the yard back at Freeport. He thought about the *Helena*, their own submersible that was still not quite ready for sea because their mechanic had not yet completed fitting the explosive collar.

The explosive collar!

Marsh sat bolt upright. Could he do it, he wondered?

He opened the valves on the oxygen bottle, switched to manual and immediately felt an uplifting sensation as his brain responded to the sweet, life-giving air.

'Careful, Marsh,' he counselled himself. 'It may not work.'

He thought about the collar and how it might have been disconnected. It was unlikely that it would have been done outside the cockpit because the collar was designed to form a watertight clamp that engaged on the firing socket. Once fitted there was no chance of water seeping inside

The screened, wiring circuit that connected the collar to the firing button was encapsulated and ran through the centre of the 'thorax' to the rear of the instrument panel. Therefore it would have been simpler, and quicker, to have disconnected the collar inside the cockpit.

Beside the firing panel was a small bank of capacitors. When the circuit was energized by pressing the first button, it initiated a charge to the capacitors. After a ten-second delay, the firing circuit would be closed and a red light would come on above the firing button. When this was pressed, the capacitors would discharge down the firing lines, into the collar and detonate it. The shaped charge inside the collar would explode and sever the cockpit from the submersible.

All Marsh had to do now was to figure out a way of reconnecting the collar to the firing panel.

He needed a tool or something with which he could remove the front of the firing panel. He looked around the interior for something he could use. The smooth, contoured features stared back at him. Everything in there had been designed for ease of handling, simplicity. No sharp objects. Helen had proclaimed it was the only place she could safely work where she wouldn't snag her tights.

He ran his hands beneath the seat, then opened up a small, virtually unnecessary toolbox and found it was empty. It didn't surprise him. He continued the search and thought about Richard III who offered his kingdom for a horse. What Marsh would have given for a simple screwdriver.

He sat there for a while thinking furiously, playing with the watch on his wrist, then realized he might have the answer there in his hand, or, more correctly, on his wrist.

He removed the watch and placed it on the floor, then stamped on it with his foot. It smashed immediately and he picked it up. Ignoring the little shards of glass, Marsh pushed the entire works through the back of the watch. As they popped out, the steel back dropped on to the floor. This was to be Marsh's screwdriver.

One by one, even with his hands trembling and sweating, Marsh removed the facia screws from the panel until it swung free and revealed the wires in the firing loom.

It was as he had suspected; the loom had been cut!

Marsh began working on the cotton bindings of the loom until he could strip away the braided steel armour, exposing the cables. He then began to strip back the insulation of the two cables leading up to the capacitor bank.

Marsh knew that all the return circuits in the *Challenger*'s systems were coded blue and that none of them were switched. After twenty minutes, with his fingers raw and bleeding, he had managed to connect the return cable from the capacitors to the blue cable running from the firing panel. Then he gently lifted the power cable from the panel and touched it against the exposed copper wire that supplied the bank of capacitors. Nothing happened for a moment, and then he heard the sweet, soft, high-pitched whine rising in crescendo as the capacitors charged up.

Marsh was almost crying by now and shaking nervously. Sweat poured from his forehead into his eyes. He stopped, took in several deep breaths and then let the power cable drop away from the charging circuit.

The capacitors were now full charged.

At the rear of the firing panel, Marsh could see the braided metal firing lines which ran through the loom to the explosive collar. He reached in and pulled them clear and looked at the severed ends. He knew he still had time before the charge in the capacitors began to decay, but his fingers were sore, making him wonder how much time he had before the strength in his hands began to decay too. And his eyes were stinging now because of the sweat running from his forehead.

Using the watch back again, he paired back the insulation to expose their bright, copper conductors He attached one to the capacitor bank and brought the other cable to within a fraction of the cables that ran from the firing button.

His hands began to shake again. He breathed in, concentrated and carried on. Marsh knew it was vital that once he had made contact, he had to keep the cables together long enough for the energy now stored in the capacitors to discharge along the firing lines to the explosive collar.

Then he was ready.

And he prayed.

Oh, how he prayed.

Slowly, he brought the ends together and held them fast. There was just time to reflect that he was not strapped into his seat when he heard the dull 'crump' as the shaped charge in the collar exploded and severed the thorax from the *Challenger*.

For what seemed like an eternity, nothing happened. Then the bubble moved and began to lift. Slowly at first, it shook off the pull of gravity and the pressure from the sea above it as the air inside exerted its own force and went in search of its own pressure level above that black, forbidding sea.

It moved up rapidly, gaining speed and momentum at the same time. It also began to roll to one side as Marsh lost his balance and fell. As he tumbled he could just see the *Challenger*, clamped to the sea bed and looking like his launch platform. It faded from view as the gathering light intensified until the cockpit bubble broke through the surface like a shot from a cannon.

It spun in the air and crashed down on to the surface. Marsh felt a terrible blow to his head as the bubble fought back against the pull of the sea and bobbed upright.

Marsh's last memory of that moment before he passed out was of the blessed, beautiful sky; beautiful but menacing with huge, black clouds.

The bubble settled and canted over gently under the pressure of the wind. The automatic beacon switched on, punching out its distress signal on the international distress frequency. And the Gulf Stream current carried the odd-looking craft towards the Florida Channel and the vast, open reaches of the Atlantic Ocean.

CHAPTER EIGHTEEN

On the bridge of the *Taliba*, Captain de Leon glanced up from his map table as the F-16 flashed by in the distance. To him it was just a silhouette; a momentary transition of life in an otherwise empty, darkening sky. It jogged his memory and he thought about the hurricane. They were running from it, but the wind was well up to gale force and he wondered what conditions would be like on the rig.

He left the bridge and went to his cabin. There was little he could do or even needed to do. The officer of the watch was quite capable. He thought he would freshen up and probably return to the bridge within the hour. Then he could fret about the gathering storm.

Taliba had been battened down for storm conditions and the helicopter had been made ready to fly off if Khan thought it prudent to do so. It looked so vulnerable, shackled to the forward heli-pad. De Leon gave it little more thought as he pulled off his shoes and lay down on his bunk. Within a few minutes he was asleep.

The officer of the watch had been on the bridge, thinking about the gathering storm and what it meant to their brief spells ashore. None for the men, or himself for the foreseeable future; they were safer out at sea, running from the hurricane.

As he paced up and down the bridge he glanced occasionally at the radar screen. When he saw the blip at first, he ignored it. But on his second pass along the bridge, he looked again. He frowned and studied it a little more carefully. The bearing on which the trace was moving would bring it directly over the *Taliba*. Whatever it was, he reasoned that it was significantly slower than an aeroplane so it was probably a helicopter.

In this weather, he wondered? Only fools and birds would want to be airborne with a hurricane on their tail.

He screwed his face up and walked away, sniffing sharply, ignoring it. But, as he came by the screen again, he knew that he could not ignore it. He picked up the bridge phone and pressed the button that linked him directly to Captain de Leon's cabin.

'Are we expecting company?' he asked, when the captain came on the line. He received a negative reply. 'Only we have what appears to be a helicopter coming our way. It's on radar.'

De Leon put the phone back, slipped on his shoes and went to the bridge. He studied the trace on the screen, larger now than when the officer of the watch first looked. He nodded absently in agreement and picked up the bridge phone.

Hakeem Khan was working on some paperwork when the phone rang beside him. He picked it up.

'Khan.'

'Sir, this is Captain de Leon. Could you come up to the bridge please?' he asked. 'We have something I think you should see.'

Khan put on a waterproof jacket and rubber-soled shoes, put his paperwork away and was on the bridge within minutes of de Leon's phone call. The exertion had left him wheezing and quite breathless. He had his hand over his heart. De Leon showed him the contact on the screen.

'Whoever they are, they will be here in about eight minutes,' Khan observed as he studied the screen. He drew a deep breath, long and hard, knowing instinctively that the contact was hostile. Now that he was so close to completing his task, he could not help but hold the fatalistic view that he could still be stopped, even at his eleventh hour.

'Is the helicopter ready?' He asked suddenly. De Leon nodded.

'Good. Have Malik meet me on the heli-pad in five minutes. I will fly to the rig from here.' He straightened up and went towards the bridge door. He paused and turned towards de Leon.

'Change course. Lead them off. If there is no danger, resume your present heading and meet me at the rig.'

He hesitated as if there was something else he wanted to say. Then he wished de Leon good luck and left the bridge.

Once inside his cabin, Khan hurriedly gathered together the papers he had been working on and stuffed them into a briefcase. Then he went up to the control console that he had so brazenly showed to Helen and unlocked a panel door.

Behind the door was a timer which Khan set to ten minutes. Then he rotated a Castell key which was set into a lock and pushed it forward. He closed the panel door and locked it.

He glanced around the cabin, satisfied. The *Taliba* would not fall into the wrong hands. In ten minutes the keel would be blown from the hull and *Taliba* would sink to the bottom of the Caribbean like a stone.

Inside the Sea Stallion helicopter the Navy Seals sat in their seats staring ahead of them, each with their own thoughts. Santos had told them why the mission had to succeed; failure was not an option. Because the mission was of the highest priority, air-to-air refuelling had been laid on should the Sea Stallion look like it was about to exceed its 550 mile nautical range. The helicopter had been flying steadily for over thirty minutes now and was slowly beginning to feel the effects of the strengthening wind.

Francesini sat with the Seals. He had a headset on and was able to listen in to any talk from the helicopter crew and also Lieutenant Santos. Much of the chatter was of no interest to him until he heard the tone of the pilot's voice change.

'Sir, *Taliba* is changing course.' The pilot of the Sea Stallion helicopter spoke to Francesini over the headphones. Francesini got up from his seat and leaned over the pilot's shoulder. The pilot touched the radar screen with the tip of his gloved finger.

'Look's like someone is leaving too.'

The fluorescent blip that the pilot was pointing at, broke into two; one smaller than the other.

'Chopper!'

'Follow the *Taliba*,' Francesini ordered.

Behind him the Seals sat patiently, all with their own thoughts. They were dressed completely in black and only their faces showed through their headgear. Around their waists they carried knives, stun grenades and pistols. And each man was clutching an automatic weapon. None of them showed rank or service insignia.

'*Taliba*!'

Francesini peered through the patch of windscreen being cleared by the wipers. In the murk he could se the white ship standing out clearly against the dull, grey sea. The whitecaps and spindrift whipped across the bows of the ship. He turned to the men behind him and held up two fingers.

'Two minutes!'

Captain de Leon could see the helicopter now. He knew why Khan had left but did not know the sentence of death the madman had passed on them all. The helicopter was almost certainly hostile and in their present position, de Leon and his crew were vulnerable.

He reached for the bridge handset and thumbed the speech button.

'Your attention please! Your attention please!'

The words rattled out of the deck speakers and were whipped away by the howling wind. Below decks his voice bounced around the bulkheads.

'The *Taliba* is likely to come under hostile action within two minutes. No man is to take action unless he feels directly threatened. Please remain below decks. I repeat ...'

The message rumbled on to its end and de Leon replaced the handset.

The Sea Stallion came straight at them. It slowed to a hover above the bridge and two dark figures dropped down on ropes. De Leon was looking up above him, as though willing himself to see through the deck-head yet not realizing what was happening.

Suddenly both doors on either side of the bridge flew open and two black figures rushed in. They were brandishing automatic weapons.

'Nobody move!'

The order was quite unmistakable and needed no repeating. De Leon said nothing. Through the windows of the bridge he could see the Sea Stallion hovering above the heli-pad and the remainder of the raiding party dropping on to it.

Within seconds the helicopter had moved away and taken up station about thirty metres off the starboard quarter.

'You, slow engines!'

De Leon reached for the engine room telegraph and signalled the order to slow engines. Almost immediately the *Taliba* began to lose way.

Lieutenant Santos felt the change in speed and sprinted down the stairs to the lower accommodation deck where he knew he would probably find Marsh and Helen. He had one man with him.

He reached Marsh's cabin door, remembering its location from his previous visit. He tried the door and was surprised to find it unlocked. He stepped inside quickly, but he could see there was no reason to linger. He had no time to dwell on the fact that Marsh was not there.

He then signalled his fellow Seal to work with him and they opened each cabin door. One would kick the door open; the other would go in, weapon raised and ready to fire. They flushed out a few crew members who gave no resistance at all. Then they found Helen's cabin. The door was locked.

Just then the scuttling charges blew, sending a shudder through the whole of the ship as the explosion ripped the bottom out of the hull.

Even though the *Taliba* was slowing, the effect was devastating. It was like hitting a brick wall. The ship stopped as the sea crashed into her open belly and she dipped her nose into the windswept ocean.

Lieutenant Santos and his colleague picked themselves up, the assault forgotten. They both realized exactly what had happened. And as they struggled to their feet, they knew the ship would be gone in less than a minute.

Helen had listened to all the commotion, knowing what was happening because of de Leon's broadcast. She could see little through the porthole of her cabin so had to content herself with hoping and praying that she would escape this hell hole she had been confined to.

As she listened to the sounds of Lieutenant Santos and his fellow Seal getting into each cabin and shouting at the crew, she could only stand, her hands clasped together almost in an attitude of prayer, but paralysed in fear.

Then the scuttling charges went off and Helen was thrown to the floor. She screamed out, knowing with fearful certainty what had happened. She scrambled to her feet and began pounding on the cabin door, shouting at the top of her voice. She could hear voices ordering everyone to abandon ship. She could imagine someone shouting that it was every man for himself.

She hurled herself at the door again and beat furiously at it with her closed fists. Then the ship lurched and threw Helen away from the door. She screamed out and fought against the pull of gravity. Suddenly the cabin door gave way beneath a huge, crashing boot and an enormous figure stepped into the cabin, lifted her up effortlessly and put her over his shoulder.

'Lieutenant Santos at your service, ma'am. Now let's get the hell out of here.'

As Santos stepped out on to the badly listing top deck, he knew there was no time to consider the best alternatives. He launched himself, with Helen still over his shoulder into the sea. As they hit the water and went under, he pulled Helen in close and kicked out for the surface.

Helen felt the water close over her and was astonished at its coldness. After the warmth of her cabin, the sudden drop in temperature was almost like being in the Arctic and the shock of it went through to her very core. She could feel Santos's strong arms support her as he kicked up with powerful scissor strokes. As they broke through the surface, Helen gasped and shouted at him.

'Leave me, I can swim! I'm OK, I can swim!'

Most of what she said was blown away by the howling wind.

'Stay close then!' Santos shouted at her. 'It's your only chance.'

Above them the helicopter hovered downwind as a crewman kicked a dinghy from the open door. It tumbled down on a line and inflated the moment it hit the water. Santos swam towards it with Helen doing her best to keep up with him.

The crewman in the helicopter had attached a line that was clipped securely to the helicopter so that the dinghy did not get blown away by the strong winds.

The wind battered Santos remorselessly as he swam towards the raft. From time to time he disappeared beneath the waves only to surface again without check. Helen continued to swim behind him, but the gap between them was increasing.

He reached the boat and lunged for the grab line attached to the side. Kicking hard with his legs, he pulled himself into the dinghy. Then he turned round and waited for Helen.

He could see her head and arms battling against the sea and the wind. Her efforts seemed pitiful against the rumbling surf and howling gale. Its fury seemed to be hurled at her frail figure, and Santos began to fear for her safety.

He glanced up at the crewman in the helicopter and made a slashing movement with his hand across his throat. The crewman acknowledged and released the rope holding the dinghy. As the dinghy began to move with the wind, Santos grabbed an oar from its stowage and began steering the dinghy towards Helen.

Helen began swimming at an angle that she hoped would bring her in line with the dinghy. As they came together, the rubber of the boat nudging Helen's face, she felt her strength leave her and slipped beneath the surface.

Santos leaned forward and reached out for her. Their arms locked and he pulled hard, lifting her into the dinghy where she collapsed in a coughing fit. Not giving her a chance to feel relieved or to feel sorry for herself, Santos unshipped another paddle and shoved it at Helen.

'Row!' he shouted.

Helen looked up, a little disorientated, but quickly realized what was expected of her. She had little strength left but she had courage, so she knelt against the side of the dinghy and drove her paddle into the sea with all the might and strength left in her body.

The pilot of the helicopter acted very professionally although he watched in horror at the events unfolding beneath him.

He thumbed the speech button on his headset.

'Homestead, this is Sea Horse One. We have a problem.' He kept the helicopter hovering about twenty metres above the surface of the water. '*Taliba* destroyed by unknown explosion. Bodies in the water. Request assistance, immediate. Over.'

The reply came back instantly.

'Seahorse One, this is Homestead. We copy request for assistance immediate. Scrambling Search and Rescue Chopper now. Contact frequency two, two niner decimal five. Repeat: contact frequency two, two niner decimal five. Good luck. Over.'

'Homestead we copy.' He repeated the frequency and contacted the search and rescue helicopter.

Lieutenant Santos had seen a second dinghy tumble from the heli- copter, but still tethered. One of his men scrambled into it as it inflated and quickly released the rope tethering it to the helicopter. He then set about getting as many survivors into the dinghy as possible.

As the two dinghies moved through the water, they managed to pick up several swimmers. Among them was Captain de Leon. He looked pale and disillusioned, but said nothing to Helen because they were now joined in the dramatic, unifying battle for survival.

MICHAEL PARKER

Despite the strong winds, they were able to send the more seriously injured up to the Sea Stallion by use of the winch man. The rescue work was extremely slow and tedious with the ever present risk of losing sight of other survivors in the stormy sea. It was obvious the group was being scattered and drifting apart. And bobbing heads could be seen as much as one hundred metres apart.

It was twenty minutes after the helicopter pilot had put out a distress call that the Search and Rescue Helicopter from the Homestead base arrived. After that the rescue became more co-ordinated, releasing the first pilot of the harrowing burden of choice; choosing who would stay in the water and who would be picked up.

The two machines worked well, circling the area, picking up those swimmers who were furthest from the dinghies. The wind seemed to increase in strength and frustrate their efforts. Added to the down-draught from the helicopter blades, it made it hell for everyone. At one stage, the downdraught almost overturned one of the dinghies, threatening to pitch everybody on board into the water.

Forty-five minutes after *Taliba* went down, Lieutenant Santos scrambled on board the Sea Stallion helicopter. He turned and glanced at the angry sea below and just caught a glimpse of the dinghies being swept away by the raging wind.

The sea was empty now, the dinghies gone. The helicopter winch man pulled the sliding door shut.

'OK!' he shouted above the noise of the helicopter. 'Let's go home!'

Khan watched the rig come into view as Malik guided the helicopter towards the overhanging heli-pad. The wind pushed and pulled it mercilessly, but slowly, inch by inch, Malik brought the helicopter safely on to the pad.

Khan breathed a sigh of relief but felt the pain around his heart and massaged his chest softly. He wondered how long he could go on. He glanced at Malik, the man's face set grimly in an expressionless feature.

'Allah is still with us, Malik. He is still with us.'

Malik turned his head a little and looked impassively at Khan.

'Then may Allah give you strength to finish the task.'

After bringing the helicopter down safely, Malik killed the engine. The blades spun for a short while and then stopped. Through the cockpit windows he could see the landing area was covered with a net of strong rope, put there for safety reasons. Once the helicopter was safely on the pad, two of the rig's crew threw lashing hooks over the skids. Malik waited until they had secured the helicopter before opening the door. He immediately moved round to Khan's side, head bent against the wind and helped him out.

Although the wind buffeted them considerably, they seemed to be in little danger of being hurled over the side. They made their way quickly up to the oil rig's accommodation deck, followed by the two men who had seen them on to the rig.

Once they were inside, into the relative peace and calm of the building's lounge area, Khan collapsed into a nearby chair. Malik asked one of the men to bring some water. The moment it arrived, Khan reached into his pocket and took out two of his heart pills. He swallowed them hastily.

'Malik,' he gasped, looking up, 'how long before the satellite will be in position?'

Malik spoke to one of the two men. He picked up a wall phone and dialled the control room. After a short conversation and a short silence, he replaced the phone and turned to Malik.

'Two hours,' he told him.

Khan closed his eyes. 'Praise Allah,' he intoned. 'In His wisdom He has given us time. We will see the end of the Great Satan yet.' He struggled to his feet. Malik helped him.

'Our enemies will never win against the forces of Islam. May Allah be praised.'

On the journey back to the Homestead Air Reserve Base, Helen sat in an extremely uncomfortable seat not designed for sitting in over periods extending more than a couple of minutes. She felt exhausted and tried to close her eyes and sleep. But sleep would not come. Her eyelids fluttered, closed and then opened again. During one of these moments she noticed Francesini. He had his hand to his earpiece and his face was screwed up into an impossible frown. Then his eyebrows lifted and his mouth opened. She could see him mouthing the word 'What?', but gave it no thought. Then he glanced at her and she thought she saw him smile. No, it wasn't a smile, it was something more; relief perhaps? He shook his head gently and leaned back against the wall of the helicopter, and she swore she could see him chuckling. She wondered just what there was to make someone laugh at a time like this. She let the thought drift from her mind and tried to sleep.

When the helicopter landed at the base, the military police were on hand to take into custody Captain de Leon and his crew; those who were fit enough to walk. Francesini disappeared very quickly, as did Lieutenant Santos and his men. Helen was taken to the base hospital for an examination, along with the others who could be described as walking wounded.

She had been at the facility for little more than twenty minutes, in a side room, when Francesini knocked and walked in. Helen was wearing a hospital gown and lying on top of the bed.

'How are you feeling?' he asked.

'Terribly sad,' she told him. 'They killed Marsh, you know.'

He nodded. 'Look,' he said, walking towards the bed. 'I had to see someone just now, that's why I couldn't come with you.' He hesitated as though lost for words. 'But things crop up unexpectedly. You've been through a rough time, but there's somebody here who wants to talk to you. Think you can take it?'

She shrugged and sat up. 'After what I've been through, I don't think a little conversation will hurt.'

Francesini turned and called out. The door opened. Helen couldn't see who had come in because Francesini was standing in the way. Then he moved.

'Hallo, Helen.'

It was Marsh.

CHAPTER NINETEEN

Helen did not want to ride in that monstrous helicopter again. The thought of rough ride, the discomfort, the noise and the memory of why she had been in the helicopter in the first place was enough to make her promise herself she would never fly in one again. Until now.

Marsh sat in the Sea Stallion helicopter oblivious to the noise and the people around him except Helen who was sitting beside him, clutching his hand in a grip so fierce that it spoke a thousand words. Her fear transmitted itself to him through her flesh. It wasn't fear of death any longer, but fear of losing him. That more than ever weighed her down like a powerful burden and, as each thought came into her mind about the terror Marsh must have experienced in the *Challenger*, it turned her inside out. It was almost as if she had been there herself.

When Marsh walked into the hospital room where Helen had lain, Francesini had wanted to remain there for a few moments and watch the sheer joy and immense relief spread through them both, but he knew it would have been churlish of him to do so. He left after a moment and waited outside in the corridor.

Helen had clung to Marsh as though her life had depended on it. The joy, relief, disbelief, all rolled into a mixture of emotions that took away her ability, albeit briefly, to think of anything else but Marsh. In the end it was Francesini who had to prise them apart. He gave them sufficient time and then came back in.

'We have a job to do,' he told them.

Marsh had been debriefed swiftly by Francesini and had been able to tell the CIA man that he believed he knew where Khan had flown to. It was when Francesini had told him that Khan had fled the

Taliba. Marsh knew it would be the rig. It was the only place Khan could be. He had remembered hearing a voice in the background during the second dive, coming over the sonar link between the *Taliba* and the *Challenger*. Someone had said, 'It's the rig, sir.' Nothing else. Then there was the unusual approach to the well-head; the faint, almost imagined outcrop of rock which he now realized was an anchor or a pylon. And finally the fact that he had caught sight of something as *Challenger* had been swung out for that dive. *Taliba*'s position had practically obscured his view, which was why he thought it was a ship. But it had been a rig: a semi-submersible oil rig.

A raiding party had been hastily assembled comprising ten, well-armed marines together with Lieutenant Santos and his Seals. Marsh, Helen and Francesini were riding in the Sea Stallion with the marines. Lieutenant Santos was in a Sea King helicopter with his men.

The reason Helen was there was because Marsh had flatly refused to allow Francesini to keep him and Helen out of the assault operation, despite the fact that they were both civilians. Francesini had been quite philosophical about it and agreed. He realized that they both had a right to be there at the end after what they had been through; particularly Marsh.

These thoughts ran through Marsh's mind as he sat beside Helen. The clamour of the turbine and the howling wind failed to penetrate Marsh's inner soul, into that sanctum that had seen the Devil and supped at his table. He glanced at Helen and gave her a tight, nervous smile. She smiled back at him and squeezed his hand.

The discussions beforehand were all based on what Helen had told them, Marsh's experiences and the report given to Francesini by the expert, Professor Schofeld at the Woods Hole Institute. Francesini had contacted the Kennedy Space Centre who told them that there were too many satellites tracking across the Gulf of Mexico to give an accurate assessment of which satellite Khan would use to trigger the bombs, but any time within the next sixty minutes could be considered to be zero hour.

The assault plan was simple enough: Lieutenant Santos and the Seals would drop from the Sea King helicopter first and make directly to the control room. The marines would come in behind the Seals in the Sea Stallion and sweep the rig to flush out any member of the crew who harboured aspirations of heroism. Marsh and Helen had both been offered a weapon but had refused. Marsh had never fired a gun in his life and Helen had no wish to.

Suddenly the helicopter dropped and Marsh felt his stomach lurch as the pilot brought the aircraft down to a level which would get them low enough to confuse the oil rig's radar. Marsh could feel the fear crawling round in the pit of his stomach as the wind hammered them with such an incredible force that he was convinced they would all be dashed into the sea.

Everybody knew the hurricane was moving towards Florida and its peripheral winds were reaching out towards them. Marsh could feel the helicopter moving awkwardly, like a carriage riding over cobblestones.

The dark clouds had blotted out the sun for so long that it was as if night had crept up on them like a ghost. It was dark and they came out of the black sky; their dull silhouettes merged with the sea and sky. Both helicopters flashed over the wave tops with little room to spare.

Francesini's headset burst into life in his ear.

'Rig on radar, sir.'

He grimaced. 'Signal Homestead,' he ordered with deep reservation. 'Have them scramble the F-16s.'

This part of the plan had been the most difficult and heart-rending to assess. In the end it was a decision taken reluctantly. All those involved in the raid on the rig were told about it and given the opportunity to opt out. There were no takers.

Three F-16s were now under orders to attack the rig if the assault failed and no signal received to say the assault had been successful. Only if the signal of their success was received would the attack be called off.

Francesini could see the rig glowing faintly in the darkening sky, its lights picked out by the harsh storm clouds behind it as he looked through the cockpit.

'Two minutes,' the pilot said.

On the rig, Malik checked his watch for about the tenth time in as many minutes. Khan had been watching him. He looked up at the clock on the wall.

'We have ten minutes yet.'

'Why not programme the computer now?' Malik asked. 'Why must you wait until the satellite is in the exact position?'

Khan explained. 'If I programme the computer now it would be like sending an open message to the Americans.'

He wished it was simpler because he, too, was feeling the tension. The pain around his heart was increasing to a degree that it began to trouble him immensely.

'We know that when the satellite is in position, the transfer of information will last for micro seconds. The Americans will never pick it up.'

'And you're not prepared to risk it now?'

Khan shook his head. 'We know the Americans are on to us. If I open up the computer link now, it will be transmitting to an empty sky. Their listening stations will be on to us in minutes and they may even be able to jam the signal. No,' he said finally, 'we must wait.'

Malik knew Khan was talking sense. There was sure to be an AWAC on patrol now above them somewhere, and if they picked up the signal, not only could they block it, but they could send patrolling aircraft to attack the rig. No, Khan was right: they had to wait.

'But we could go up to the control room,' Khan suggested. 'They will have battened down against the storm. It should be quiet and peaceful enough.'

He stood up and reached for his briefcase. He thought about taking two more tablets but thought better of it. He would take a couple later.

They stepped out on to the open catwalk in the lee of the accommodation block. As they turned the corner, the wind slammed into them with such a force it threatened to lift them up and pitch them into the angry sea.

Khan stopped and backed into the lee of the building.

'It's too risky!' he shouted. 'We'll have to go under the platform.'

They turned back and followed a route which took them down a staircase leading to a protected gallery from where the drilling crew operated. Normally the main riser, the eighteen-inch diameter pipe drilling section would descend from there, through the open gallery floor and into the sea. Because of the weather conditions, the pipe had been withdrawn and all that remained was a black void.

The wind inside the gallery crashed around the walls and the thick,

Perspex glass windows, but its ferocity was tempered and nowhere near as fierce as on the open deck. They walked quickly, using the handrails for support.

Malik walked in front of Khan and, as he reached the foot of the stairs that led to the upper platform, he saw something move outside the windows on the far side of the gallery. He stopped and Khan walked into him.

'What is it?' Khan shouted.

Malik didn't reply at first, but stared fixedly at the far windows, a deep frown coming on his face. Suddenly he whirled round and almost screamed at Khan.

'We're being attacked! There!'

Khan looked across the gallery and just caught sight of the Sea Stallion helicopter moving slowly towards the upper decks of the oil rig.

'They won't know,' Malik shouted desperately. 'They won't know.'

He glanced hurriedly around the metal catwalks and steelwork, searching furiously along the stanchions until he saw an alarm button. It was mounted next to the drillers' control point and was for use in an emergency.

Malik brushed past Khan and ran across the gallery floor and slammed the heel of his hand at the button. Suddenly the entire rig seemed to come alive as a blaring klaxon siren came to life and filled the air with a riotous noise.

Khan knew instinctively what was happening. It was what he had feared the most. Ignoring the clamping pain around his chest he began climbing the stairs as quickly as was humanly possible for him. Malik followed. As they reached the main deck of the oil rig, they could see the black shrouded figures dropping from the helicopter.

Malik had a Stechkin automatic pistol with him which he pulled from inside his jacket and began firing. Almost immediately the steelwork around him erupted in a cacophonous noise as the Seals returned his fire.

He stopped shooting and urged Khan forward, pushing and half carrying him up the next flight of stairs to the main control room. Khan felt a massive pain lash at his heart and he cried out and fell to his knees.

'Come on,' Malik urged him, lifting him bodily. 'They will have us; it's our last chance!'

He pulled Khan round a protective corner as bullets cannoned off the superstructure. He let Khan go and returned a burst of covering fire. He looked up as Khan reached the door of the control room.

'The lights!' Malik shouted. 'Get them to douse the lights!'

He rolled over on to his stomach and emptied the magazine along the catwalk. Then he heard the stuttering sound of automatic rifle fire and knew that others had joined the fight.

The Sea King landed on the heli-pad as all the lights went out.

Helen could not control the trembling that ran riot through her body. She had never known fear like it. The noise of the fire-fight had already penetrated the interior of the helicopter and suddenly they were in darkness. She felt the helicopter bounce on the landing pad and settle, and then the wind punched itself into the interior as a crewman slid the door open.

'Now listen up!' someone shouted. 'When you hit the deck, grab hold of the net. Wait until the chopper has lifted clear of the rig before you let go of the rope. And don't move until you're told to!'

Helen found herself tumbling out of the door into that incredible wind. Marsh pushed her to the ground and she could feel the coarse hemp beneath her. His mouth pushed up against her ear.

'Stay with me!' he shouted.

She nodded but he didn't see it.

Suddenly a marine sergeant sprawled alongside them. 'Listen up. My orders are to get you up to the control room.' The wind whipped the words away and they could barely hear him. 'When we go, stay close.' He waited until the Sea King drew away from the rig, then he hit them both between the shoulder blades and almost drove the breath from their bodies.

'Let's go! Let's go!' he shouted. 'All the way!'

At Homestead Air Reserve Base, the bird colonel charged with the mission to destroy the oil rig glanced over his shoulder, left and right at his wingmen. He gave them a salute and applied the full power of the F-16s' Pratt and Whitney engines. The aircraft trembled under the power of the jet's reheat exhaust until he released the brakes, the seat slammed into his back and the aircraft accelerated along the runway.

The two wingmen rolled with him at speed down the runway and soon the tarmac was flashing by beneath them. As the nose came up, he lifted the undercarriage and let the reheat fire him up towards their formation height. At 2000 feet he levelled and let the wingmen form up on him. Then the three aircraft turned and headed out over the angry sea.

At that point, Birdman, the mission leader in the lead jet, thumbed his transmit button and spoke on a radio frequency connecting him directly to the Sea Stallion helicopter.

'Sea Horse one, this is Bird one. How do you read? Over.'

'Bird one, this is Sea Horse one. Charlie Tango. Over.'

Birdman looked down at his knee pad. On it were written three letters: C, T and R; Charlie, Tango and Romeo. The first two letters were the code to authenticate the call from Bird One; the Sea Stallion helicopter. The third letter, Romeo would not be used unless the mission had to be aborted.

Birdman was satisfied.

'Roger that, Sea Horse one. Birds one, two and three are flying. Out.'

The three F-16s climbed from their 2000 feet level and roared up to 30,000 feet to get above the storm. Once above it, the formation leader set the co-ordinates, checked the 'time-on-target' with his wingmen and offered up a short prayer.

'OK, guys, this is it,' he called over his radio. 'Let's go hunting!'

Marsh followed the marine sergeant in the darkness, clutching Helen's hand tightly. He caught brief glimpses of the soldier's silhouette against the flickering lights of muzzle flash and ricocheting bullets. The rig seemed to be lit up like a Christmas tree with flashing lights.

Although the crew on the rig were well armed, none of them was really prepared for this kind of professional assault. Many of them had come straight from their rest rooms or places of work without the benefit of camouflage clothing or even a prepared plan of action. Against the Seals and the marines, they stood little chance.

The wind screamed and hammered at the sergeant and his two charges as they made slow progress up the stairs. It seemed to toy with them. One moment it would slacken and eddy to a soft swirl; then suddenly it would rise up into a gigantic fury. High in the derrick tower the wind tore at the rigging lines and the whole rig seemed to shake and resonate beneath the savage fury of the wind.

They reached the top of the stairs and huddled against a wall for protection. In the flickering light the sergeant's eyes seemed to detach themselves and float before them.

'I hope this damn rig can stand up to it,' he shouted. 'She's beginning to move.'

It was true; Marsh could sense the enormous strain on the anchor chains. They vibrated with a hum that echoed through the deck plating. Much more, he thought, and the rig would start dragging its anchors.

The battle to get into the control room had reached something of an impasse as the Seals were forced to keep their heads down because of the covering fire coming from the men defending the rig.

The sergeant motioned to Marsh and Helen to stay put and not move.

Lieutenant Santos crouched on the upper platform cursing his luck. He had seen Malik and realized it was him who was orchestrating the defence of the control room. And he guessed that Khan was already inside, feeding the figures into the rig's computer.

'I'm going up top!' he shouted to his men. 'Hold their attention.'

Santos knew his way around oil rigs. It was not because rigs were his particular *forte*, but he had conducted so many classroom scenarios in rig protection, and had participated in active exercises, that he had come to know many rig layouts. And this rig was no different.

He left his position and clambered down to the lower gallery. The roaring of the wind and the sea combined with the cathedral-like space induced in him a complete sense of detachment. It was as though he had moved into another world.

He felt his way round the gallery catwalk using faint illumination from the insipid daylight to help him pick his way round the steel structure. He found the stairwell he figured would take him directly to the rear of the control-room deck.

At the top he peered cautiously along the deck until he was certain nobody was there. He was on the far side of the rig, away from the immediate fire-fight.

There was a catwalk from his position to the platform on which the control room was standing. Part of it was sheltered from the wind. But, as he stepped into the wind, it struck him so fiercely that it threatened to pitch him off the catwalk and into the steelwork below.

He turned and backed into it, using the handrail to steady himself and edged toward the control-room deck. He could sense, rather than see the long, empty drop below him, but chose not to dwell on it. His immediate thought was to get to the control-room safely before any of the rig's crew spotted him.

He sensed Malik before he saw him.

It was the uncanny sound in that roaring wind of a footfall on the steel plating. He spun round and saw the looming figure of the Arab coming towards him.

Santos had his weapon slung over his shoulder. He had put it there because he needed both hands free to negotiate the rig in that fearsome wind.

Malik was holding the Stechkin pistol in his hands. He lifted his arm to fire but the wind caught him and pushed him off balance against the inner rail of the catwalk. Santos seized the moment and launched a kick at Malik, using the handrails to support him. His boot connected and caught Malik a glancing blow to the chest, but Malik fired a round and Santos felt the sting as the bullet tore into the top of his shoulder.

Malik came forward, seeing that he had wounded the Seal. His clothes billowed out transforming him into a colossal, nightmarish figure. He pointed the gun at Santos and, even as his hand wavered in the wind, Santos knew he wouldn't miss at that range.

The shot came just after Santos rolled himself into a ball and hurled himself at Malik's midriff, thrusting his good arm upwards to ward off Malik's arm. Malik tried to club Santos but the Seal's weight brought them both crashing down on to the deck.

Malik fell on top of Santos. The American knew he would not win a physical contest with the Arab because of the wound in his shoulder, but if he was damaged physically, he wasn't damaged mentally. His brain was still quick and he was trained to react to any situation,

As Malik landed on top of him, Santos rolled his body towards the edge of the catwalk. Before Malik could figure out what was happening, the Navy Seal used his own body as a roller and pitched him towards the lower gap in the safety rail.

Malik grabbed for the handrail, but the combined force of the wind and Santos's rolling motion beneath him, caused him to miss it. Santos stopped and pushed Malik forward. He saw the Arab's legs thrash the air and then there was nothing: not even the sound of his deathly screams as he plummeted eighty feet into the angry sea below.

Khan was unaware just how close the Seals were to the control-room, because he had two things on his mind: one was to programme the computer, and the other was the searing pain across his chest and down his arms. He was leaning against the computer table, sweat breaking out on his brow. Alongside him were two engineers and although they were both carrying arms, they were not mentally equipped for a fight with America's finest.

Khan felt the rig lurch again and his heart protested. The pain squeezed his chest and he instinctively brought his hand up to it. He massaged the area around his heart and prayed that he would be given the strength to last.

'How much time?' he gasped.

'Three minutes. The satellites will be in the vector in three minutes.'

He slipped the disc into the computer's disc drive, waited until the command came up on the screen and began feeding the figures in. As he watched the screen, small beads of sweat ran down his face. He looked grey and ashen.

The pain continued to nag at him, reminding him that he didn't have much time. The sounds of the fire-fight outside had subdued and the eerie silence was broken only by unclear scuffling noises.

Suddenly there was a terrific bang on the control-room door.

'Open up, Khan! Now!' the voice commanded. 'If you don't open the door now, we will blow it and all of you in there will be killed. Now, open up! It's over!'

Khan ignored the voice and looked at the engineer.

'How much time?'

'Now. The satellite is in position now.'

Khan felt his knees sag and the sweat began to pour from him. He punched in the commands, running his fingers over the keyboard clumsily, making mistakes and having to correct them. Eventually the screen flashed and asked him to verify the command. He fed in the verification again as more banging came at the door. The screen told him to wait and he moved his trembling fingers towards a combination dial mounted next to the screen.

There was a sudden clamour outside and an ear-splitting noise filled the control-room as the Seals fired their weapons at the steel door. The bullets were leaving walnut size impressions around the lock, but the door did not yield.

The firing stopped as suddenly as it had begun. Khan looked over at the deadlights covering the windows, fearful that the Seals would come in that way. Then a short, high-pitched 'bleep' drew his attention back to the screen; the satellite had accepted the command and opened the firing channels. He set the dial and put his hand on the Castell key. All he had to do was push and turn it. This would then complete the uplink and the bombs would be armed. And nothing on earth could stop them.

'Khan, this is Marsh!'

Marsh's voice came through the steel door like a lance, arrowing in on him. It wrapped itself round his heart and began to crush the life from him.

'No!' he gasped breathlessly. 'No, Marsh, you're dead!'

His fingers closed into a fist as his muscles began to contract with the seizure. He fought hard, trying to push the key, but his arm began to quiver violently and he felt the strength leaving him.

'You're dead, Marsh,' he cried soundlessly. 'Dead!'

The breath locked in his throat and he began to topple. The door crashed open and the Seals poured into the room. Khan twisted round as the screen continued to blink at him, asking for the final command. He saw Marsh's reflection in the screen, a dead man walking. Then his heart stopped and he fell to the ground, dead.

The F-16s dropped to their attack height of 1500 feet. The two wingmen formed up on the lead aircraft. Birdman thumbed his transmit button.

'Target twelve o'clock, ten miles.'

Both wingmen acknowledged.

'Roger, Birdman. Have visual.'

Both his wingmen had the rig on their radar screens.

'Eight miles.'

Birdman looked down at his knee pad and then at the TV screen as the rig came up. It was an intensified image. He toggled a switch to move between radar and TV monitoring which came through the moving head of the Maverick missile slung beneath his wing. Selecting TV now for better definition, he moved the target acquisition square around the screen.

'Contact, six miles!'

He locked the missile's TV head on to the rig. Reached down to the 'final arm' switch and moved it to the 'armed' position. The Maverick was now ready for firing. He knew his wingmen would be going through the same procedure.

All missiles were now live.

'Four miles.'

He felt the skin tighten on his face as the F-16s flew across the surface of the grey sea, moving in for the kill. It was a beautiful target. He was ready to take out the control-room and upper superstructure while his wingmen would launch their missiles at the legs of the rig to send it to the bottom of the sea.

'Two miles.'

Suddenly a voice buzzed in his ear.

'Birdman, Sea Horse one.' It was the Sea Stallion. 'Code Romeo. Abort, abort.'

For a moment, Birdman sighed. But he recognized the confirmation code and his professionalism and training kicked in.

'Roger. Code Romeo. Aborting mission.'

He cursed and then smiled, disarmed the missile and called his wingmen.

'You heard that guys. Code Romeo. Mission aborted.'

'Birdman roger. We understand Romeo. Aborting mission.'

'OK, guys, let's go home.'

They screamed across the top of the oil rig, rocking their wings in recognition, turned as one and sped across the angry sea for home.

CHAPTER TWENTY

Marsh looked across the table at Francesini. The man seemed content with life, as though a great weight had been lifted from his shoulders. The gardens of the Caravel Club in Freeport were a perfect setting for the occasion. A warm sun shone down on them while a gentle breeze blew in from the Gulf to caress the islands. It instilled a warm tranquillity in him that Marsh found most rewarding.

With Marsh and Francesini were Helen, Admiral Starling, the island Police Commissioner and Inspector Bain, lording it over his guests. They were all wearing casual clothes, no suits or uniforms. It added to the calming effect and made the storming of the rig seem like a bad dream.

They had come close to failure. So close it was almost unbelievable. Even with Khan lying dead on the floor of the control-room, no one had thought to power down the computer because of the chaos that reigned. It was only the lightning reaction of one of the Seals that had saved them. One of the engineers with Khan had made a lunge for the Castell key only to be killed with a fast, clean shot. The speed of the kill numbed Helen for a moment, and then she suddenly stepped forward, spun the combination on the lock, and fainted.

The recollection of it all made Marsh smile inwardly. There had been bedlam after that. Lieutenant Santos came staggering into the control-room nursing a broken shoulder and screaming instructions to contact the helicopter and get the attack called off. Within seconds it seemed, three F-16s roared over the top of the rig and had them all diving for the dubious cover of the control-room floor.

Now they were here enjoying a cool, refreshing drink in the Bahamian sunshine. Enjoying the free world, he mused ruefully. If it could ever be free after the colossal events they had been through. He was certain that all they had achieved was a lull in the never-ending conflict between fanatical terrorists and the free world.

'I was convinced you knew what Walsh was involved in,' Francesini was saying. 'I even had you as a member of the opposition at one time,' he told him.

The irony was not lost on Marsh. 'Well, you could say I was, after all I did end up working for them, didn't I?'

They all laughed.

'Better stick to fishing trips in future,' Francesini joked.

Helen glanced at Marsh. 'I expect that's all he'll want to do after this.'

Admiral Starling cleared his throat and pulled a couple of envelopes from his pocket. He gave one each to Marsh and Helen.

'No fishing trips yet, I'm afraid. These are commissions to retrieve the bombs. We'll need your submersible, of course, and your expertise.'

Marsh opened his envelope and read through the contents. He whistled softly through his teeth; the remuneration was extremely generous. More than enough to get the yard back on its feet again and back into business.

'Is this by way of saying thank you?'

The admiral nodded. 'If something had gone wrong, thousands upon thousands would be dead by now. Who knows how many would have suffered the long-term effects of Khan's deadly fanaticism? You two became unwitting pawns in a dirty and very dangerous game. Even now we cannot admit officially that it happened.' He shrugged. 'We can always explain terrorist behaviour when they ply their deadly trade publicly. But there are times when we have to keep the lid very tight on some of their tricks. Can you imagine the outcry and panic if it got out into the public domain that there are three nuclear bombs sitting out there? So, yes, we are saying thank you and asking for your commitment and your silence.'

'Asking?'

Starling grimaced. 'Well, insisting actually. I'm afraid it has to be that way.'

Marsh folded the envelope and pushed it into his pocket.

'Well, our business needs the work and it won't hurt to get a healthy bank balance again. All we'll need now is an experienced diver, but what about his silence?'

Francesini leaned forward. 'We have an experienced diver and I am sure we can count on his silence.'

'Who is it?' Marsh asked. 'Do we know him?'

Francesini grinned. 'Batista.'

Marsh and Helen sat bolt upright in their seats immediately. 'Batista?' they echoed together.

'That's right. He's a professional and worth his weight in gold in such an endeavour. After all, who could be better? He put the bombs there; he can get the damn things out again. And remember, the fewer people who know about this, the better. Batista has every reason to keep silent; his life wouldn't be worth squit if his involvement in this got into the public domain.'

'I thought he would be going to prison,' Helen protested.

It was the inspector who answered. 'Why? He hasn't really committed a crime. Oh sure, he is responsible for a certain complicity, but all this was in international waters. What would a judge give him? Couple of years?'

'So it's bargaining time, right?' asked Marsh.

'Quite,' answered Bain, 'but you could always drown him when it's over.'

Helen stood up. The others got up out of courtesy. 'Well I'm sure you'll all work out the details,' she said. 'But for now I think I would like some time with Marsh. We have a great deal to talk about.'

They all shook hands and Helen and Marsh took their leave. Out of sight of the others she squeezed his hand.

'Let's go somewhere quiet and more private.'

She led him through the flowered walkway to the car. Marsh followed contentedly, the past events forgotten, and only the future with Helen on his mind.

The Devil's Trinity was a thing of the past. Now they could start living again.